IN CUSTODY

Books by
Anita Desai

For Adults
Clear Light of Day
Fire on the Mountain
Games at Twilight and Other Stories

For Children
The Village by the Sea
The Peacock Garden

ANITA DESAI
In Custody

Heinemann : London

William Heinemann Limited
10 Upper Grosvenor Street London W1X 9PA
LONDON   MELBOURNE   TORONTO
JOHANNESBURG   AUCKLAND

First published 1984
Reprinted 1984
© Anita Desai 1984
SBN 434 18635 X

Photoset in Great Britain by
Rowland Phototypesetting Limited,
Bury St Edmunds, Suffolk
and printed by St Edmundsbury Press,
Bury St Edmunds, Suffolk

To Alicia Yerburgh
With affection and gratitude

'. . . they should take, who have the power
And they should keep who can.'

Rob Roy's Grave
William Wordsworth

CHAPTER ONE

His first feeling on turning around at the tap on his shoulder while he was buying cigarettes at the college canteen and seeing his old friend Murad was one of joy so that he gasped 'Murad? You?' and the cigarettes fell from his hand in amaze-ment, but this rapidly turned to anxiety when Murad gave a laugh, showing the betel-stained teeth beneath the small bristling moustache he still wore on his upper lip. 'But I have a class just now, Murad,' he stammered as Murad squeezed his shoulders tightly as if he did not intend to let go.

'Stop worrying about your class,' Murad said, drawing him close to him and laughing into his ear. 'I've come all the way from Delhi to see you – can't you give me half an hour of your time?'

'But it's Monday – not on Monday, Murad.'

'Oh, so friendship is only for Sunday, is it? Is that friendship?' Murad boomed.

They walked away from the canteen, across the dusty field that separated the corrugated iron shack of the canteen from the brick building of the college where Deven taught. Deven was aware that many of his students had observed this encoun-ter with his old friend and were staring openly, some even smirking at the sight. He tried to wriggle out of Murad's grasp unobtrusively so as not to offend him.

'Just one more class, Murad,' he pleaded, 'then I'm free to go home.'

NEWPORT CENTRAL

'Home? Who wants to go home?' shouted Murad. 'We're going out to lunch. We're going to lunch in the best restaurant in your great city. If I come all the way from Delhi to see you, then you can at least give me a good lunch,' he added in a petulant voice.

'Of course, of course,' Deven assured him, feeling guilty at his lapse in hospitality. 'Here, have a cigarette, I bought two.' He fumbled in his shirt pocket for them and handed one to his friend.

'Still a two-cigarette man, are you?' Murad laughed, holding one between his fingers and waiting for Deven to strike a match. As there was a March wind tearing across the open field and whirling dust and dry leaves around violently, this was a lengthy, fumbled business. When it was done at last and they strolled on, Murad said insolently, 'A full-fledged lecturer in a college, an important citizen of Mirpore, and still can't afford a whole packet of cigarettes? You seem to be where you were in your college days. What's the matter?'

'No, no,' Deven hastened to explain. 'My wife has told me not to buy a packet at a time. She says if I have to go out to buy just one at a time, I will make smoke less.' He tried to laugh, as at a pleasant joke. 'Women are always trying to make you smoke less, drink less. You know.'

'Oh, so you do still drink, do you? I'm glad to hear that,' Murad gave a yelp and another clap on Deven's shoulder. 'Will I get a drink with my lunch?'

Deven was shocked. He looked furtively to the left and the right. They were walking up the stairs to the main hall. Anyone could have heard, even someone on the staff, or the principal himself. His eyebrows crept together in a furry scowl. 'Please, Murad, leave me now,' he muttered anxiously, hunching his shoulders and clutching his books to his chest. 'I must go to my class.'

'Even a visit from an old friend you have not seen for years will not make you give up your damned class?' Murad shouted, pretending to be outraged. 'Perhaps I should not have come. Why did I bother to catch a bus and travel all the way in this heat to see an old friend who doesn't even care?'

Deven felt uneasy, certain that Murad had reasons for this that he had not yet divulged. Determined not to go another step with Murad at his side, he stood at the top of the stairs and begged, 'Please, Murad, wait in the canteen for me. Have a cup of tea there. I'll join you after my class.' Then he swung away with such desperation that he dashed right into a group of girl students also coming up the stairs and caused much offence, affront, tittering and giggling which Murad stood and watched with a grin.

Recoiling from them, Deven made his way down the passage to his classroom and arrived at the desk beside the blackboard as if at a refuge, panting with exertion and relief. Here he could turn his back to the class and pretend to write something on the blackboard while he composed himself and tried to construct an authoritative teacher-self out of his jolted nerves and distracted ways. Why should a visit from Murad upset him so much? There was no obvious reason of course – they had known each other since they were at school together: Murad had been the spoilt rich boy with money in his pocket for cinema shows and cigarettes and Deven the poor widow's son who could be bribed and bought to do anything for him, and although this had been the basis of their friendship, it had grown and altered and stood the test of time. But Deven did not like him appearing without warning during college hours and disturbing him just when he needed to concentrate; it was very upsetting. Now, instead of going home to lunch, he would have to displease his wife by keeping her waiting, and not turning up, and instead spend far too much money on a restaurant meal for Murad. He pressed his hand to his shirt pocket where he kept his money ever since a pickpocket on the bus had stolen his wallet. There was not much to feel in the pocket except for one crumbling cigarette: it was the end of the month after all and he had had to give Sarla more household money just that morning. How would he manage? He could not bear to think of Murad flashing those brightly coloured teeth in another derisive grin and saying, 'Oh, still a two-cigarette man?'

Why should Murad not pay for the lunch after all? Not

only was he the son of a wealthy Kashmiri carpet dealer in Delhi – although he claimed to have been disowned by him he still lived in his house – but he was also the editor of the magazine he had persuaded his father to buy for him, and of which he liked to say he had made a great success. It was true that he had never paid Deven for the book reviews he had printed in an issue six months ago or for the poem he had accepted and was to publish in the next one. Perhaps he had forgotten. Perhaps he had come to Mirpore to pay him.

Suddenly and savagely Deven wiped out whatever he had written on the blackboard along with this foolishly sanguine idea, and turned to face the class that had been gathering behind his back with much scraping of chairs and shouting across desks. It was not wise to allow himself such indulgence in fantasies of sudden wealth, unexpected cheques, acceptance in the literary circles of the metropolis, so enticingly close. Childish, he snapped at himself with a small jarring sound of his teeth that some of the students closer to him seemed to hear for they looked up at him enquiringly. He was too old now, he went on scolding himself obsessively, and had had too bitter an experience of life to set any value upon such puerile fantasies.

'Withered as the last leaf upon the tree,
Shaken by the chill blast of winter,'

he murmured to himself for he was much given to reciting poetry aloud, a habit he had been told his schoolteacher father had also had and which he therefore felt entitled to inherit.

The students in the first row or two were staring openly at him now. He became aware of their curious waiting faces at last and squared his shoulders to meet their looks. The expression he saw – of boredom, amusement, insolence and defiance – made him look away quickly and focus his eyes upon the door at the far end of the room, the door that opened on to the passage, freedom and release. He had for years been practising this trick of ignoring his class and speaking to himself, or someone outside, invisible. That was what made

12

him a boring teacher who could not command the attention, let alone win the regard, of his unruly class.

'Last time I asked you to read as much as you could find of Sumitra Nandan Pant's poetry,' he began, pitching his voice too high in order to make it carry to that invisible student outside the door, the ideal one. Now it cracked. 'I hope you have done it,' he squeaked, and the class dissolved in laughter.

'Don't laugh,' he said, putting down the tumbler of cold buttermilk. 'This is not the capital, after all, it is only a village.'

'So this is village fare we are getting, is it?' grimaced Murad. 'I must take care not to visit your village again.'

'Oh, it is not so bad,' Devon protested. 'Try this radish,' he coaxed. 'We have good fresh vegetables here at least.'

'Raw radish – the food of cows, and pigs,' groaned Murad, but took it all the same and appeared to eat it with relish, making loud crunching sounds.

Fortunately the small restaurant in the bazaar was packed with lunch-hour crowds and what with all the talk, the roars of laughter, the loud sounds of eating and the clatter of tin dishes and ladles and spoons, Deven was not afraid of his friend's derogatory remarks about the cuisine being over-heard. It was true that this was not a very good place to eat; being next to the bus depot it catered chiefly to bus drivers and passengers in a hurry which made the service hurried and slapdash. It must seem very mean in comparison with the restaurants of Delhi but he could not possibly afford a meal in Kwality or Gaylord, the two best restaurants, both air-conditioned and exorbitant, on the main road where the bigger shops and offices were, and perhaps it was not a bad idea to show Murad that he was not at all well off and could afford only this simple meal of potato curry and fried *puries* in a grimy bazaar eating-house. He gazed into the mirror that hung behind Murad's head and watched the customers move in and out of the roses and vines engraved along its edges while Murad finished the plate of raw radishes.

To his surprise, Murad seemed to be aware of the message he was trying to convey to him silently. Helping himself to the potato curry and bread, he grumbled, 'It is too bad how badly our lecturers are paid. How can the intellectuals of this country do any worthwhile work if no one shows them any respect or compensates them for all the suffering they have to undergo for the sake of art?'

Deven nodded and nodded with great vehemence, quite overcome by his friend's unexpected sensitivity to his situation and by his compassion. It was rarely that one heard such sentiments from any but similarly hard-up colleagues. Helping himself to the last spoonful of curry in the bowl – the helpings were very small, he noted regretfully – he sighed and said, 'Yes my friend, now you have seen how hard it is to survive in this position. If I knew a way to change my situation, I would do it but – what is there to do?' Then an idea struck him as sharply as a slap on the head. The boldness of it quite embarrassed him but it was the end of the month after all, and the bill for this meal would clear out his pocket and leave him with nothing for tea or cigarettes for the rest of the week. The desperation of his circumstances made him say something he never would have otherwise. All through his childhood and youth he had known only one way to deal with life and that was to lie low and remain invisible. Now he leaned forward on his elbows and said emotionally, 'If only we got payment for the articles and reviews that we write for magazines and journals, that would be of some help.'

But now Murad was no longer being sensitive or compassionate. He was feeling inside his mouth with a finger for something that had made his face darken and frown with anger. Extracting it, he placed it on the edge of his plate and glared. Had he heard Deven at all? Raising his head, he glowered at Deven as if it was he who had placed the stone in the bread for him to bite. 'Nearly lost a gold cap,' he said furiously. 'Everybody thinks it an easy thing to bring out a magazine,' he went on. 'Nobody knows of the cost involved. Every month there is a crisis – the printing press refusing to print unless past bills are cleared, the distributor refusing to pay for last month's supplies of copies, the telephone bill, the postage . . . Such expenses. What can you know about it?' he challenged Deven aggressively. 'Worries, worries, worries. And where are the readers? Where are the subscriptions? Who reads Urdu any more?'

'Murad, your magazine must be kept alive for the sake of those who do still read it,' Deven said fervently.

'That is what I am doing,' Murad glared at him. 'Now I am planning a special issue on Urdu poetry. Someone has to keep alive the glorious tradition of Urdu literature. If we do not do it, at whatever cost, how will it survive in this era of – that vegetarian monster, Hindi?' He pronounced the last word with such disgust that it made Deven shrink back and shrivel in his chair, for Hindi was what he taught at the college and for which he was therefore responsible to some degree. 'That language of peasants,' Murad sneered, picking his teeth with a matchstick. 'The language that is raised on radishes and potatoes,' he laughed rudely, pushing aside the empty plates on the table. 'Yet, like these vegetables, it flourishes, while Urdu – language of the court in days of royalty – now languishes in the back lanes and gutters of the city. No palace for it to live in the style to which it is accustomed, no emperors and nawabs to act as its patrons. Only poor I, in my dingy office, trying to bring out a magazine where it may be kept alive. That is what I am doing, see?' He threw another proud and angry look at Deven and spat out a small piece of chewed matchstick in his direction.

'I know, I know, Murad,' Deven sighed. 'How happy I would be to join you on the staff, work for you, for the journal. But I can't give up my job here. I had to take it when it was offered. I was married, Sarla was expecting, you know . . . '

'How could I know,' Murad said. 'Am I supposed to be responsible for that?' He laughed crudely.

Deven pretended not to hear. He went on trying to win Murad's sympathy. 'I could not have supported even myself by writing in Urdu, let alone Sarla and a child. I can write Urdu now only as my hobby.'

'Only your hobby,' mocked Murad. 'Can you serve a language by taking it up "only as your hobby"? Doesn't it deserve more? Doesn't it deserve a lifetime's dedication – like mine?' he demanded.

Deven lifted both hands in the air with a helpless gesture of accepting all Murad had to say, accepting and admitting defeat.

Then Murad unexpectedly barked at him, 'So, what about sending me something for my special number on Urdu poetry, hunh?'

Deven's hands fluttered on to his knees as he melted at the suggestion and felt a glow creep through him at the thought of writing something in the language which had been his first language when he was a child in the half-forgotten, unsubstantial city of childhood, and which was still his first love. The glow was also caused by pride, of course, at being asked to contribute a piece by the editor of what he took to be a leading Urdu journal. That was what Murad had assured him it was and he was happy to believe it. 'Will you print my poems if I send them to you – the remaining ones in the sequence?'

'No. Who wants to read your poems?' Murad said at once, abruptly. 'I have enough poems for the issue already. As soon as I sent out the circular announcing it, contributions started pouring in. Poems, poems, poems. Everybody writes them, I tell you,' he complained, plucking at his hair in mock distress. 'I had to stop them. I had to pick and choose. Only the best, I said. Firaq, Faiz, Rafi, Nur . . . '

'Nur? He has sent you some poems?'

Murad looked evasive and shrugged. 'Poor man, he is very old and ill. I have said I will only publish new work, not excerpts from old collections, and he has written nothing new. He is finished.'

'But no special issue on Urdu poetry would be complete if it did not have some verse by Nur,' exclaimed Deven, scandalized. 'Old, new, it doesn't matter – you must have Nur.'

'Of course I must have Nur,' responded Murad, looking

suddenly smug. 'Nur will be the star of the issue. The light that blazes in the centre and sends its rays to all corners of the world where his verse is known – in Iran, Iraq, Malaysia, Russia, Sweden – do you know, we have sent his name to the Nobel Prize Committee for its award for literature once again?'

Deven nodded. They did this every year, he knew. He himself was convinced that one day the response would come from Stockholm, and shake the literary world of India to its foundations. He felt it beginning to shake already, under his feet. The two o'clock bus from Moradabad roared by. When it had passed and he could make himself heard, he asked, 'So you will print some of the old poems after all? The great Rose poems, or the Winter ones? You know – ' and he made ready to declaim his favourite lines, the ones that contained all the enchantment and romance he had ever experienced in his life.

But Murad cut him short by leaning forward on his elbows and speaking almost into his ear. 'No, I won't, Deven. I don't print stale old stuff in my journal. Even if I have to wait two, three, four months before I get all the material I want, I get it – then I print. I want a full feature on Nur – Nur in his old age, the dying Nur before he is gone, like a comet into the dark. I want you to do that feature.'

'I?' breathed Deven, so overcome that he quite forgot for the time the noisy surroundings, the empty plates, even the foul breath from Murad's mouth so close to his face. It was the comet he was seeing, swift and pale in the dark like a bird of the night.

'You go and see Nur,' Murad continued. 'You know his work well – oh, as well as anyone, I suppose. You wrote a book about him once, didn't you?'

'A monograph, yes. Will you publish it?' Deven asked breathlessly, thinking that when a comet appeared all kinds of strange happenings might occur. For a moment he became confused and thought it was not Nur who was the comet but Murad who had come from Delhi to visit him, to show him a light: he was willing to believe anything.

But Murad snapped crossly, 'No, I won't. Of course not.

17

I don't want to become bankrupt. I want to bring out my journal. That is what I'm talking about, idiot. Try and listen. Be serious. I want you to track him down in his house in Chandni Chowk –'

'Oh, they say he does not like visitors,' Deven said quickly. The comet was something to be feared, he just remembered, it was a bad omen, not lucky. He could not have said why but he was frightened.

'Look, will you do this feature for me or not?'

'Of course I will, Murad.' He became meek. He hung his head, looking at his fingers clutching the edge of the table. On each fingernail a pale cuticle loomed bleakly.

'Then do as I say. Find him. Go to him and interview him. Discuss the Urdu scene with him. Ask him for his new work. He must have some, dammit, and I want it. I need it for the special issue, see?'

CHAPTER TWO

The bus soon left Mirpore behind. It came as a slight shock
to Deven that one could so easily and quickly free oneself
from what had come to seem to him not only the entire world
since he had no existence outside it, but often a cruel trap, or
prison, as well, an indestructible prison from which there was
no escape.

Although it lacked history, the town had probably existed
for centuries in its most basic, most elemental form. Those
shacks of tin and rags, however precarious and impermanent
they looked, must have existed always, repetitively and in
succeeding generations, but never fundamentally changing
and in that sense enduring. The roads that ran between their
crooked rows had been periodically laid with tar but the dust
beneath was always present, always perceptible. In fact, it
managed to escape from under the asphalt and to rise and
spread through the town, summer and winter, a constant
presence, thick enough to be seen and felt. During the monsoon, always brief and disappointing on this northern plain
more than a thousand miles from the coast, it turned to mud.
But the sun came out again very soon and dried it to its
usual grey and granular form. The citizens of Mirpore, petty
tradesmen rather than agriculturists, could not be blamed for
failing to understand those patriotic songs and slogans about
the soil, the earth. To them it was so palpably dust.

History had scattered a few marks and imprints here and

there but no one in Mirpore thought much of them and certainly gave them no honour in the form of special signs, space or protection. The small mosque of marble and pink sandstone that had been built by a nawab who had fled from the retaliatory action of the British in Delhi after the mutiny of 1857 and wished to commemorate his safe escape to this obscure and thankfully forgotten town, and also to raise a memorial to the grace of God who, he believed, had made it possible, was now so overgrown by the shacks, signboards, stalls, booths, rags, banners, debris and homeless poor of the bazaars that it would have been difficult for anyone to discern it beneath this multi-layered covering. Its white marble facings had turned grey and pock-marked through urban pollution, the black marble inlay had either fallen out or been picked out by sharp instruments held in idle hands, the red sandstone of the dome had turned to the colour of filth from the smoke of open fires, the excreta of pigeons, and the ubiquitous dust of Mirpore. It was by no means forgotten, it was still used, five times a day the priest gave the call to the faithful, and many men came in, washed in the shallow pool and knelt and prayed in the small courtyard amongst the brooms and cooking fires, but not one of them thought of it as an historical landmark or remembered the man who had built it or his reasons for doing so.

The temples were more numerous but had no history at all. There was literally not a man in Mirpore who could have told one when they were built or by whom. If one enquired, one might be told that a bright pink and white concrete structure with a newly-painted clay idol and fluorescent tubes for lights was five hundred years old; not strictly true of course but when one considered that its site might have been used for prayer that long, it was not all that false either. The temples had the same kind of antiquity that the shacks of the poor had, and the stalls of the traders – they were often wrecked, rebuilt and replaced, but their essential form remained the same. There were also small stone shrines, mere apertures in walls, or half-smothered by the roots of rapacious banyan trees, that might have been truly old, but although

20

some might have been able to provide them with legends, none could supply them with a history. The fact was that no one knew the difference.

Lacking a river, the town had an artificial tank in which people bathed and from which they fetched water although there was no water to be seen in it, only a covering layer of bright green scum on which bits of paper, rags and flowers rested as on a solid surface. There were wells, too, in which the water was even more successfully concealed. Mirpore spared no effort to give an impression of total aridity. Lately a canal had been dug to water the fields of an agricultural college but it was dug behind the houses that lay on the outskirts, hidden by their walls, and few town dwellers knew of its existence. Their lives were lived almost entirely within the bazaars that joined – and separated – the different religious shrines.

Naturally the area around the mosque was considered the 'Muslim' area, and the rest 'Hindu'. This was not strictly so and there were certainly no boundaries or demarcations, yet there were differences between them that were not apparent to the eye but known and observed by everyone, so that pigs were generally kept out of the vicinity of the mosque and cows never slaughtered near a temple. Once a year, during the Mohurram procession of *tazias* through the city, police sprang up everywhere with batons, sweating with a sense of responsibility and heightened tension, intent on keeping the processions away from the temples and from hordes of home-less cows or from groups of gaily coloured citizens who unfortunately often celebrated Holi with packets of powdered colours and buckets of coloured water on the same day as that of the ritual mourning. If these clashed, as happened from time to time, knives flashed, batons flailed and blood ran. For a while tension was high, the newspapers – both in Hindi and Urdu – were filled with guarded reports and fulsome editorials on India's secularity while overnight news-sheets appeared with less guarded reports laced with threats and accusations. Then the dust of Mirpore rose and swirled and buried everything in sight again; the citizens of Mirpore

21

returned to their daily struggle to breathe. The Hindus slaughtered pigs in their own quarter, the Muslims took to slaughtering buffaloes in place of cows, realizing that the latter would have been tantamount to suicide. The few Christians of the town ate the meat of both and attended the one small whitewashed brick church set in a cemetery shaded by dusty *neem* trees.

But where was the centre of this formless, shapeless town on the plain that had not even a river or a hill to give it any reason for its existence? Was it the main bazaar, skirted by mosque, temples, stores, shops and cinema houses, or was it the shabby municipal park where concrete benches stood in a circle around an empty fountain painted blue – again, Mirpore's addiction to total dehydration – and broken bricks edged flowerbeds that contained empty tins and paper bags but no flowers? Here, through parched hedges of oleander and the yellowed foliage of *neem* trees, the bungalows of some of the town functionaries, such as the sub-divisional officer and the superintendent of police could be seen, as well as the Public Works Department's rest house, the college where Deven taught, and some of the schools. These educational institutions were named after, respectively, Lala Ram Lal, Mahatma Gandhi, Swami Dayanand, Annie Besant, bluebells and sunshine. Except for the latter, none had ever visited Mirpore but their fame and the power of their images had not left the town unimpressed, for Mirpore was isolated but not cut off from the world, as Deven had come to believe. It had its railway station, after all, at one end of the bazaar, and the bus depot at the other, and the constant comings and goings of trains and buses gave it an air of being a halting place in a long journey, a caravanserai of a kind. People went up to Delhi to consult doctors in the big hospitals there, present petitions to various government departments, appear in the courts, sell goods or else take delivery of them. Others merely passed through, peering out of smeared train windows and wondering how much longer it would take to Delhi, or reaching out to buy oranges, lengths of sugar cane, dry gram or the particular sweet for which Mirpore was known. (This latter consisted of a shiny yellow stuff that was shaped into balls on which flies crawled as if in animated illustration of the laws of gravity.) Then they would move on, unreluctantly. This had the effect of making Mirpore seem in a state of perpetual motion. There was really more of bustle than doldrums and it was often deafening. Yet the bustle was strangely unproductive – the yellow sweets were amongst the very few things that were actually manufactured here; there was no construction to speak of, except the daily one of repairing; no growth except in numbers, no making permanent what had remained through the centuries so stubbornly temporary – and it was other cities, other places that saw the fruits of all the bustle, leaving the debris and the litter behind for Mirpore.

Its solidity, its stubborness had formed a trap, Deven felt, and yet it was so easy to leave it behind. No sooner had he got into the bus that waited at the depot between the grain and vegetable markets, than it started off with a snarl and jerked its way over the railway crossing, edging out of the way a herd of sluggish buffaloes, a bullock cart loaded with sugar cane and several bicycles, every one of which seemed to carry not only a bicyclist and a milk can but also an aged mother on the carrier seat, and then rumbled past the graffiti-scarred yellow walls of the Lala Ram Lal College, its dust field and barbed wire fencing, past the red brick walls of the Swami Dayanand Veterinary and Agricultural College which seemed to have no human population but was set in surprisingly lush grounds of green, waving grain and bougainvillaeas that ran rampant along the boundary fence, several outhouses full of mud and dung and domestic beasts, and then it was out in the countryside.

Of course the stretch of land between Mirpore and the capital was so short that there was no really rural scenery – most of the fields looked withered and desolate, and tin smokestacks exhaling enormous quantities of very black and foul-smelling smoke, sugar-cane crushing works, cement factories, brick kilns, motor repair workshops and the attendant teashops and bus-stops were strung along the highway on both sides, overtaking what might once have been a pleasant agricultural aspect and obliterating it with all the litter and paraphernalia and effluent of industry: concrete, zinc, smoke, pollutants, decay and destruction from which emerged, reportedly, progress and prosperity. There were many huge signboards proclaiming this hard-to-believe message, with pictures of small, smiling families and big tractors and tyres.

Deven was determined, however, to enjoy it purely for its novelty. As a student he had known the countryside only as a background for an occasional picnic with his friends: they had gone out into it on their bicycles, bought sugar cane from some surly farmer and sat in the shade of a ruined monument to chew it and sing songs from the latest cinema show and talk lewdly of cinema actresses. That countryside had had no more connection with the landscape celebrated in the poetry he read than the present one. Then, after he graduated and married and came to Mirpore to teach, it became for him the impassable desert that lay between him and the capital with its lost treasures of friendships, entertainment, attractions and opportunities. It turned into that strip of no-man's land that lies around a prison, threatening in its desolation.

Now he peered at it through a glass pane filmed with dust and gave an apprehensive shiver, just as a released prisoner might. This made his pale green nylon shirt crackle with latent electricity, reminding him how it had arrived, with his wife, after her last visit to her parents' home in Haldwani, an ingratiating present to their sullen son-in-law who had to be placated and kept contented if their daughter was not to suffer from ill treatment. He had tossed it on to the floor in an obligatory fit of temper – the meek are not always mild – saying the colour was one he detested, that the buttons did not match, that the size was too large – how could they have chosen such a cheap garment for their son-in-law? Did they think him worth no more than this? Sarla had picked it up, folded it silently and put it away in a shoe-box – for malice is often mute. This morning he had ordered her to take it out for him to wear on his trip to Delhi. He had tried to ignore her smirk as she shook it out and laid it across his bed. Now he fingered the buttons he had said did not match and stared through the streaked and stained windowpane at a grove of *neem* trees outside, an occasional Persian wheel and slow, dragging buffaloes, and tried to convince himself that he was actually on his way to Delhi to see a poet, his hero, and talk to him. Nothing in his life had prepared him for an occasion of this scale. Neither the bus drive nor the nylon shirt helped.

His large, turbanned neighbour, noticing his occasional tremors of apprehension, offered him some peanuts in a paper bag, asking at the same time, 'Going to Delhi?'

Deven refused the peanuts but had to admit to the latter since the bus went nowhere but to Delhi where it turned around and brought back another load of passengers to Mirpore.

'I am also going,' his neighbour confided with some pride, spreading out his thighs in an expansive gesture. 'My nephew's first birthday. His mother said come, you must come, it is the first birthday. So I closed down my shop for the day, gave up a day's earnings to go. You know what sort of people we are – ', he put his hand on his shirt pocket, pressing it with spread fingers. 'When it is a choice between head and heart, we always choose heart, na? Not much head after all,' he guffawed and crunched down upon a peanut shell, cracking it open .

He was about to give a full account of his business when the bus swerved suddenly and wildly to avoid a stray dog slouching across the road, struck it on its hindquarters, sent it rolling and howling into the roadside ditch and plunged on through a bank of yellow dust, leaving the occupants choking, coughing and crying out in protest, anger, warning and commiseration.

It made Deven give another, more violent shiver. Again the nylon shirt responded wih an electric crackle, as if it were an embodiment of Sarla's malice and mockery. His fear and loathing of acts of violence and pain were overcome by irritation. It was sadly disappointing to him that he was not travelling up to Delhi on this important occasion in a style more suited to a literary man, a literary event. He had never found a way to reconcile the meanness of his physical existence with the purity and immensity of his literary yearnings. The latter were constantly assaulted and wrecked by the former – as now in the form of the agonized dog, the jolting bus, the peanut-crunching neighbour, the little tin box in which Sarla had packed his lunch and which he kept wrapped in a news-paper, the smallness of the sum of money he carried in his pocket: all these indignities and impediments. How, out of such base material, was he to wrest a meeting with a great poet, some kind of dialogue with him, some means of ensur-ing that this rare opportunity would not also turn to dust, spilled blood and lament?

He turned and peered out of the window to see if the dog lay on the road, broken, bleeding, or dead. He saw a flock of crows alight on the yellow grass that grew beside the ditch, their wings flickering across the view like agitated eyelashes.

'It seems to be dead,' he murmured, unable to contain his unease. Was it an omen?

'Fortunate for the dog if it is,' said his neighbour philo-sophically, and drew a deep breath that made the mucus gurgle in his large nostrils. It might have been done in sorrow, or in satisfaction; it was hard to tell from his impassive expression. 'Birth and death, and only suffering in between,' he added, quite cheerfully. This seemed to have no relation to what he had told Deven previously of his life. 'When God calls us away,' he went on , 'it is a blessing.'

The lack of connection between the man's thought and speech made a break in Deven's own line of thought. He surprised himself by suddenly quoting aloud some lines of Nur's that rose in his mind, the ones about the first white hair on a man's head appearing like a white flower out of a grave. Having recalled these lines, he went on:

> 'Life is no more than a funeral procession winding
>   towards the grave,
> Its small joys the flowers of funeral wreaths . . . '

Silence followed this quotation while the bus bumped loudly and ground and overtook a bullock cart and a lorry while the two men, sitting uneasily side by side, tried to adjust them-selves to the exacting presence of poetry between them.

'Ha, that is wonderful,' said the turbanned man, slowly shaking his head as if it had received a blow. 'You are a poet,' he added respectfully, turning to look at Deven with open curiosity. He had a cast in one eye that made him look as if he knew something that Deven didn't, and that put Deven on the defensive.

'No, no,' he muttered, 'only a – a teacher.' Hunching his shoulders, he relapsed into his usual anxious and sullen persona.

This information appeared to make his neighbour distinctly uneasy. His large, heavy buttocks shifted away from Deven's meagre shanks. He neither spoke to Deven again nor offered him any more peanuts. Instead, he turned his garrulous atten-tion to the man across the aisle from him who had a milk can wedged between his feet, a dusty turban wound round his head, a green eye-patch covering one eye, and with whom he fell to discussing the rising prices, the increase in lawless-ness and the last harvest.

Excluded, Deven stared out at the white dust and the yellow weeds, the leafless thorn trees, the broken fences, isolated tin and brick shacks and the scattered carcasses of cattle that littered the landscape and yet rendered it more bleak and more bare under the empty sky. His chin sank low as he wondered what had made him set out this morning with such confidence and excitement. Now he was convinced that Murad had not meant any of what he had said, that he would let him down as so often before and that he would not meet the illustrious poet after all. How could he, insignificant and gullible nobody that he was? And if he did, if somehow such a miracle did come about merely to prove him wrong once again, then what could he possibly say to him? Why had he not been content to recite his verse, draw solace from it and impress others with the source of his solace? What mad-ness had drawn him out to undertake this journey into what could only be disaster?

He hung around the Inter-State Bus Terminal on Ring Road for a long time, not daring to enter the city walls and search out Murad's office in Kashmere Gate and so set in motion the events of the day to which he knew he would not measure up. What vainglory to have accepted Murad's challenge, to have agreed to a task for which he was not qualified, for which he had neither the experience nor the confidence. He realized that he and Murad were no more than a pair of undeveloped, clownish students who could not hope to pass the examination of life. Clowns: that was how Nur would see them when they impudently burst upon him, uninvited, self-invited, and put to him their presumptuous questions and requests.

This reminded him – he clutched at his pocket – was the questionnaire still there? The questionnaire he had been working on night after night ever since Murad's visit? Yes, he could feel the wad of papers under his fingers, consoling in their number and solidity. He was a scholar after all, and a lover of poetry. There was that. Sighing, he drew out a cigarette from between its folds and went towards a teashop to light it at the smouldering length of rope that hung from one of the door posts precisely for this purpose.

Seeing him there, the teashop owner called, 'Come in, come in. Don't stand outside. You need a cup of tea after your long journey, my son,' and although Deven had resolved to spend nothing on extras, to keep to only the most essential expenditure, he was led by the teashop owner's suggestion just as helplessly as he had been led by Murad's, and he shambled in to sit down on a wooden bench along the wall and accept a glass of sweet, milky tea: he did, after all, need something to see him through the most momentous day of his adult life. Certainly he had never felt more inadequate and the measure of his inadequacy must be in proportion to the importance of the task that had been set him. By whom? By Murad of the betel-stained teeth, the toothbrush moustache, the fiddling, shifty, untrustworthy ways? Impossible. He saw the hand of God as clearly as if it were the shaft of dust-laden light filtering through a hole in the corrugated iron roof of the teashop and striking the handle of a ladle with which the owner was stirring a great pan of steaming milk upon a small charcoal fire.

When he had drunk to the bottom of the glass, he saw a dead fly floating in the dregs of his tea.

The gasp he gave was only partly of horror at the teashop owner's filthiness and the wretched standards of hygiene in his shop. Or even from a fear of typhoid and cholera. It was the revelation that all the omens of the day had come together and met at the bottom of the glass he held between his fingers. In it lay the struck dog, the triumphant crows, the dead fly – death itself, nothing less. Coming together in the separate prisms of the fly's eye, drowned but glittering in the tea, it stared back at him without blinking.

Putting down the glass, he got up and crept out of its way quietly while the teashop owner shouted jovially at the passengers who were tumbling out of the next bus: 'Come this way, friends, come this way. Here you will find *pakoras* fried in purest oil, sweets made of purest milk, and the tea with most sugar. This way, friends, this way!'

Murad came charging down the steep wooden staircase to meet him on the pavement outside the drycleaner's shop where Deven was still studying the clutter of signboards above the door, saying, 'Snowflake Dyers and Cleaners', 'K. K. Sahay & Sons – Printers and Publishers since 1935', amongst a plethora of others, all equally aged and faded. Murad arrived at his side, gasping for breath: it seemed he had either been watching for Deven from an upstairs window or had posted someone else to do so. But who else would have recognized him in this city? He had not returned to it since he left after his graduation when, one might have said, the dew was still fresh on him, while now he was, or at any rate felt, withered and grey. Murad stood breathing hard, holding on to the doorpost on either side of him. Did he not want Deven to see his office, evaluate the degree of the success or failure of the journal and ascertain if Murad really was in a position to commission poets and scholars to write for him?

Deven had to have verification. He said testily, 'What is all this hurry?'

'Of course there's a hurry,' Murad gasped. 'Didn't I tell you – the appointment is for three o'clock? There's just time to go and have lunch.'

'I've had my lunch,' Deven said loudly and positively: he was not going to be taken in by Murad again, so soon after the last time.

'Tea then,' Murad pleaded.

'I've had tea, too,' Deven insisted. 'Let us go and see Nur!'

Murad's shoulders sloped precipitously and he seemed to be having some trouble with his right eye: he kept dabbing at it with a corner of a large and dirty green handkerchief. Stooped and sniffling and silent, he set off, pushing his way through the lunch-hour crowds of Kashmere Gate, and Deven had to hurry after him. But when Murad stopped, it was only at an electrician's shop to ask if some repair work to an electric lamp had been done. Deven stood beside the gutter, trying to avoid being pushed in by the crowds, while Murad argued heatedly with the electrician who had been interrupted while eating his lunch out of a small tin box and was not very polite either.

'Once you put something into the hands of these rogues, you can just say goodbye,' Murad said bitterly, turning away when the electrician shouted loudly over his shoulder for a glass of buttermilk, and starting back the way he had come.

'But, Murad – where is Nur's house? Aren't we late?'

'Late? Who says we are late? Do you think that old man has any idea of time? Let him wait,' said Murad, showing yet another switch of mood as if playing with some interior kaleidoscope. Deven had been watching these shifts and switches helplessly since their schooldays in the back lanes of Darya Ganj but found himself still amazed and enraged by them.

'We can't let him wait,' he said with some heat. 'He mustn't be kept waiting. We are to be there at three – is it far?'

'Who knows?' Murad shrugged with maddening non-chalance. 'He lives somewhere in the bazaars of Chandni

Chowk – it's not a quarter I know,' he added loftily, with a sniff and a dab at his eye.

'But then – how are we to go there? I thought you must know it,' Deven cried in dismay. He often had nightmares in which he struggled towards an unspecified destination but was repeatedly waylaid and deflected, never in any stretch of sleep arriving at it any more than he did in waking. His feet seemed to be enmeshed in the sticky net of the nightmare that would not let him escape at any level of consciousness.

Just then an ash-smeared *sadhu* wearing a python draped over his neck and shoulders and a garland of marigolds on top of his head but nothing on the lower regions, thrust his begging bowl at Deven's face and stood firmly between him and Murad. Deven looked helplessly into the bowl which made the *sadhu* rattle the few coins he had there loudly as if he were addressing a deaf man. Intimidated, Deven took out a coin from his pocket and dropped it in so that he would be left alone. He waited cautiously to make sure the python would not rear suddenly at him and strike – who knew what the creature had been taught to do by its savage trainer? – then ran after Murad who was slipping through the crowds as if the way was greased.

'That snake scared you, didn't it?' Murad grinning at him sideways, mischievously, when he caught up with him. 'What a fool you are to give it money – don't you know their fangs are removed and they are harmless?'

'Pythons are not poisonous – any child knows that,' Deven replied with dignity, glad of an opportunity to recover some. 'I just had to get rid of the *sadhu*. What are you in such a hurry for now? You said Nur doesn't care about time.'

'But I have to get back to the office, don't I? D'you think I earn my living by loitering in the streets? I've work to do.'

'Look, Murad,' Deven said heatedly, 'you are supposed to take me to Nur. That is what you called me to Delhi for and I have spent my free day and a good deal of money on the bus fare for this purpose. Now you tell me you are not going to take me to him.'

'I'm not stopping you. Go. Why must I take you? Are you

31

a baby? Are you frightened of him? D'you think he might be a python?' Murad gave a jeering laugh. 'Go, go and see him, interview him, write an article for my paper – I will see it, I will print it. But I can't nurse my contributors as if they are babies, can I?'

'Then give me his address,' Deven said furiously, 'and I will go myself.'

'Don't shout,' Murad said with a sudden grin, slowing down and taking his arm. 'Don't shout in the street. This is not your village, you know. People don't need to shout as if they are at opposite ends of a potato field. You are in a city now. Better act like a city dweller if you want to work for my paper. Come along with me to my office and I'll write out a letter of introduction for you and send along my office boy to show you the way. Will that do, my lord?' Deven couldn't tell whether his grin was malicious or merely mischievous. Not being able to tell made him helpless.

'All right,' he muttered, just as he had done when, as schoolboys, Murad had come to stand outside his house and bellowed an invitation to join a cricket game in the fields below the city walls. Reluctantly, because he was no sportsman and saw both bat and ball as unnecessary and hostile, he had changed from his pyjamas into his shorts and gone down only to find Murad strolling away, whistling and pretending that now there had been such a delay he did not feel like playing after all. Enraged because he had been made to change and give up his reading, he had turned hysterical in his insistence that they go and join the game. When he had got him thoroughly maniacal, Murad would suddenly grin and agree to go along. Deven remembered the shifting expression on the boys' faces as Murad approached – his inconsistency and contrariness threatened the precise rules and progression of their games, leading them inevitably to collapse in temper, tantrums and uproar. He could see Murad had not changed, yet he had no alternative, having come so far, but to say 'all right'.

At least he would see Murad's office and find out how much of his description of it was truth and how much fantasy.

So he followed Murad doggedly along the pavement, edging past the bicycle repair shops, the fried fritter stalls and the shoeshine boys and lottery ticket sellers, weaving through crowds of office-goers returning after their lunch and housewives with large shopping bags and bemused afternoon faces. He was thinking that the great city was no different from his own small town and that the dissimilarity lay only in scale: this was certainly larger, noisier, more crowded and chaotic, but that was all, and it was the scale and not the unfamiliarity that made him feel so small, weak and inadequate, when they arrived at the staircase beside the drycleaner's shop that bore the sign 'K. K. Sahay & Sons, Printers and Publishers since 1935', but nothing closer than that to paper or periodical. So he was relieved when he found, at the head of the stairs, not only the dark, clattering and clanking printing works but also a corner that seemed actually to belong to Murad. Here were desks, shelves, even a clerk rolling up magazines in brown paper and addressing them in sticky black ink, as well as an office boy squatting on his heels and washing some cups and spoons in a bucket of water that had already seen much washing. This office appeared to spill out on to the wrought-iron balcony where files and bundles of magazines were stacked high against the railing. Bamboo screens hanging by strings from the rafters had been lowered and attached to the railing to prevent them from being blown out into the street below by the dusty gusts of March wind, but all the same there was a great deal of litter blowing around in restless eddies.

Deven could not help staring open-mouthed at these arrangements. They were not at all what he had imagined – and no one could possibly have been impressed by the scene, yet the very fact that it existed seemed a miracle and he stood summoning up gratitude for the fact out of the conflict of disappointment and amazement.

Murad was clapping an elderly, bewhiskered man on the shoulder as he stooped over a tray of newsprint, grinning proudly at Deven and saying, 'This is my landlord, my patron, my mentor – Mr V. K. Sahay, son of K. K. Sahay, the founder of the best Urdu printing press in Delhi. When I told him I was going to start a high-class Urdu magazine, he offered me a part of his premises, he was so impressed – nah, V. K. Sahib?'

The old man squirmed and gave a vague smile, settling the spectacles on the bridge of his nose with a nervous push of his ink-stained fingers. 'That is not quite the way I remember it, Murad-*bhai*,' he murmured. 'Wasn't it you who – '

'Of course he hasn't given me an electric point for a lamp or a fan yet,' Murad interrupted quickly, 'and it seems he is slowly edging me out on to the balcony now that he is getting more and more orders and becoming a success – '

Now it was the printer who interrupted him. 'It is the UP Government schools' text books, Murad-*bhai*, a very big order, you know, and they have to be ready before the new term begins. When I have them out of the way, you will get more room.'

'For six months you have been saying that.' Murad gave his shoulders one last squeeze and then let him go. 'Come, Deven, now let me see what I can do for you. These writers, these contributors,' he threw over his shoulder at the old man, 'they never leave an editor in peace, and one has to look after them, nah?'

Deven sat bemused upon a wooden stool in the shadows, watching Murad pass through one act after another like some chameleon giving a bravura performance. Considering the full range of his moods and shifts in temper, his contradictions and discrepancies, he wondered why he had trusted his word, taken it seriously enough to use his one free day to catch a bus to Delhi and let himself in for making a fool of himself in the presence of no other than the greatest living poet of Delhi, his hero since childhood. Ought he to approach him with a letter of introduction from so unworthy a go-between as Murad? Was that not a kind of sacrilege to the life of his imagination, his mind?

Murad was bent over the desk, writing out a letter on a large sheet of paper with many a flourish, knowing he was being watched, studied. Handing it over at last and instructing

the small office boy to show him the way, he gave Deven a
hint of a wink, as though admitting it was a practical joke he
was playing. He covered it up immediately with a corner of
his dirty green handkerchief but Deven turned grey with
apprehension.

He stood hesitating, wondering if he ought to go. But
when Murad looked at him in inquiry, he said only, in a
mumble, 'I'll leave this here – pick it up later,' and dropped
the tin box containing his lunch on the stool from which he
had risen, then left holding only the newspaper wrapping.

CHAPTER THREE

If it had not been for the colour and the noise, Chandni
Chowk might have been a bazaar encountered in a nightmare;
it was so like a maze from which he could find no exit, in
which he wandered between the peeling, stained walls of
office buildings, the overflowing counters of shops and stalls,
wondering if the urchin sent to lead him through it was not
actually a malevolent imp leading him to his irrevocable
disappearance in the reeking heart of the bazaar. The heat and
the crowds pressed down from above and all sides, solid and
suffocating as sleep.

With the accuracy of his malevolence, the boy suggested
'Cold drink?' at a stall where poison-green and red sherbets
in bottles topped with lemons and carrot juice in damp,
oozing earthen jars were in great demand.

Deven shook his head contemptuously and they walked on
down the sari lane where lurid Japanese nylon saris covered
with octopi and spiders of flower patterns and nets of gold
and silver embroidery flashed from doorways like gaudy but
shimmering prostitutes propositioning the passers-by, while
the rich soft traditional silks were folded and stacked in sober,
matronly bales at the back. Shopkeepers eyed them casually
but did not rise from their bolsters or cease to pick their toes,
in order to attract their attention; they were so obviously not
worth any.

They turned into the food lanes where there was little

36

custom at this hour and flies were allowed to nuzzle the pyramids of crystallized fruit undisturbed and milk steamed and bubbled in drowsy pans.

They walked past shady-looking and evil-smelling shops where herbal medicines and panaceas were being wrapped in paper packets by men who looked too ostentatiously like quacks, past booths in which astrologers and palmists and soothsayers had spread out the exotic tools of their trade - elaborately illustrated scrolls, mynah birds in cages, birthstones and gems in open boxes – and pavement stalls where scarves and handkerchiefs and underwear were heaped in mounds of starched cotton, or thick glasses and enamel plates balanced on each other in precarious display, and came out into a circle lined with silversmiths and jewellery shops.

Here Deven halted in despair. He knew he could not be near the poet's residence in this pullulating honeycomb of commerce. Spreading out his arms, he told the boy, 'We must be lost. This is not the right place. It is no use to go further. I'm not going on.' His desperation made the blood beat in his ears so that he didn't hear the frantic ringing of a bicycle bell and was very nearly run over by a cycle rickshaw heavily loaded with parcels heading for the railway station. Its driver, acrobatic as a monkey with a red cap, managed to swerve in time, doing no more than running over Deven's foot, but his parcels slid off the slippery rexine seat and were scattered over the street. Deven was so dazed by this near-accident that it took him a while to realize he was being accused of having caused it, and abused filthily and loudly. The boy was helping the rickshaw driver collect the parcels but when Deven bent to help, he was shoved aside by a blow from his elbow and forced to move on. Breathlessly they hurried down a narrow lane that was lined with nothing but gutters and seemed to serve as a latrine for the entire neighbourhood. The high green walls that threw it into deep shadows belonged to a hospital of *ayurvedic* medicine. It was as gloomy as a prison.

Deven broke into a hobble in order to get to the end of it

without inhaling the sickly air there. The boy pursued him, panting, 'Cup of tea? Here's a teashop – have a cup of tea at least, sahib.'

'No, no tea,' Deven hissed at him. 'I want to get to Nur Sahib's house by three o'clock. Where is it? Do you know where it is or not?'

'Very far,' said the boy, gazing back at him steadily and standing firm outside the tea stall where packets of tea and baskets of eggs dangled in the sooty doorway in invitation. 'It will be better to have some tea and a rest first.'

'*No* rest, *no* tea,' Deven bawled at him, bending down to bare his teeth in the boy's face.

The boy shrugged but his expression did not change. Stepping over a flowing gutter, shoving aside a great humped bull that was quietly munching paper bags from an open dustbin that lay on its side, spilling its contents across the gutter so that it was blocked and had begun to flood, he turned a corner into another lane. On one side of it stretched the high wall of the gloomy green hospital and along the other was a row of small, tightly shut wooden doors set into straight, faded walls. There was no signboard on any of them but the boy went up to one and beat on it with the palms of his hands till, after a long interval, it was opened.

Then Deven knew it was not the familiar nightmare because if it was, the door would have remained shut.

Before he could make out who had opened the door and now stood behind it, he heard an immense voice, cracked and hoarse and thorny, boom from somewhere high above their heads: 'Who is it that disturbs the sleep of the aged at this hour of the afternoon that is given to rest? It can only be a great fool. Fool, are you a fool?'

And Deven, feeling some taut membrane of reservation tear apart inside him and a surging expansion of joy at hearing the voice and the words that could only belong to that superior being, the poet, sang back, 'Sir, I am! I am!'

There was an interval and then some mutters of astonishment and horror at this admission. In that quiet pause, pigeons

38

were heard to gurgle and flutter as if in warning from the wings.

'Shall I let him in?' called the opener of the door, still hidden behind it. It was a female voice, high-pitched and frayed with irritation.

'Bring him then,' moaned the poet in the upper reaches of the building which rose in tiers around a small inner courtyard where a tap dripped, a broken bicycle lay and a cat slept.

'I have been dreaming of fools,' the voice above went on muttering. 'I am surrounded by fools. Fools will follow me, pursue me and find me out and capture me so that in the end I myself will join their company. Bring him up then, bring him up,' and again Deven felt another warm, moist tide of jubilation rise and increase inside him at being recognized, named and invited into the presence of a man so clearly a hero. On tiptoe, trembling a little, he stepped over the high threshold into the house, then stopped, remembering the boy who had brought him here and the need to dismiss him. Surely he ought to be rewarded for his part in what had turned out to be a gloriously successful pursuit. His face lit to a radiance, he smiled at the boy and thrust the folded newspaper wrapping into his hands with benign absent-mindedness, then turned back into the house and, rejoicing, obeyed the wave of the henna-painted hand from behind the door and began to run up flight after flight of wooden stairs from which dust rose at every step.

It was to him as if God had leaned over a cloud and called for him to come up, and angels might have been drawing him up these ancient splintered stairs to meet the deity: so jubilantly, so timorously, so gratefully did he rise. This, surely, was the summons for which he had been waiting all these empty years, only he had not known it would assume this form. In his mortal myopia and stupidity, he had expected it to come from Sarla when he married her, or from the head of the department at his college who alone could promote and demote and alter his situation in life, or even from Murad who, after all, lived in the metropolis and edited a magazine. The poetry he had read and memorized lay beneath all these

39

visible tips of his submerged existence, and he had thought of it more as a source of comfort and consolation than as a promise of salvation. He had never conceived of a summons expressed in a voice so leonine, splendid and commanding, a voice that could grasp him, as it were, by the roots of his hair and haul him up from the level on which he existed – mean, disordered and hopeless – into another, higher sphere. Another realm it would surely be if his god dwelt there, the domain of poetry, beauty and illumination. He mounted the stairs as if sloughing off and casting away the meanness and dross of his past existence and steadily approaching a new and wondrously illuminated era.

Although there were no angels singing 'Hallelujah! Hallelujah!' in accompaniment, the pigeons cooed loudly with agitation and the old man could be heard muttering incredulously, 'Fool, says he's a fool – hah!' and Deven took that as sufficient invitation to enter.

The room in which the poet lay resting, like a great bolster laid on a flat low wooden divan, was in semi-darkness. Not only were the bamboo screens hanging in every doorway let down to keep out the sun that beat upon the top floor of the building most fiercely, but the walls were lined with dark green tiles that added to the shadowy gloom. The few pieces of furniture – a single armchair with elongated arms that seemed designed for some earlier, larger species of man, a small gate-legged table piled with very shabby books, a revolving bookcase with more of them, several solid cushions and bolsters cast upon the cotton mats on the floor, were like objects carved out of this murkiness, heavy and palpable with gloom.

In the midst of all the shadows, the poet's figure was in startling contrast, being entirely dressed in white. His white beard was splayed across his chest and his long white fingers clasped across it. He did not move and appeared to be a marble form. His body had the density, the compactness of stone. It was large and heavy not on account of obesity or weight, but on account of age and experience. The emptying out and wasting of age had not yet begun its process. He was still at a moment of completion, quite whole. This gave him the power and the dignity to be able to say to the intruding stranger, in a murmur, 'Who gave you permission to disturb me?'

'Sir,' croaked Deven, fumbling in his shirt pocket for Murad's letter, 'I have a letter here – '

'Couldn't it wait?' sighed the old man in a fading voice. Was he drifting back into sleep? There was an age, after all, when the difference between sleep and waking became very faint and could be crossed at ease, continually.

'Sir, I have come to Delhi only for one day. I must return to my college in Mirpore,' Deven stammered. 'I have a letter here from Murad Beg – editor of *Awaaz* – '

'Can't you see, it is too dark for me to read? I am resting. I don't know where my spectacles are. Read it to me. Now that you have ruined my sleep you might as well read it to me.'

Deven unfolded the letter, trying to hush the loud crackling made by the sheets of paper, and then tried to read audibly and smoothly Murad's floridly written letter of introduction. It flustered him to have to read the flattering names Murad had called him, just as the wheedling, begging tone of his request for an interview made him uncomfortable. A poet of such godlike magnitude ought to have been presented with a prayer or a petition but not with flattery or bribes.

It made the old man on the bed curl up his lips and make a spitting sound through his beard. He unclasped his thin fine fingers with their pale, fish-like skin and fish-like spattering of the brown freckles of age, and waved them dismissively. 'That joker – he should paint his face, wear a false nose, and perform in a travelling circus,' he said derisively. 'Are you a part of his circus?'

'No, no, sir,' Deven protested, still standing stooped over the letter in his hand, not quite read to the end. 'I sometimes – he sometimes asks me to contribute to his magazine. He has asked me to interview you for the special issue on Urdu poetry. It is a great honour for me, sir, a great privilege. I mean, if you allow me – ' he added quickly, looking anxious.

41

Should he have told the poet about the monograph he had written on him and that still awaited publication? Or would the poet consider that presumptuous rather than flattering? He hesitated.

The house was very still, miraculously silent. The tall hospital walls cut it off from the hubbub of the bazaar, Deven supposed. All he could hear were the pigeons complaining to and consoling each other up on the dusty ledges of the high skylights, and the laboured sound of the poet's breath, snarled in his throat with some elderly phlegm.

'Urdu poetry?' he finally sighed, turning a little to one side, towards Deven although not actually addressing himself to a person, merely to a direction, it seemed. 'How can there be Urdu poetry when there is no Urdu language left? It is dead, finished. The defeat of the Moghuls by the British threw a noose over its head, and the defeat of the British by the Hindi-wallahs tightened it. So now you see its corpse lying here, waiting to be buried.' He tapped his chest with one finger.

'No, sir, please don't talk like that,' Deven said eagerly, perspiration breaking out on his upper lip and making it glisten. 'We will never allow that to happen. That is why Murad is publishing his journal. And the printing press where it is published is for printing Urdu books, sir. They are getting large orders even today. And my college – it is only a small college, a private college outside Delhi – but it has a department of Urdu – '

'Do you teach there?' A wrinkled eyelid moved, like a turtle's, and a small, quick eye peered out at Deven as if at a tasty fly.

Deven shrank back in apology. 'No, sir, I teach in – in the Hindi department. I took my degree in Hindi because –'

But the poet was not listening. He was laughing and spitting as he laughed because he did it so rustily and unwillingly. Phlegm flew. 'You see,' he croaked, 'what did I tell you? Those Congress-wallahs have set up Hindi on top as our ruler. You are its slave. Perhaps a spy even if you don't know it, sent to the universities to destroy

42

whatever remains of Urdu, hunt it out and kill it. And you tell me it is for an Urdu magazine you wish to interview me. If so, why are you teaching Hindi?' he suddenly roared, fixing Deven with that small, turtle-lidded eye that had now become lethal, a bullet.

'I studied Urdu, sir, as a boy, in Lucknow. My father, he was a schoolteacher, a scholar, and a lover of Urdu poetry. He taught me the language. But he died. He died and my mother brought me to Delhi to live with her relations here. I was sent to the nearest school, a Hindi-medium school, sir,' Deven stumbled through the explanation. 'I took my degree in Hindi, sir, and now I am temporary lecturer in Lala Ram Lal College at Mirpore. It is my living, sir. You see I am a married man, a family man. But I still remember my lessons in Urdu, how my father taught me, how he used to read poetry to me. If it were not for the need to earn a living, I would – I would – ' Should he tell him his aspirations, scribbled down on pieces of paper and hidden between the leaves of his books?

'Oh, earning a living?' mocked the old man as Deven struggled visibly with his diffidence. 'Earning a living comes first, does it? Why not trade in rice and oil if it is a living you want to earn?"'

Crushed, Deven's shoulders sagged. 'I am – only a teacher, sir,' he murmured, 'and must teach to support my family. But poetry – Urdu – these are – one needs, I need to serve them to show my appreciation. I cannot serve them as you do – '

'You don't look fit to serve anyone, let alone the muse of Urdu,' the old man retorted, his voice gaining strength from indignation. Or perhaps he was wider awake now; he sounded upright even if he was still reclining. 'Sit down,' he commanded. 'There, on that stool. Bring it closer to me first. Close. Here, at my side. Now sit. It seems you have been sent here to torment me, to show me to what depths Urdu has fallen. All right then, show me, let me know the worst.' He rolled out the syllables, in a lapidarian voice, as if he were inscribing an epitaph. 'I am prepared for suffering.

43

Through suffering, I shall atone for my sins.' He groaned. 'Many, many sins,' and shifted on the wooden bed as if in pain.

Deven, to his astonishment, heard himself repeat the poet's familiar words as he had heard his father recite them to him when he had sat beside him on the mat in the corner of the verandah of the old house. *'Through suffering I shall atone for my sins.'* He repeated it twice, and then, as if unwinding a kite's thread from the spool that his memory still held, he went on reciting that great poem of Nur's that his father had loved to recite and that he still read, ceremoniously, whenever he felt sad or nostalgic and thought of his father and his early childhood and all that he had lost. It rose above him into that upper realm occupied by poetry and hovered over their heads, an airborne kite.

> 'Many sins, and much suffering; such is the pattern
> Fate has traced on my tablet, with blood. . . .'

His voice grew steadier as he found his memory not failing him but flooding in confidently and carrying him along on its strong current. He could almost feel the smoothness of his father's reed pens which he played with while he listened, and smell the somewhat musty, but human and comforting, odour of his father's black cotton coat with the missing buttons and the torn pockets, thickly darned at the corners. A tender, almost feminine lilt entered his voice with those memories and the poet listened engrossed, now and then joining in with his own cracked voice as if he had forgotten the lines and was happy to be reminded.

> 'My body no more than a reed pen cut by the sword's tip,
> Useless and dry till dipped in the ink of life's blood.'

He broke off, chuckling. 'Your pronunciation is good. Very clean, chaste. Do you remember more?' and Deven, swaying upon the stool, recited on and on in a voice that grew increasingly sing-song. As he continued, he began to be overcome by the curious sensation that he was his own mother, rocking back and forth on her heels as she half-sang, half-recited a story in the night, and that the white bolster-like figure on the bed beside him was a child, his child, whom he was lulling to sleep. He understood completely, in these minutes, how it must feel to be a mother, a woman. He had not known before such intimacy, such intense closeness as existed in that dark and shaded room where his voice merged with those of the pigeons to soothe the listening, lulled figure before him. He was also aware, with the welling up of a drop of sadness that now rose and trickled through him, moistly, that this moment that contained such perfection of feeling, unblemished and immaculate, could not last, must break and disperse.

When the mat in the doorway was lifted aside by a boy in striped pyjamas and a vest bringing in a tumbler of tea, that miraculous intimacy came to an abrupt end. It was not to be recovered. Nur angrily sent the boy away again to fetch tea for the guest but other people began to come in who must have been in the building all that time, asleep or biding their time, and took the bringing in of tea as a signal to come swarming up the stairs, into the room, filling it with noise. Deven looked across at the figure on the bed, helplessly, regretting that he had not even discussed the proposed interview with him. Now others demanded his attention while someone thrust a metal tumbler of scalding tea into Deven's hand. He nearly dropped it in agony, then recovered himself and clutched it with blistering fingertips while waiting for an opportunity to have another word with Nur.

There seemed little chance of that since the servant boy was demanding to know what Nur wanted for his dinner tonight, whether it was to be prepared at home or ordered from the bazaar; a child – too young to be his son, Deven thought, and wondered if it could be a grandchild – wandered around, whining petulantly for some money but when he was given it, flung it upon the floor and cried; then there were some young girls who came to pick up the crying child and carry him off, and were evidently surprised to find the room full of men for they hastily covered their heads with their veils and hurried away, grumbling at the invasion; also several loutish young men who stated they had been waiting downstairs to be summoned, had been playing cards at which all claimed to have lost money and demanded their host make up to them for their losses since he was responsible for them. Deven was scandalized by their audacity but the poet did not mind at all. Laughing, he reprimanded them for their dissolute habits and threatened them with expulsion from his home which was, he said, a temple of domesticity as they could see.

'Since when has Nur become the resident of such a temple?' challenged one of the men, pock-marked and not so young. 'We met in a temple of another sort. Have you forgotten?'

Deven flushed; it was not possible to misunderstand their innuendoes, they grew more blatant and ribald by the minute. It was the kind of talk Deven heard plenty of in and around the college, and had had much of when he had himself been a student, but he was not used to hearing it in the presence of the aged whom he had been brought up to consider very near sacred. The frequent use of the word temple made it still more blasphemous.

When he could stand it no longer, he got up to go. This movement attracted Nur's attention and he raised his hand to stop the chatter and asked Deven to help him out on to the terrace, 'to escape from these – these devils from the gambling dens and drinking houses of my past'. Deven came forward eagerly to support him but the poet, after placing his hand on Deven's shoulder, grew angry when it became clear that Deven did not know the procedure, the routine, and left behind such essential aids to his comfort as a footstool and a favourite bolster, so that the servant boy had to be sent for after all and Deven made to feel inadequate. When the boy appeared, more sullen than before, Deven tried to help him gather all the necessary cushions and bolsters to carry out to the terrace but found himself either ignored or rudely pushed out of the way. Was he wanted or not? he wondered.

46

Then his bewilderment and resentment were sent spinning with a few hard words from the poet that he brought out of the depths of his being as if they were the bile that had collected there. 'Wait till you are my age,' he spat, 'you – you boy without hair. Wait till you experience the afflictions I know. I sit upon them daily – not my crown but my throne of thorns. That is what piles are, my friend – oh, the pain, the suffering – ' he nearly wept, standing there in the middle of the room, wringing his hands while he waited to be led out.

Deven hung his head, then lowered himself on to his knees beside the bed, running his fingers over the poet's slippers and trying not to hear the poet's curses, wondering what he could pick up and offer.

When he got up from his knees, he saw the servant boy had led Nur out, the mat in the doorway was rolled up and the afternoon light stood there as solid as a pane of glittering glass. He hurried out after them to find the poet could proceed no further – a flock of pigeons had swooped down out of the coppery sky and blocked his way with their hurtling wings and violently struggling bodies. He stood there in the centre of their frenzy – slate, chocolate and snow – and the birds not only seethed around him but perched and teetered on his bald head and hands, furiously scrabbling with their hooked claws, raw and pink, and their gluttonous beaks as if they would tear the flesh from his bones and devour it if he had nothing else to give them. Their greed was monstrous, they coated him with their gluttony.

Deven stumbled forward to rescue him, but the poet did not want to be rescued. He merely cried out weakly to the servant boy to give them grain and Deven was relieved to see that they unfastened their hooks from his flesh and swarmed after the boy and his tin can of grain that he flung through the air and scattered over the terrace for them.

Deven waited till they had removed themselves to a distance, then hurried to Nur's side and asked solicitously, 'Sir, have they hurt you?'

The poet stood still for so long, still slightly trembling

from the assault, that Deven thought he was staring at the spectacle of the pigeons' frenzied feasting, but after a while he turned his head slowly towards Deven and gave him a strange look from his cataract-curtained eyes. 'Who would have thought,' he muttered, dry-lipped, 'that one day the bird, symbol of flight and song, would cease to be a poet's inspiration and become a threat?'

The words were spoken so slowly and with such precision that Deven could see them being etched in elegant hieroglyphs upon the copperplate of the Delhi sky. He stood open-mouthed, wondering how to console the poet for the inexorable procession of time, but when he spoke all he stuttered was, 'Sir, will you please let me interview you for Murad's journal?' and then stood aghast at his own clumsiness.

The old man made no answer however. He suddenly launched himself into one of those curious, bandy-legged, stiff-jointed but swift and precipitous passages that the old are capable of on occasion and, arriving at the edge of the couch that had already been prepared for him, he lowered himself and sat stroking his knees and looking as if he were seriously thinking of an answer. But before he could actually give one, an ancient gnome of a man with wild white hair tied up in a cotton scarf hobbled across the terrace and came chuckling towards him. The poet saw him and let out a groan of protest but the old man only giggled and laid him down on the couch with a gentle push, then rolled up his sleeves and began to massage him, pummelling and pounding him and making him gasp and choke. All the time the gnome laughed and sang snatches of song and kept up such a barrage of talk that Deven could do nothing but stand silently to one side, waiting for this act in the poet's routine to come to an end. The pigeons seemed to have accepted the end of theirs and were busily settling on ledges, in wooden crates, baskets and on bamboo poles, tucking their feet under their wings and their beaks into their feathers, as if withdrawing their weapons in truce, shifting and grumbling till darkness drew a cover across them and put them out for the night. Deven, listening, gathered that the gnome was a professional masseur

Nur had known in his more athletic years, who still served a large community of wrestlers and athletes whom Nur apparently knew for they gossiped about them, the matches they had won or lost, their fortunes and physiques. In between his cries of pain and pleasure, Nur said enough to make it clear to the incredulous Deven that he was, or at any rate had been, a connoisseur of the sport and kept very much in touch with what went on in the *akhadas* on the banks of the Jumna.

'But Bhim Singh, the greatest of them all, *he* is finished, *his* career is over,' pronounced the gnome, sitting back on his heels and rolling down his sleeves to show that the session was over.

'He can never be finished,' Nur protested. 'I've felt his muscles – like rocks, like boulders.'

'Yes, but the Bombay cinema has finished what even a steamroller could not. They have given him a contract to act in a film about a champion, and he has signed, the fool,' cried the gnome, picking up his bag of bottles and tins of oils and lotions and hobbling away while Nur continued to lament, 'The fool, the fool . . .'

Immediately the servant boy appeared as if summoned by name and helped him rise from the low bed, then led him back into the house for a bath. It seemed the poet led a life as busy as that of a whole hospital. Wondering if there was any point in waiting longer, Deven sank on to a rug spread out on the terrace in sheer despair. No one paid him any attention although more and more people began to come out of the room and up the stairs and spread out on the terrace and filled the space there as if it were a public park or a promenade to which they were accustomed to repair at this hour when the white-hot sky became blotched with the city's soot and faded to grey and then to mauve and finally to an uneasy, disturbed darkness. It could not become wholly dark because then the shops and cinema houses and restaurants and streets of the bazaar below lit up for the night and the sky was tinged sporadically red and orange and yellow and violet, like an old hag at a fair crazily dancing a dance of seven veils. The noises of the street and its traffic intensified as well and through the steady rumble coiled and uncoiled the long steely loops of song blaring out of a cinema house at the end of the street. The rooftop did not really raise one above the din of the streets; it was as if they were inside a balloon, floating above but remaining enclosed.

Deven sat cross-legged upon the mat, crushed by an excess of noise, light and people, trying to be unobtrusive himself and succeeding with no effort at all. He was uneasy about the lateness of the hour and the atmosphere of perpetual wakefulness, yet he felt reluctant to leave without seeing Nur once again and making one more sincere and positive effort to arrange the interview. He could not waste the day and return to Mirpore without having accomplished even so much; nor could he face Murad again without showing himself capable of having made such an attempt. Yet his hopes of a dialogue about poetry in the centre of all this garishness began to seem, even to him, quite grotesque.

Nur did eventually reappear, freshly bathed and looking truly poet-like in fresh, starched white muslin clothes, loose and flowing and free, but he was greeted with a jubilant shout of welcome, half-mocking and half-admiring, and his time and attention were entirely monopolized by his evening visitors, all of them far more at ease, familiar and capable of engaging his attention than Deven was. He remained hanging upon the fringe, looking hungry and desolate, while others reached out for glasses and drink, toasted each other, quoted poetry, burst into song and engaged in ribald repartee. It was clear to Deven that these louts, these *lafangas* of the bazaar world – shopkeepers, clerks, bookies and unemployed parasites – lived out the fantasy of being poets, artists and bohemians here on Nur's terrace, in Nur's company. Some might have written lyrics of the kind that blared endlessly from the cinema, or jingles for the radio; some might have acted small roles in a local theatre during a festival. Certainly they spoke as if they belonged to a world of hectic activity on the fringes of art and creativity. This did not surprise Deven; it was exactly the kind of circle he had been familiar with as a student, but what

50

was astonishing was that the great poet Nur should be in the centre of it, like a serene white *tika* on the forehead of a madman. It was not where Deven had expected to find him. He had pictured him living either surrounded by elderly, sage and dignified litterateurs or else entirely alone, in divine isolation. What were these clowns and jokers and jugglers doing around him, or he with them?

Could he, did he, approve of it all? Deven wondered. It was impossible to tell, for the old man either lay against the bolsters on the couch, groaning, or sat up to drink from a glass held out to him by the servant boy, then doubled over, his head bent almost as low as his knees, and groaned again. Deven thought he must be ill, or in pain, or grievously tired, yet he kept holding out his glass to be re-filled when it was empty, and later, when trays of food were brought up by several young men in filthy pyjamas, tattered vests and with waiters' napkins slung over their shoulders, he became quite alert and bright-eyed, demanded to inspect all the dishes before they were passed around and then ate what seemed to Deven unwise quantities of very rich and greasy dishes of biryani, and highly spiced kebabs, korma, kofta and dal.

Nur eating was not at all a dignified or impressive sight: he plunged his hands into the food, lowered his face into it, lifted handfuls to his mouth from where it dropped or leaked on to his lap. The small kneeling boy was kept busy with a towel and several napkins but did not seem to be succeeding at all in keeping him sightly. Deven tried to avert his face and concentrate on the plate of food which someone had thrust roughly at him and which he had gratefully accepted, realizing that he had not had anything since tea that morning at the bus terminal and was hungry almost to the point of tears. While he ate, he was aware that it was entirely the wrong sort of food for his rather delicate digestive system and that he would regret it all within a few hours, but Nur suddenly lifted his head, with grains of rice and drops of gravy sticking to various portions of it, and called across to him, 'How do you like our Jama Masjid cooking, my friend? Kings and poets alike have sampled it. Is it anything like what you get in your

51

college hostel?' and Deven was so taken aback and so flattered that he had been remembered and not only he himself but his humble origins as well, that he nodded and ate with reckless rapidity to show how much he appreciated the favour.

But the poet's attention had already wandered – there were so many others to attract it, more loud and brazen than Deven could be even in his most heated dreams. It was amazing how many people wanted to recite their verse to him rather than listen to him recite his, Deven noted bitterly, while others seemed to believe that he needed a clown to entertain him and joked and gestured with crude abandon. Then there were those who argued heatedly and so fluently as to suggest they had been through these debates many times before and Nur had always played the arbitrator. No one would have thought such an old and frail man would have so much energy to expend on so many others and their preoccupations and demands, yet now the energy seemed to be there although Deven would never have believed it earlier when the old man lay on the bed in the darkened room, half-asleep and barely able to respond.

Perhaps the rooftop of his house caught some of the electricity that seemed to rise from the city, its sparks flying from the wildly circling and flashing neon signs that lit up the sky, its cacophonous noises from the traffic in the streets, the shops in the bazaar and the cinema soundtrack, now reaching its deafening climax in which songs, screams, gunshots, armoured tanks, galloping horses and hysterical laughter and weeping all joined together in an incredible chorus. It seemed to excite him, made him raise his voice above it and, in a way, even blend with it.

Deven sat gloomily with his back against the parapet, wondering how, out of all this hubbub, the poet drew the threads and wove his poetry or philosophy. Yet, when he paid attention to his talk, he discovered that it was, after all, about his poetry.

'Cowards – babies,' he was taunting a group of young men who stood around unsteadily, glasses tilting and dribbling in their hands. 'You recite verses as if they were nursery rhymes

52

your mother had composed. I tell you, we must get over this rolling of Urdu verses into little sugar pills for babies to suck. We need the roar of lions, or the boom of cannon, so that we can march upon these Hindi-wallahs and make them run. Let them see the power of Urdu,' he thundered. 'They think it is chained and tamed in the dusty yards of those cemeteries that they call universities, but can't we show them that it can still let out a roar or a boom?'

Here a young man with yellow teeth and red eyes made a rude remark. Those who heard it, laughed. Nur seemed not to object but to agree. 'Yes, all right, that will also be a kind of assault – on their noses anyway. Yes, let Urdu issue from any orifice as long as it drives them away. But make its presence felt,' he thundered, thumping down his glass on his knee so that the liquor flew from it.

'Nur Sahib,' responded a tall man who swayed on his feet as if only tenuously tethered to the roof, 'Nur Sahib, I am telling you the time for poetry is over. To feed the Hindi-wallahs with Urdu poetry is like feeding cows with – hunks of red meat. Turn to journalism instead, Nur Sahib. Reach out to the people directly. We have a message for them. Tell them in plain speech. Use your powers for the purpose of – attack and vengeance!'

'Wah, wah, very fine, very fine,' mocked a young man sitting cross-legged on a mat. 'He calls for attack thirty years after his claws have been extracted and his teeth filed. You are laughable, my friend, laughable. How do you expect to attack? With what weapons – with metaphor and alliteration? If you want arms, you had better cross the border and go find them in Pakistan. Here we live as *hijras*, as eunuchs.'

Deven watched Nur's face with curiosity. He could make nothing out of that tortured, scowling expression behind the ruffled beard. Turning his head to one side pettishly, he growled at the servant boy, 'More biryani,' and it seemed to Deven that the conversation had taken a turn that displeased the old man and that he did not wish to continue.

But after he had downed another helping of biryani and drunk another glass of country liquor, Nur was once again

53

taking vigorous part in the conversation. It was obviously one that was repeated night after night, everyone spoke as if on cue, fluently, and there was a lack of spontaneity, a staleness. There was the India camp and the Pakistan camp, the pure-Persian camp and the demotic-Hindustani camp. They quarrelled and mocked and taunted and lost their tempers, but as if acting assigned roles. There was no evidence of anyone persecuting anyone else or of winning anyone over to his side through argument or persuasion. The dialogue was as stale as the rice and gravy lying on tin trays all over the terrace. Nur sat hunched, listening, while he picked his teeth and occasionally spat into the tin spittoon under the divan. Then, raising his shaggy head so that it looked severe and granolithic, he interrupted the babble to say, 'Wrong, wrong, for thirty years you have been wrong. It is not a matter of Pakistan and Hindustan, of Hindi and Urdu. It is not even a matter of history. It is time you should be speaking of but cannot – the concept of time is too vast for you, I can see that, and yet it is all we really know about in our hearts,' he pressed his hand to his chest and there was comparative silence now for him to speak into. In that silence, Deven's heart gave a series of knocks. It gave him a sense of victory and triumph that Nur had so effectively stopped the raucous babble around him and placed the whole argument in perspective. That, he saw, was the glory of poets – that they could distance events and emotions, place them where perspective made it possible to view things clearly and calmly. He realized that he loved poetry not because it made things immediate but because it removed them to a position where they became bearable. That was what Nur's verse did – placed frightening and inexplicable experiences like time and death at a point where they could be seen and studied, in safety. His joy at this recognition made his heart beat a tattoo inside his chest so that it was a minute or two before he could calm himself and listen to Nur again. Looking up, he saw to his alarm Nur pointing at him as if he had all along been aware of him in that dark corner. 'He has come to speak for me,' Nur said. 'Through his throat, my words will flow. Listen and tell me

54

if my poetry deserves to live, or if it should give way to – that fodder chewed by peasants, Hindi?' he spat at the man who had disparaged his vocation.

Deven responded with such an expression of terror that those who noticed laughed. He felt as if Nur had noticed his childish moment of satisfaction and decided maliciously to wreck it. All his joy and the regard and the honour he had accorded Nur dispersed as if over the ledge into the night. Nur was inviting him to join the fray, allowing the sublime concept of time to dwindle into the mere politics of language again. He could not possibly have opened his mouth or uttered a word. He knew he ought not to have stayed, listening to this kind of talk, he a Hindu and a teacher of Hindi. He had always kept away from the political angle of languages. He began to sweat with fear.

'What is the matter?' Nur mocked, glaring at him with small bloodshot eyes. Why did he choose to pick on Deven, the only one who had remained silent and not expressed any opinion at all? 'Forgotten your Urdu? Forgotten my verse? Perhaps it is better if you go back to your college and teach your students the stories of Prem Chand, the poems of Pant and Nirala. Safe, simple Hindi language, safe comfortable ideas of cow worship and caste and the romance of Krishna. That is your subject, isn't it, professor?' He threw back his head and cackled with laughter but the rest fell silent. They all stopped talking and arguing and laughing and turned to look at Deven with a curiosity they had not felt before.

'I am no poet, only a teacher,' Deven mumbled, but no one heard.

Then, unexpectedly, he was saved by the tall man who would not sit but teetered and swayed above them, his head framed by a neon sign that flashed 'Atlas Bicycles, Nation's Favourite' in letters of acid green. 'Have you heard Sri Gobind's latest poem cycle?' he bawled. 'They are saying in the bazaar that it will win the Sahitya Akademi award for Hindi this year. For Urdu we can of course expect the same verdict as usual: "No book was judged worthy of the award this year." Why such treatment for Urdu, my friends?

55

Because Urdu is supposed to have died, in 1947. What you see in the universities – in *some* of the universities, a few of them only – is its ghost, wrapped in a shroud. But Hindi – oh Hindi is a field of greens, all flourishing, and this is its flower,' he cried, and throwing back his head, recited fulsomely:

> 'Sun, moon, stars, sky,
> Planets, clouds, comets, I,
> God made them all as he made me,
> A star too I must be.'

While the others laughed, Nur gave him a bloodshot look, saying, 'Do you think they have nothing better to recite in the bazaars of Delhi? I tell you there are better things to be heard in the streets of *my* Delhi. Even the hit song from *Sholay* is better. And wait till you hear my Chunna sing it. Call that boy,' he suddenly ordered the servant boy who sat on his heels, dozing. 'Bring him to me,' he shouted, giving the boy a shove that sent him toppling.

'He is sleeping,' the boy protested indignantly.

'What he is doing is immaterial. It is what he will grow up to do that I am interested in. The son of a poet must grow up to be a singer of songs. Go tell his mother to wake him and bring him here – I want him to sing for my friends. Friends, I want you to listen to a child sing a film song rather than listen to – to these – these –' he waved his hand helplessly at the gathering around him.

'No, Nur Sahib, how can you say that? Are you angry with me for reciting Sri Gobind's immortal verse? All right, I will give it up – I will throw it away with all these dirty dishes,' said the tall man, casually kicking out at a heap of tin trays so that they went slithering across the terrace, scattering rice, gravy and tin spoons as they went.

Someone lifted his glass high over his head, saying, 'Yes, smash it all up, smash it,' and dropped the glass with a crash. Another got to his feet and wove his way to where Nur sat, shouting, 'Nur Sahib, I will sing for you. Hear me sing the song I wrote for *Azadi* – only the damned director stole it and used it without paying me a *paisa*,' and instead of singing he began to cry with a great heaving of shoulders and rubbing of eyes. Laughing, his companions crowded around him and patted him violently on the back, calling, 'Here, give him a *paisa*, poor fellow,' and, 'Here, Bobby, here's twenty *paise* for your song. Now sing.' 'Yes, sing,' they all bellowed.

Deven, who was watching with his back tightly pressed into the wall as if he hoped it would give way and allow him to escape, saw the crowd before him part and Nur emerge through a crack and go stumbling away without anyone's noticing. 'That damned, stupid, disobedient – ' he was muttering to himself. 'I'll go myself and fetch – fetch – '

The others were still laughing and thumping Bobby and did not seem to notice that he was no longer in their midst. Perhaps this was his usual manner, and time, of departure. After watching for a moment or two to see what direction the old man was taking, Deven started to follow him, in an instinctive choice of the poet's company, however terrifying, rather than that of the rabble. As he lifted the bamboo mat in the lighted doorway and saw Nur slipping out of the other door, he heard their voices behind him:

'If you won't sing your song, you'll have to listen to Gobind-ji's':

> "Butter, milk, curds, ghee,
> Sweets, drinks, food for me –
> God made them all and God made me,
> Butterballs all, butterball me."

Dropping the mat in place, Deven hurried through the empty room, wondering how the old, helpless man could have moved with such speed. If only he could catch up with him, he might have a word with him about his poetry after all, and the interview. Desperately he called out his name: 'Nur Sahib!' and ran out on to the veranda to search for him.

Deven never quite believed what happened next. He was so confused and shattered by it that he did not know what it was that shattered him, just as the victim of an accident sees and hears the pane of glass smash or sheet of metal buckle but cannot tell what did it – rock, bullet or vehicle. The truth was that he did not really want ever to think back to that scene. If his mind wandered inadvertently towards it, it immediately sensed disaster and veered away into safer regions.

All he was willing to admit, even to himself, was that it was the sound of a child crying that led him along the veranda and down the stairs to a lower floor. Doors opened on to the unlit verandas all around the silent well of the courtyard where one bare electric bulb burned. From some of the doorways, light fell through the curtains or bamboo mats that hung there. Others were solidly, impassively dark. Some rustled with furtive life, concealed by darkness. Others seemed dead, or asleep, or empty. Deven tiptoed past them, peering in through his spectacles, his heart thumping against his ribs like a fish in a trap. The child wailed and wailed in one of the rooms. Then a woman began to scream, rapidly and hysterically. There was a sound of protest, possibly from Nur – certainly in an aged and weak strain. The woman's voice rose sharply. It was cut short by a howl so appalling that Deven raced forwards and flung open a closed door, certain he would find the poet in a pool of blood, a dagger through his heart, his son weeping beside the corpse.

He fell with a cry upon the body that lay upon the floor. It lay face downwards, arms and legs spreadeagled across the thick mattress unrolled upon the terrazzo floor. Then there was another howl but it did not come from the prostrate body, it came from the figure that stood over it, a small shaking creature in white, draped in a silver shawl from which ringlets of gleaming black hair escaped and danced upon a forehead as white as chalk, made still paler by contrast with the kohl-ringed eyes and the blood-red mouth. Deven sat back on his knees, open-mouthed with terror at this apparition of fury and vengeance.

58

'Get up!' she screamed. 'Get *up*! Go and have Ali clean you. How can you wallow in such filth, such muck? See what you have done to my room, in my room – see!'

'No, no,' begged Deven, but his voice was only a whisper as he reached out trembling fingers to stroke the great back of his fallen hero, trying to find life.

The figure on the mattress gave a heave and then began to quiver with sobs that sounded like small, squelching giggles. It was crying; it was alive. 'It was a pain,' he wept, 'a pain in my stomach, *janum* – I swear – I am ill, these ulcers of mine – '

'Ulcers? Then why did you drink? Why do you nightly have that rabble up there in your room, drinking? It isn't ulcers that has made you vomit on my floor, it is *drink*.' She shook with outrage, a fierce and infuriated apparition in white and silver. Bending, she half-lifted the fallen figure from the mattress in an effort to thrust it out of her offended sight, but Deven clasped his arms around the fallen poet, trying to achieve an exit more gently, less violently, whereupon she turned round and screamed, 'If you want to be his servant, then *you* clean it up. Listen to me, will you? Leave that – that poor beast on the floor and go and clean it up, I tell you.'

Releasing the poet, Deven looked up at her, helplessly.

'What is the matter?' she cried. 'Aren't you willing to do that for your – your *hero*? All of you who come to see him and lead him on with your hero-worship, do you care for *him* or for the food and drink with which he pays you to come – '

'What are you saying?' Deven hissed in horror at her perverse interpretation of the soirée upstairs. 'We come to pay our respects, out of regard for a – a great man, a poet – '

'How? How?' she hissed back at him, and her scarlet lips were speckled with spit, he saw. 'He *was* a poet, a scholar – but is he now? Look at him!' She pointed dramatically at Nur who was huddled, whimpering, on the mattress, holding his knees to his chest and rocking from side to side in agony. 'Do you call that a poet, or even a man? All of you – you

59

followers of his – you have reduced him to that, making him eat and drink like some animal, like a pig, laughing at your jokes, singing your crude songs, when he should be at work, or resting to prepare himself for work – '

Deven dropped his eyes and his head sank in admission of this indubitable truth. His submission seemed to enrage her and throw her into another paroxysm. Marching across the room to a shelf where books and papers were stacked, she began to fling them at him, saying, 'See what you've done to him? See what he's done in my room? Am I to stand for this in my room, in my house? Did he marry me to make me live in a pigsty with him? Am I to live like a pig with all the rest of you?' With each question she flung another handful of papers at Deven and when he was deep in them, turning his head from side to side to avoid their impact, growing giddy and muddled and frantic as more and more descended on him, she screamed, 'Don't you see? It is *there*!' and pointed at a pool of yellow vomit in a corner of the room. He stared across it and only then noticed the crying child – the little fat boy who had thrown down the coins the poet had given him, now sitting against the wall with his legs stretched out before him and his fists thrust into his eyes, howling with sleepiness and terror. Following the direction of Deven's eyes, she too stared at the child, then swooped down upon him and picked him up in a fierce embrace. 'See what my child has to witness – the depths to which his father has been brought by you – you – '

'No, no,' Deven protested, and to remove any such signs of the poet's degradation, he grabbed some handfuls of paper she had flung at him and, crawling forwards to the tell-tale stain, began to scrub the floor with them, made desperate in his movements by the sobbing of the terrified child and the retching of the poet at the other end of the room as well as the outrage that the woman exhaled as though she were a fire-eater in the middle of a performance.

'Take it away from here,' she commanded, standing by the bookshelf and holding the child as if out of the swill. 'Go fetch water. Wash the floor. I want it washed and polished.

I will have my room clean, my house clean. D'you hear? D'you think I entered this house to keep company with swine?'

'No, *janum*, no,' wept the poet, in between retching sounds that were tearing him to pieces. 'I tell you – I had this pain here – my ulcers – '

'Don't talk to me!' her voice rose hysterically. 'Don't talk to me about ulcers. It was drink, it was your party, your friends, your horrible, inferior life – '

'He is ill,' Deven protested, and crept towards the door with the dirty sheets of paper in his hand. 'Please, please, he is ill, and aged. I beg you – '

'Ill? He is *foolish*, foolish to spend time with you, to have friends like you, to ignore his wife and child – ' here the woman stopped her high-pitched abuse as her voice broke, and she turned her face away as if to hide a moment of weakness. Deven took her momentary inattention as an opportunity to slip out of the room with the sopping bundle of paper, desperate to get rid of it.

For a while he stood on the veranda outside, in the dark, a little to one side of the lighted doorway, struggling to control his breathing while he listened to the voices continue inside – the one accusing, the other placating; the one harsh, the other helpless – and the child's crying reduced gradually to watery hiccups and occasional wrenching sobs. He wondered if he ought to return, to bring about justice and mercy. But the papers between his fingers oozed and stank. He stared at them in repulsion, not quite certain how he came to be holding them. He almost threw them over the railing into the courtyard below but it was obvious that there were people at every door, in every nest of shadows, listening and watching for it to be safe to come out and resume whatever was the normal life of this household. So he clutched them tightly in order to overcome his own repulsion and then did what every instinct in him told him to do – raced down the veranda, hurled himself down the stairs, broke through the door into the lane, and there dropped the disgusting parcel into the gutter, and fled. He was at the end of the lane, at the corner where the street light blazed with normality, before it occurred to him that those papers he had thrown away might have been inscribed with Nur's verse.

Those were the two moments of the evening that stayed, that even his conscience or his memory's selective talents refused to let go – the moment when he had stood above the well of the courtyard, listening to the voices inside, and the moment he had erupted out of the house, dropped the papers and run. What exactly had happened in between? There were times when he remembered a totally different scene: how he had marched in and thrust away the vengeful figure of a white and silver witch, how he had raised Nur in his arms and seen to his ills and rescued him from them . . . but then his congenital inability to satisfy himself with fantasy would apply a brake, the wild careening of his imagination crash to a halt, and he would be faced with that one truth again – how he had abandoned the poet in his agony, desecrated the paper on which he wrote his verse, and run.

Even to remember it made his breath come short and fast.

CHAPTER FOUR

Dawn was breaking at the end of the road as Deven rattled homewards in the bus. At least, that was how the poets described it, he thought bitterly as he looked through the dust filming the windowpane at the sooty darkness lightening to grey as if the soot and smuts were being dissolved in dishwater. Shapes began to emerge out of this watery murk, dim and formless to begin with, then gradually assuming the lines and dimensions of trees, houses, smokestacks, shacks. Dawn and poetry, he thought as he spat out a shred of tobacco from his mouth that felt painfully unclean at this hour of morning, all that was simply not real, not true; it was humbug, hypocrisy and not to be trusted. If it were true then it would have stood the test of actual experience, and it had not. Oh, it had not, it had not. Henceforth he would avoid that mirage, that dream that so easily twisted into nightmare. Any reality was preferable, he told himself, even if it was the smeared window of a country bus bumping along the rutted road homewards.

He groaned aloud and rolled his head about on the palms of his hands in a very real agony.

An early milkman sitting across the aisle asked kindly, 'Are you ill, son? Are you sick?'

Deven rolled his head from side to side in denial, then raised it and stared stoically out at the yellow roadside with its barbed wire fence trampled into the dust and emaciated cattle slowly heaving themselves up from the shelter of thorn trees where they had slept, and swaying across the barren fields in search of fodder, like some prehistoric beasts who have not been informed that they are now outdated. After the nightmare he had lived through, the still calm of this morning scene seemed to him positively idyllic. He stared and stared, noting every signboard and landmark along the way – 'Mita Sugar Factory', 'Friends Cycle Repairs', 'Modi Tyres and Tubes', a grove of blackened acacia trees, a tumble of broken mud huts, 'Punjab Eating House: Hot Food Cold Drinks' – and they struck at his eyes and the aching temples that were the legacy of a sleepless night, like small vicious pebbles. There was no idyll that could not be broken.

His head swayed with sleep on its thin stalk. He would have liked to close his eyes, lean an ear against the rattling side of the bus, and sleep a little, but dared not. He knew what figures would come scrambling out of the dark to assault him – the woman with spittle-flecked red lips which had parted to scream abuse at the poet; the rolling white bolster on the floor that was the poet, rolling and rolling towards him till it struck him below the knees and brought him down into the gutter that was blocked with sodden, stinking papers inscribed with his verse . . . He lifted up his feet in fear that they might wrap themselves around his ankles – he could smell them still – poetry for ever mixed with vomit in his mind. What was more, he would always feel responsible – at least partly – for the defacing of that poetry. And yet, how could he be, when he loved poetry so, *had* loved poetry above any reality?

'Here, son, a pinch of tobacco – try it and see how you feel,' coaxed the kindly milkman, leaning across the aisle to him with a small flat tin that he opened with one green fingernail to offer the tobacco.

Deven shrank back, muttering his thanks and refusal awkwardly. He would have preferred being ignored to any kindness now.

'Clears the head,' urged the man, 'makes it spin around so you think it's coming right off – then you stop feeling giddy and you find it's been cleared, made as good as new.'

64

'No, no,' Deven raised his voice angrily, and turned resolutely to the window. He heard the tobacco tin snap shut.

Here was the oasis of the Agricultural College at last, with its fertilizer-fed greenery, and the railway track, the granary and the bus depot, the waiting crowds and their luggage, the barrows of fruit and peanuts for the travellers, the cacophony of the bazaar so familiar to him. As he rose and stumbled out of the bus on bent, disobedient legs, he saw the face of one of his students going past on a bicycle. In the moment that they stared at each other with mutual shock, a verse of Nur's fell into Deven's mind as casually as a discarded bus ticket:

Night ends, dawn breaks, and sorrow reappears,
Addressing us in morning light with a cock's shrill crow.

For a while he stood there as if his limbs had been filled with cement. He was pushed from both sides by passengers who were getting off and those who were getting on, but could make no move in either direction. Then he shook his head, wincing to feel large-sized stones rattle inside it, and told himself he must decide where to go, what to do next. This initial uncertainty was followed by a rapid decision: he could not go home and face Sarla's stony face, her sulks or her open fury; it would be better to go straight to college. There would be no one there so early in the morning. He would go to the washroom and put his head under the tap. He would go to the canteen and have a cup of coffee. He would go to class, give his lecture, stumble a little perhaps but climb on to the familiar track again eventually. No doubt something or someone would come along to give him a push and send him moving along it. Once back on it, he would never stray again. Never, oh never. And, hunching his shoulders to protect his ears, his head, he left the crowd.

When he did get home, Sarla was standing in the doorway with her arms and her sari wrapped about her shoulders and her face bent under the thin straggling hair as she talked to a neighbour outside – the picture of an abandoned wife. The neighbour was one Deven particularly disliked – the widowed mother of a colleague of his, stout and shapeless in her white widow's sari, and a face that was both sanctimonious and martial, like a hatchet in the hands of a fanatic.

As he pushed open the gate with its familiar rusty sound of protest, both women raised their drooping heads and stared at him as if he were a stranger, an interloper. Then Sarla twitched a fold of her sari over her head. She didn't normally cover her head when he appeared; it was evident that she was preparing for a scene. He tried to smile, then lifted his hand to cover his mouth because he felt he shouldn't.

Mrs Bhalla started to sidle away in her characteristically deceitful manner. As she edged past him at the gate, she said, 'I told Sarla not to worry, my nephew saw you getting off the Delhi bus in the morning when he was going to the homoeopathic clinic for his father's medicine. That was at six o'clock I told her.'

'Ye-es, I missed the last bus at night,' he said hoarsely, 'and caught the first bus in the morning and – and decided to go straight to college.'

'But a message you could have sent,' said Mrs Bhalla in her sweetest, most wheedling tone. 'It is a small thing only, but means much to the poor ladies waiting at home.' She gave Sarla a benign smile. '*Accha*, sister, then I will go,' she sighed, and disappeared around the corner on her shuffling widow's feet.

Sarla abruptly detached herself from the doorpost and turned to go in, holding the fold of her sari firmly over her head as if she were in mourning or at a religious ceremony. Sighing, Deven followed. He knew this manner would be his punishment for many days to come. The tedium of it settled upon him like a grey, crumbling mildew. He felt aged and mouldy. He was sure his teeth had loosened in the night, that his hair would come out in handfuls if he tugged it. That was what she might well do, he feared, to teach him not to venture out of the familiar, safe dustbin of their world into the perilous world of night-time bacchanalia, revelry and melodrama. Now he would sink back on to the dustheap like a crust thrown away, and moulder. It was not only all he deserved but all he was fit for and therefore could expect from life, from fate. Justice was not unrelated to fate, after all; was not that the teaching of – of . . . ? He couldn't remember. But what vainglory it had been to try to find an entry into Nur's world – the world of drama and revolving lights and feasts and furies; how inadequate he had proved to its demands and expectations. No, all he could measure up to was this – this shabby house, its dirty corners, its wretchedness and lovelessness. Looking around it, he felt himself sag with relief and gratitude. At the same time his shoulders drooped in defeat.

Deven had been more a poet than a professor when he married Sarla – he had only been taken on as a temporary lecturer and still had confidence in his verse – and for the wife of a poet she seemed too prosaic. Of course she had not been his choice but that of his mother and aunts, crafty and cautious women; she was the daughter of a friend of an aunt's, she lived on the same street as that family, they had observed her for years and found her suitable in every way: plain, penny-pinching and congenitally pessimistic. What they had not suspected was that Sarla, as a girl and as a new bride, had aspirations, too; they had not understood because within the grim boundaries of their own penurious lives they had never entertained anything so abstract. Sarla's home had been scarcely less grim but on the edges of it there flowered such promises of Eden as could be held out by advertisements, cinema shows and the gossip of girl friends. So she had dared to aspire towards a telephone, a refrigerator, even a car. Did not the smiling lady on the signboard lean seductively upon her crowded refrigerator, promising 'Yours, in easy instalments'? And the saucy girl in the magazine step into a car as though there were no such things in her life as bills, instalments or debts? Her girl friends had a joke about it – 'Fan, 'phone, frigidaire!' they would shout whenever anyone mentioned a wedding, a bridegroom, a betrothal, and dissolve in hectic laughter.

While her mother collected stainless steel cooking pots and her sisters embroidered pillowcases and anti-macassars for her, she dreamt the magazine dream of marriage: herself, stepping out of a car with a plastic shopping bag full of groceries and filling them into the gleaming refrigerator, then rushing to the telephone placed on a lace doily upon a three-legged table and excitedly ringing up her friends to invite them to see a picture show with her and her husband who was beaming at her from behind a flowered curtain.

But by marrying into the academic profession and moving to a small town outside the capital, none of these dreams had materialized, and she was naturally embittered. The thwarting of her aspirations had cut two dark furrows from the corners of her nostrils to the corners of her mouth, as deep and permanent as surgical scars. The droop of her thin, straight hair on either side of her head repeated these twin lines of disappointment. They made her look forbidding, and perhaps that was why her husband looked so perpetually forbidden, even if he understood their cause. He understood because, like her, he had been defeated too; like her, he was a victim. Although each understood the secret truth about the other, it did not bring about any closeness of spirit, any comradeship, because they also sensed that two victims ought to avoid each other, not yoke together their joint disappointments. A victim does not look to help from another victim; he looks for a redeemer. At least Deven had his poetry; she had nothing, and so there was an added accusation and bitterness in her look.

Usually he was enraged by her tacit accusations that added to the load on his back. To relieve it, he would hurl away dishes that had not been cooked to his liking, bawl uncontrollably if meals were not ready when he wanted them or the laundry not done or a button missing or their small son noisy or unwashed; it was to lay the blame upon her, remove its clinging skin from him. Tearing up a shirt she had not washed, or turning the boy out of the room because he was crying, he was really protesting against her disappointment; he was out to wreck it, take his revenge upon her for harbouring it. Why should it blight his existence that had once shown promise and had a future?

But now the blight settled on his own existence and he submitted to it; it suited his mood, it seemed fitting. Sprawled upon the broken cane chair in the veranda, he listened to Sarla moving about the house inside, and watched his son playing on the steps. They were busy, he idle. They were alive, he in a limbo. If he made no effort to rise from it, there he would remain.

'Manu,' he called at last, softly, moved by his own isolation into making his first overture since his crestfallen return.

If Manu heard, he made no response, merely wiped his nose with the back of his hand and continued to play with a tin top on the stairs.

'Manu, son,' called Deven again, sorrowfully. 'Come to Papa. To Papu.'

Now Manu looked up from under his dusty thatch of hair at the unexpected appeal in Deven's tone.

'Come, talk to Papa, son,' Deven coaxed, moving his legs to make a lap. 'Tell me about your school.'

Silence from Manu; only a twitch of a finger, nervous.

'Show me your books,' Deven went on trying. 'Where are they?'

Suddenly a voice came from the dim room behind them. 'Go fetch your books,' Sarla called. 'Show them to your father.'

Both Deven and his son gave a jump, her voice sounded so close; then the child climbed up the steps and went in to fetch his school bag while Deven sank back into his chair, weak with relief that the punishment period was over. Tension had snapped. It lay in dead coils at his feet, exhausted.

He smiled at Manu as he came back across the veranda, lugging his school bag sullenly for he seemed to have preferred his father to remain in eclipse. He looked unwilling and apprehensive while his father drew out the limp, greasy exercise books and opened them with every expectation of pleasure, if not pride. But it would have been difficult if not altogether impossible for a poet and a lecturer at a local college to take any pride in the filthy, scrawled pages, stained by erasures and slashed by an angry red pencil, the dismal marks, the sharp comments in the margins. A cry of protest rose to Deven's lips, and died. He was aware that this was not an occasion for parental censure. He was also aware of Sarla's watchful presence in the room behind them, hidden but listening. He knew he had too often already said, 'When I was a boy, I tried to please my father by bringing home good marks, neat copybooks and fine handwriting. He never gave me rewards but it pleased him – he felt proud. I wanted my father to be proud of me.' He knew how Sarla curled her lips up at that, how his son sulked, and how unbearable that was. So he only sighed.

'And what have you been reading?' he tried again, heroically. 'This book? Ah, very good, it is very good,' he chuckled, looking through a book of rhymes about peacocks and crows, tortoises and hares, monkeys and crocodiles – that bestiary which pranced through every childhood, which he remembered from his own and fully endorsed as a proper background to his son's. Or did he? Staring at the classic opposition of different species that made for the bright energy of the primary colours of the illustrations, he hesitated and a shadow fell across his face as he saw superimposed upon them pictures that seemed to fall out of his heart like badly concealed cards at a game: pictures of a thin, vividly-painted face taut and dragged out of proportion with disgust and rage; of a twisted figure bent in pain on the floor – and upon these pictures a third one, older and more faded and yet as fraught with pain, a picture of his father, emaciated with illness, shrivelled upon a pallet on the floor, holding a tattered copy of poems in his hands and reading from them with an expression of ineffable joy, poems that were inscribed, strangely enough, upon the other two cards, so much more harsh and livid in their fresher colouring. What made all these dissimilar memories come together to form one image?

Rising from his chair, he stammered, 'Let us go for a walk. Come, Manu, come and walk with me.' He put out his hand blindly and the boy cautiously inserted one finger into his father's fist and felt it tighten. Then they went down the steps and through the gate on to the road, the mother in the house watching in astonishment and coming as close to that mother in the glossy magazine as she was ever likely to come.

Deven and the boy walked down the road between the small yellow stucco houses that belonged to the same grade of low-paid employees as he did and which were all waiting for a coat of paint some day when the funds were collected for such an unlikely project. In the meantime they peeled and mouldered under bean and pumpkin vines and red dusty bougainvillaeas. Broken furniture spilled out of their small verandas. Strings of washing hung on lines outside. Beneath them, chickens scratched diligently and children played fiercely. Radios blared forth so that as they walked along they heard the same programme in uninterrupted instalments.

Deven breathed it all in, finding it reassuring. For once he did not resent his 'circumstances'. Their meanness was transformed for him by his new experience and the still raw wounds it had left. Also by the feel of his son's thumb enclosed within his fist. He walked along with a light step, breathing in the close stuffy air of the small colony, its odours of cooking and dust and chicken dirt and washing, as if it were invigorating. The calm exhilaration of the evening and the walk gave him an unaccustomed peace of mind, contentment with things the way they were, and a certain modest, suburban wellbeing.

He walked as if he were walking away from the debris of his Delhi trip, his visit to Nur, the failed interview – leaving it all behind. The first desolation at his loss of them was being gradually filled this evening, as an empty glass with water, with the realization that that loss had simplified his existence, reduced it once again to a pure emptiness with which he knew how to cope, having coped so long. He had made a timely escape from complexities with which he would not have known how to contend. Compared to the horror of that threat, this grey anonymity was sweet.

He told himself how lucky he was to have exchanged the

71

dangers of Nur's poetry for the undemanding chatter of a child. The boy was telling one of his monotonous stories of school life that he often prattled to his parents, only they never listened. Now Deven looked down at the top of his head and smiled when Manu told him, 'My teacher, he has hair growing out of his ears. Why does hair grow in his ears, Papa? He puts his pencil behind his ear – like this – ' Deven laughed and swung the boy's hand – 'and when he is angry he takes the pencil and throws it – like this.' The boy flung out his fist and a crow rose from the barbed wire fence and flew off with a squawk. Manu's face reddened with surprise and pride at the effect his story was having. For almost the first time in his life since the early days of infancy which he could naturally not remember, he had a feeling of power, of being able to impress people and influence events. He rushed along at his father's side instead of dragging behind as was more usual with him. The boy, who was so often querulous with hunger and sleep by the time Deven came back from work, seemed quite unlike the protesting, whining creature he usually was; he too seemed to find something pleasant and acceptable in the uncommon experience of a walk with his father.

When his mother took him for a walk, it was invariably to the market or to a friend's house, but his father seemed to be launched upon a more adventurous expedition. They had left behind the colony of low-grade employees' quarters. They were walking past the back of Lala Ram Lal College and its barbed wire fencing through which could be seen the dusty empty playing fields where no one ever played and the row of whitewashed huts where the non-teaching staff lived amidst buffaloes, washing, string cots and buckets of water. Then the path veered away from the barbed wire fence that marched through rough grass and patches of saltpetre, and ran down to the canal that separated the town proper from the chemically lush grounds of the Agricultural and Veterinary College whose purple bougainvillaeas crept down to the canal bank and flowered profusely behind clumps of pampas grass. Here the path narrowed to a muddy track that was used by

72

the college servants who came to squat behind the bushes and the buffaloes that came to drink. The clay had dried and was pleasant to walk on as it cracked beneath their feet. The canal was narrow but deep and never ran dry, even in the hottest weather. Pampas grass grew thickly along the bank and buffaloes and bees stirred in the reeds at its edges.

'Look at the parrots,' Deven instructed his son and pointed at a flock that exploded out of an acacia tree and streaked over the fields, acid green against the pale yellow of the western sky.

'I know a song about a parrot,' Manu claimed at once, and launched lustily into a nursery rhyme familiar even to Deven who laughed with delight at being reminded of its simple nonsense. 'My father taught me that,' he said lightly. It was perhaps not strictly true, he could not honestly claim to remember, but it could be true because he did remember it and felt his father's apologetic smile somewhere in it. His father, who had been a chronic sufferer from asthma, and whose career had foundered upon his invalidism, had appeared always to be apologizing to his wife who had expected more from a husband and felt grievously disap- pointed at the little he had made of his life; as a child Deven had barely understood this but now that he himself occupied a not very dissimilar position at home, he felt protective towards the dead man, and in his imagination glorified and deified him as he had not done when he was living. At magical moments like this the fantasy took on the stuff of truth. It positively glowed – like the sunset.

Then the flock of parrots wheeled around, perhaps on finding the fields bare of grain, and returned to the tree above their heads, screaming and quarrelling as they settled amongst the thorns. One brilliant feather of spring green fluttered down through the air and fell at their feet in the grey clay. Deven bent to pick it up and presented it to his son who stuck it behind his ear in imitation of his schoolteacher with the pencil. 'Look, now I'm master-*ji*,' he screamed excitedly.

Yes, that was the climax of that brief halcyon passage. It was as if the evening star shone through at that moment,

73

casting a small pale illumination upon Deven's flattened grey world. Of course it could not be maintained, of course it had to diminish and decline. Yes.

When they got back to their house – DII/69 in that colony named after a leader of Harijans – the careful brown paper parcel that Deven had been making of the evening and tying up with care, came apart. Sarla handed him a postcard that had arrived by the evening post with fingers damp from a bucket of washing. 'Here,' she said with an eloquent sniff. She had read it, obviously. He took it and knew his doom had searched him out and found him after all.

'Dear Sir,' said the small, precise handwriting, in English. 'I'm happy to learn of your decision to work as my secretary. Please report earliest date convenient. I am wanting to dictate some poems to you. Murad Sahib is wanting to publish same. Time is fleeting. Yours faithfully . . .' The name was signed in elegant, elaborate Urdu.

CHAPTER FIVE

'This is what I don't like about you,' Murad said, making a
face around the toothpick he had inserted between his lips.
'Always saying no, I can't, how can I, I am afraid, I will be
hurt, I will be killed – '

'I am not saying that,' protested Deven, holding his head
in his hands with despair. 'I am only saying I have my job, I
can't lose my job, my salary. I have my family – a wife, a
son. I can't let them starve – '

'Who is saying they will starve?' Murad feigned bewilderment. 'Here you are getting extra work, and you are howling
about starvation.'

'Murad, it is not work I can do, I am telling you only. I
don't even live in Delhi. I have no time.'

'Then you should have told me that long ago instead of
saying you wanted to write for my magazine. You have no
time. All right. Go back to your village, rot there with your
buffaloes and your dung heaps. Why come and pretend you
are a poet and have written things to be published in my
magazine? Go away, don't waste my time – there are many
better poets than you to be found in the streets of Delhi.'

But this was too categorical for Deven who always shel-
tered in ambiguity. 'Listen, I did say I would write for your
paper, yes. I said I would interview Nur. An interview with
Nur, that was all I promised. For that I travelled to Delhi, I
went to see the man in his own house, and allowed myself

to be dragged into his kind of society. For an *interview*. How could you imagine, how could you tell him I was going to be his secretary and take dictation from him? You think I will give up a job in a foremost college of North India, give up my salary, provident fund, pension, housing and medical allowance to be that – that madman's secretary – fill his inkpots, take down his curses and abuses? How could you tell him such a thing, Murad, *how*?'

'There are many people who would consider it an honour, a very great honour,' said Murad, severely, looking at Deven with contempt while he dug inside his mouth with a tooth-pick. 'I know five, six people who would be happy to go and fill his inkwell and sharpen his pens, thinking it a golden chance to learn the art of poetry from a great master. You are forgetting our Indian tradition, Deven. You are forgetting the *guru-shishya* tradition – how the *shishya* sits at the feet of his *guru*, for years, years – sometimes till his own hair is white – happy only to learn, and to serve, and through service learn, before he tries to do any work of his own. But people like you – they want to travel by first class – everything easy, just go straight ahead. No time to sit at a *guru*'s feet, and study – you are only thinking of getting ahead – '

Deven interrupted with a sputter of indignation. 'I don't know why you are going on and on about this *guru* and *shishya*. I never said I was looking for a *guru*. I have given up thinking I can ever write poetry. I am only a poor lecturer, temporary, earning my living. I tell you I haven't time, I can't serve Nur, I can't go and become his secretary, and you had no business – no business, do you hear,' his voice rose and threatened to splinter, 'to tell him I would.'

Murad removed the toothpick from his mouth. 'Listen to me,' he said loudly and slowly as if talking to a moron. 'I did not tell him you would be his secretary. When I saw him at the *urs* of Khwaja Nizamuddin Auliya, I went up to him to pay my respects. Yes, I have much respect for great men like him, for poets and artists. I went and bowed to take the dust off his feet. And I asked him only if he had spoken to you and agreed to let you interview him – you remember you did not come back and tell me what had happened, you simply ran away, disappeared without a word – ' he looked more and more severe and Deven winced at the accuracy of his memory – 'and he said yes, he had agreed, that you got on very well, and that he wished you to know that he was waiting for you to come so that you could begin. That is *all*.'

But Deven did not feel reassured: there was something about Murad that did not make for reassurance. He watched, thin-lipped, while Murad cleared the teacups off his table and began to arrange his papers on its filthy top, and said weakly, 'Then he must have misunderstood me. I only mentioned the interview, I never spoke about being his secretary. He did not even say he wanted a secretary. Who has put this idea into his head if not you? Now I can't go near him – if I go to him for the interview, he may make me sit down and start working for him – '

'See!' Murad shouted, suddenly slamming the flat of his hand upon a pile of papers on the desk. 'You see what I mean? Always afraid, always saying how can I, I will be killed, murdered, caught, made to do this, made to do that. Who can make you do what you don't want to do? Have you no tongue? Can you not speak? Can you not say, Nur Sahib, I have come for the interview I spoke of the other day. Please give me two hours of your time, Nur Sahib, that is all, then I must go back to my Hindi class in Lala Ram Lal College, Mirpore, to my wife and son, to my vegetarian meal and glass of milk – '

Deven got up sadly, knowing he could expect no help here. 'No one ever listens to me,' he said pathetically, pulling down the hem of his bush-shirt, feeling the pen in his shirt pocket, smoothing down his hair. 'That is the trouble – he won't listen to me.'

Murad had buried his head in his papers busily and looked up briefly to glare at him. 'Why should he listen to you?' he snapped. 'You are supposed to go there and listen to *him*. And go at once, will you, go quickly – I've wasted enough time on you already. By now another man would have interviewed him and brought me the piece.' He picked up a pencil that was halved in the middle and blue at one end and red at the other and began to make slashing lines across the pages in front of him, very impressively.

In the final examination at school, he had scored higher marks than Deven, although he had borrowed Deven's notes and often asked for Deven's help.

Once in the lane that ran along the back of the hospital wall, there was no chance of turning and fleeing, as all his best instincts told him to, for the door leading to the house stood wide open and other people were streaming along the lane towards it as well, all the traffic going in that one direction, making a turning round and retreating out of the question for anyone as anxious as Deven to avoid collision or attention. Men in dazzling white stood posted by the door to welcome all who came, and excited children in velvet caps and satin jackets ushered them over the threshold, already buried under a hill of shoes and sandals discarded by the guests who had entered the courtyard from which all the old litter had been cleared to make room for what appeared to be a soirée.

After his first alarmed palpitations had subsided, Deven began to feel relieved at the sight of such a crowd – perhaps he would not be noticed. Surely it was Nur himself who was going to recite his poetry, he would be seated on the divan that was spread with carpets and cushions, and Deven could hide behind the people sitting cross-legged and waiting on the cotton durries and white sheets spread in the open court-yard, and the two would not need to meet at all.

He dropped on to his knees and sank down behind a row of large, well-fed, passive men with splendid caps and turbans that would surely conceal him from whoever had the place of honour on the divan. But he was not to be left in peace: more people were pouring in through the small wooden doorway, and it seemed he was in everyone's way. He found himself at first huddling and crouching and making himself as small as possible, then having to shift further up the line in order to make room for the latecomers, and finally having

78

to push back and assert himself in order to breathe. People at the back began to press forward with the words, 'Brothers, make room for us here, please move up,' and others with no speech but only appropriate gestures, forcefully made. As he found himself moving up closer and closer to the front row, his face stiffened with embarrassment and displeasure. He kept it lowered almost on to his knees and did not see the performer coming out of the lighted room to be seated on the divan and was only made aware of it by the applause and shouted welcome.

When he did look, he blinked with shock to find seated, in the centre of the divan, not Nur's aged and benign figure in white but a powdered and painted creature in black and silver, coquetting beneath a shining veil which she held in place over her forehead while she turned her face from side to side, flashing smiles at her audience and making the ring on her nose glint with delight. She sat cross-legged and comfortable on the rug, her red-painted toes waggling with pleasure at the scene of which she was the undeniable centre. Nur was there too but not on the divan: he was at the back of the veranda, on a sagging cane chair, looking like a bag, or bolster, that someone had flung down on to it. His beard looked like rather old and yellowed stuffing that had leaked out of his chest and was tumbling across it, dustily. As Deven stared, open-mouthed with shock, at him, some young men came out, stood on either side of his chair, lifted him up by his arms and laughingly coaxed him to come to the front of the audience while an urchin dragged the chair along behind him and had it ready for him to sink on to, in the front row with Deven directly behind him. Perhaps he could have hidden, Nur would certainly not have been capable of turning right around and seeing him behind that large, sagging chair, but now Deven found he did not want to hide. Remembering the scene in which he had deserted him and fled that first night of their meeting, Deven was filled with an intense need to make amends and save the poet from whatever new humiliation that painted creature on the divan had devised for him that evening.

Struggling on to his knees and feeling them tremble under him, he whispered furtively, 'Sir – I have come – Murad-*bhai* gave me your message.'

Nur tried to swivel around in his chair, could not quite manage it, so only one eye peered from a cloudy corner through the distorting lens of his steel-rimmed spectacles that were perched on the great beak of his nose, and rolled around under a withered eyelid in an effort to recollect the face tilted up to him with such pain and intensity in its expression. Then he stuttered slowly, 'Yes, yes, yes – Murad-*bhai* – is coming? I sent him an invitation too.'

'He didn't tell me,' Deven cried, stabbed to the heart by the thought that Murad had deceived him once again, had known something he had not divulged, had sent him here this evening knowing there would be this soirée that Deven had no wish and no reason to attend and never would have done had he suspected anything. 'Murad – he – had an invitation?' he stammered.

'Yes, yes, yes – I told him to bring you along. I told him to bring his friends – everyone – ' his ineffective fingers waved in the air – 'to listen to Imtiaz-*bibi*. She is going to recite her new – new – ' he stammered a bit, then turned away in irritation at his inability to remember.

'Imtiaz Begum,' called a voice from the audience, 'you are like a star fallen into the well of the courtyard from which we have come to fetch water. When will you quench our thirst? Give us the Star poems. Will you give us the Star poems tonight?'

'I can recite nothing – nothing – until my accompanists have had enough refreshments and decide to come out,' she called back, joking, in an excited, high-pitched voice that grated on Deven's ear like a fingernail on a glass pane, and a cry went up for the accompanists who now found themselves hustled down the stairs from the upper rooms and brought along like a team of oxen, or servants, to range themselves behind her on the divan and start tuning their instruments. Some of them were still wiping their mouths and dusting crumbs off their lapels. Imtiaz Begum drew a laugh when she leaned towards one of them and flicked some shreds of sweet off his shoulder, making him rear back as if stung.

'So, had your last drink to help you survive this evening?' she teased them, an awful menace under the mock sweetness of her tone, and her audience roared delightedly while the drummer and the harmonium player broke into a sweat and pretended to busy themselves with knocking the drums with the tuning hammer and strumming the harmonium. A young woman with bulging eyes staring out of the pale, triangular face of a fanatic, ran her fingers wildly over the strings of the upright *tanpura*, over and over and over, till Imtiaz Begum turned and asked her to please play in tune or not at all whereupon she stopped playing altogether and appeared paralyzed.

Someone brought a silver box of betel nuts and leaves – the smile Imtiaz Begum gave was as sudden and swift as if scissors had cut it through her face, snip-snap, and the teeth were stained red besides. Those in the front row edged closer to her and carried on their banter but after a while she began to frown and press her hand to her forehead as if it hurt. She called petulantly for a glass of water. There was a delay. When it finally arrived, she thanked the red-faced bearer with an ornateness of speech that was heavily laced with sarcasm. Her audience tittered and she threw them a contemptuous look. Her mouth trembled with tension.

Deven looked anxiously at the poet who was shifting uneasily about in the cane chair, making it creak. He raised himself on to his knees in order to ask if he wanted something too – water, betel leaves, or simply to leave? But Nur, lowering his chin to his chest, only whispered, 'It is her birthday. This is in her honour. It is an auspicious day, her birthday.'

Yes, but who was she? Why should her birthday be celebrated in this manner? How could she claim monopoly of the stage with her raucous singing that now afflicted their ears, her stagey recitation of melodramatic and third-rate verse when the true poet, the great poet, sat huddled and silent, ignored and uncelebrated, Deven asked himself, determinedly not listening with more than a fraction of his attention. She was not worth listening to, he would not listen to her, he had not come to listen to her, he grumbled to himself, and scowled at the spectators who were bobbing their heads, swaying from side to side, beating time with their hands on their knees, giving forth loud exclamations of wonder and appreciation – like puppets, he thought, or trained monkeys. Yes, why not call a monkey trainer from the street and watch a monkey perform instead? It would not be very different, and the monkey would not demand so much applause and accord.

Deven's face was distorted with dislike of the scene. He had expected to come in and be admitted into the presence of the revered poet; he had hoped to put questions to him at last, to listen, and record his words. Instead, there was the thrumming of the drums and drawling of the harmonium and above that the thin, high-pitched voice flaunting itself before the audience like some demented dervish of sound. Just as Deven had suspected, the voice proved nasal and grating, often on the verge of cracking. If the audience applauded and cried 'Wah! Wah!' it was because it often did crack, giving out that authentic sound of heartbreak that was considered indispensable to the arts of music and poetry. When Deven brought himself to listen to a line or two, it was just as he thought: she said she was a bird in a cage, that she longed for flight, that her lover waited for her. She said the bars that held her were cruel and unjust, that her wings had been hurt by beating against them and only God could come and release her by lifting the latch on the cage door, God in the guise of her lover. When would he come? She languished, panting for the clouds that would carry him to her and the rain that would requite her thirst. Oh, it was all very beautiful, very feeling, very clever. Oh, she had learnt her tricks very well, the monkey. Did she not have the best teacher in the world to put these images, this language into her head? It was clear she had learnt everything from him, from Nur, and it was disgraceful how she was imitating his verses, parodying his skills, flaunting before his face what she had stolen from him, so slyly, so cunningly.

Deven clasped his arms around his knees and found them trembling under his chin with restrained rage, with emotion. He listened to the sounds of pleasure and appreciation going up from the audience in little bright bubbles that burst in the air, and felt murderous. The women with their veils held decorously over their heads while they vigorously chewed betel leaves and cried 'Ah-ha-ha' whenever a poetic phrase particularly touched them, the children in their rippling satiny garments who jumped and sprang and clapped as if at some wedding or festival, all pressing upon him in the small, tightly-packed courtyard where the air grew rapidly more stifling, gave him the same sensation he had when his wife's family came to visit them and her sisters and aunts and cousins climbed on to a string cot in the veranda and sat with their babies and their knitting, the needles flashing as rapidly as their tongues, then fell silent when they glimpsed him hurrying down the path on his way to college with a book tucked under his arm, only to burst into titters as soon as he was out of the gate. What was this conviviality of steamy femininity that found him a figure of fun and even reduced the aged and revered figure of the poet Nur to a pathetic old cushion that spilt out old stale cotton?

This woman, this so-called poetess, belonged to that familiar female mafia, he thought, looking at her with unconcealed loathing. She would need only to shed her silver and black carnival costume and take on the drabness of their virtuous clothing. Dressed as she was, she would of course be barred from their society – they would have thought her no better than a prostitute or dancing girl. Was she one? Narrowing his eyes in order to feign worldly wisdom, he wondered at her background, at her age. Impossible to detect under that floury layer of powder and the glistening of lipstick and rouge. She could be fifty, painted to look like a summer rose, he thought derisively. Who was she and how was it that Murad had not mentioned her? Nur must have given him some explanation when issuing the invitation. Had Nur said, 'My wife will recite' or, 'Imtiaz

Begum will perform'? Why did Nur submit to her insane whim of performing in his house, the house of a poet?

He could have gone on speculating and arriving at more and more bizarre and unsavoury explanations, but she paused, there was a sudden silence in which she cleared her throat loudly, clutching her neck as she did so. With a look of her eyes, she summoned some younger women out of the audience to her side. An earnest dialogue took place between them. After much scuffling and shifting and whispering, the harmonium player rose and left the divan and his place was taken by the oldest and plainest of her women friends – a thin, stiff woman clothed in brown with her veil tightly drawn across her forehead and tucked behind her ears to make her look as if she had no hair at all. The other friends, younger and prettier and more attractively clothed, fell back with obvious disappointment, giggling to cover up their discomfiture. It was the elderly stick-insect woman who was chosen to sing. It was obvious to Deven why, and he twisted his lips in scorn at the poetess's vanity. Turning to the audience again and pointing at her throat – which was long and slim and fair, yes – she explained, 'You must forgive me – my throat – it gives me trouble. I need your help – your forgiveness.' She bowed her head. Had she been an actress once? A dancer? Where – in a brothel? She knew all the appropriate tricks. Now she began to sing in a lower key, in a sad, wilted voice, as one on whom the rain did not fall, whose lover did not come. After each phrase, she fell silent and sat brooding, picking at the rug with red-nailed fingers while her friend took up the phrase and repeated and embellished it in tragic tones. Her voice was as plain as her appearance – Imtiaz Begum could not have chosen a more apt foil. Oh she was cunning, cunning, Deven had to admit.

Suddenly Nur heaved himself out of his chair and stood tottering on the two pillars of his legs, looking as if he were about to fall. Deven scrambled to his feet to support him from behind. He was aware of the women on the divan glaring in their direction, the audience shifting and shuffling and questioning the interruption, but he ignored them and stepped over their feet and knees and shoulders to help the poet stumble away into the veranda.

'It is enough,' groaned Nur. 'I must lie down. Show me my bed.'

Deven looked around for help, knowing perfectly well he would not be able to haul him up the stairs to the top floor by himself. Seeing them stagger down the veranda with their arms around each other, some of the young men sitting at the back of the audience detached themselves from the carpets and came to their aid.

'What is it, Nur Sahib, aren't you enjoying the Begum's birthday celebrations?' asked a young man with a nasal voice like the singer's. He even had her nervous, intense face. She must have planted her relations in the audience, to lead the applause. Didn't Deven know that for a common trick? He gave him a fierce look and did not surrender Nur's arm.

But Nur groaned, 'I am tired – I want – I want – ' and stood looking around helplessly. To Deven's relief, the dirty urchin who generally served him put down a trayful of clay cups of tea that he was passing around and came to help. Together, they shoved the old man, creaking and complaining, all the way up the stairs to the room on the terrace. It was a long haul, painful and often verging on the impossible, but as the two voices rose and joined each other in a frenzied crescendo, the impulse to escape grew so strong that it helped them to achieve that impossible level. Here, although the late night show of the nearby cinema house was in full swing, its songs and dialogues and pistol shots magnified and relayed across rooftops and streets and bazaars, it seemed quieter simply because it was deserted, there was no one else there. The curtains and mats were drawn against the lurid electric lighting and kept the room as dark as a lair.

They lowered Nur on to his bed and he collapsed upon it as a dead weight. The boy disappeared into a corner and then reappeared with Nur's usual tumbler filled to the brim. He did not ask if Deven wanted one too and Nur did not appear to notice the lapse. Even hospitality was driven out of his head by the performance downstairs.

Deven sat on the cane stool as he had on his first visit, keeping his head lowered so as not to watch while the poet drank and drank. Then, wiping his mouth and throwing his head back into the high pillow, Nur sighed, 'Birthdays. I thought we had done with celebrating them, with the setting up of gravestones along the path of life. Who wants to read the dates engraved upon them? But the vanity of women – oh, the vanity! No chance to gather garlands, gifts, applause, attention can be passed by, you see. Not even the occasion of the setting up of another gravestone.' He began to laugh sadly and Deven cleared his throat, not knowing if it was proper to add his own banal comments on the matter. He had himself long ago stopped counting the years, and when asked his age had to stop and calculate: was it thirty-five or thirty-six?

'Mind you,' said Nur, surprising Deven by fixing an eye on him and speaking much more crisply of a sudden, 'she was not always like this, you know. When she first came to my house, she was happy just to sit in a corner, and listen. She told me she wrote verse – but she would not even show it to me. She said she only wanted to listen – and learn from me. She sent my secretary away. I had a secretary then but she said she wanted to work for me so she sent him away.' He closed his eyes and laughed silently, his lips peeling back from his stained gums and rotten teeth, like a mask of decay. 'You see, they are like that in the beginning, when you are alone together. But then the others came – to listen to me. They only wanted to hear my poetry. They paid her no attention. And she was not used to that. So that is how it began . . . ' He waved his hand in the direction of the performance down in the courtyard, now loud with the accompaniment of drums and harmonium, reaching for a high-pitched climax in the night. 'That is what she really wanted, you see. This house – my house – was the right setting for it. The right setting – unlike her own house which was a house for dancers, you see – although she was quite famous, you know, for her singing. She was one of the top – the top – when I saw her – ' he mumbled, still with his eyes

86

closed. 'But she was not content with that, she wanted my house, my audience, my friends. She raided my house, stole my jewels – those are what she wears now as she sits before an audience, showing them off as her own. They are not her own, they are *mine*! And she sent my secretary away too.' He gave a cry, opened his eyes very wide and held out his tumbler to be refilled. Holding it close to his chin, he began to curse the woman in the most filthy terms he could assemble with his slurred speech and sodden memory. The dark room reeked – of filthy abuse, rotten gums, raw liquor, too many years and too much impotent rage.

Deven disliked this as much as he had earlier disliked the woman and her singing. It was not a fit subject and not proper language for a poet, nor worthy of the poet. Trying to interrupt, he said desperately, 'Murad-*bhai* told me you wished to dictate something to me, sir, that you had something you wished me to take down – '

'What?' roared Nur. 'Another looter? raider? thief? Poor as I am, must I have the rags torn off my back by these vultures who can't wait till I die? Allah – oh Allah,' he began to weep, flinging himself about till the servant boy came back with an angry look and took his glass from him to refill. Then he lay against his pillows, quietly holding it under his chin, and glanced slyly at Deven to see what effect his outbreak had had on him. 'What have I to give you, my friend? Nothing, I tell you, nothing. I am a beggar myself now, all my jewels stolen away.' He gave a sudden howl, animal and ululating, making Deven freeze.

'You sent me a postcard, calling me,' Deven reminded him reproachfully.

The newly vehement tone of his voice made the poet break off his lament and turn it somehow into a laugh. 'Oh yes, yes – perhaps. That was on the day I wrote a new poem. No, not new, that is not true – it was one I wrote long ago, in college, the day my best friend died, and I suddenly remembered the first four lines of it; then it all came back to me – ' he gestured with the palm of his hand, drawing it across his eyes as if wiping a pane of glass – 'it all came back, you know – his fever, how he raved, how he died, while outside a gardener was watering the rosebed with a hose pipe and a mynah bird was singing in the spray from it, but he couldn't hear and I was telling him to listen – and I wanted someone to write it down for me while I tried to remember it all.'

Deven found himself on his knees beside the bed. He had slipped off his stool and was kneeling beside the poet. 'I will write it now,' he urged, 'if you will recite it, sir.'

Nur reflected on that for a long time, his opaque eyes turned inwards as he sipped his drink. Then his eyes rolled sideways and one of them seemed to droop out of its red socket towards Deven's tilted, waiting face. 'I have many poems,' he muttered, with a certain slyness, 'many I could tell you – never written down, or written and lost. But I am too old to go hunting them down, too broken and crushed, you see, to find all that is there – somewhere here – ' he slapped the side of his head, making it wag. 'But if the right person – the right man – came, not Imtiaz Bibi, I won't tell her, I won't let her have them – I need someone else – and if I could find someone else to sit beside me and listen, I'd have much to tell, yes,' he began to laugh softly into Deven's face. 'Much, much to tell,' he chuckled.

Deven was still on his knees, breathing painfully, trying to think what proposal he could make, how he could draw out of Nur the maximum amount, when there was a noise of slapping slippers on the tiled floor of the veranda, of papery satin slashing against swift legs, and in marched Imtiaz Begum, her face ravaged, lipstick and kohl smeared from the corners of her eyes to the corners of her mouth, her hair escaping in black bunches from under the veil on to her shoulders, and her long fingers clutching at her fluttering, metallic garments as if to rip them. Exhaustion and rage were written in her every gesture and expression.

Instantly Nur began to cringe, his lips to pout, his glass to tilt and spill across Deven's hands, folded in supplication at the edge of the bed. Deven, remaining paralyzed in that position, entered that state in which he could not credit his own eyes and ears, doubted every sound and image as it attacked him, and never could say later what he had seen or heard.

'So, this is where you have come to hide,' she began in her hoarse, exhausted voice. 'A tortoise that sticks its head in the mud at the bottom of the pond,' she taunted him. 'You couldn't face an audience that was not willing to listen to you. You couldn't accept the evidence of my success. You could not bear the sight of someone else regaling a large audience with poetry – the same poetry you used to mouth – '

'Mouth? I mouthed it?' moaned Nur, as hoarse as her.

'Yes, and see what it has earned me tonight,' she cried, letting fall the fold of her garment that she had been clutching so that rupee notes showered from it to the floor. Neither Nur nor Deven turned their heads a fraction to look at the money. Averting their eyes from it as if from something monstrously embarrassing, they sat frozen while she screamed, 'Ali! Ali! Come and pick this up and count it. Put it in a bag and give it to your master.'

'No, Ali, don't touch it!' cried Nur, turning his face aside and shutting his eyes.

'Then how will you buy your drink?' she challenged him. 'How will you pay for all those bottles Ali gets you from the corner shop? You know that is how you have ruined your voice, your song. That is why you cannot abide my voice, cannot abide to hear me sing and so you insult me by getting up and leaving my performance. You *insult* me!'

Her voice rose to such a pitch that it was about to shatter, and Deven lifted his hands to his ears before the walls cracked and the roof fell upon them, but all that happened was that the screen at the door was lifted aside and another woman entered the room. Deven looked to see if rescue was at hand, and saw an old creature wrapped in a brown cloak, her white hair combed about the sides of her face. The face was commanding, so straight in its lines, so military in its firmness. 'Run away from here, bitch,' she said in a level voice, and in a corner Ali was heard to snigger – 'and leave the old man alone. What more do you want from him? You have taken his name and his reputation and today even his admirers. Be satisfied. Leave him and go down, go dance before the public since that is your manner of earning a living – '

The younger woman who had appeared stricken by apoplexy, leapt at her with a screech. Nur's bed lay between the two, she would have to leap over him and stamp him under her feet to get at her enemy. Deven would have to protect him. He scrambled to his feet, and turned and fled.

'I had to catch the bus,' he explained. 'The last bus to Mirpore. I couldn't spend another night in Delhi without informing Sarla. She gets very worried and – '

'Oh, Deven, *fool*, you thought about your *bus* at that moment? Instead of staying to see the two women tear each other's eyes out over the great poet's body, as anyone else would have done his best to stay and witness, you ran to catch your *bus*?' Murad lay back in his chair, gasping with horror and laughter.

'I can't do this night after night,' Deven complained in an aggrieved tone. 'I have my job to think of, and my wife and son. I can't let this family's dramas and performances take over my whole life.'

'Even if it is the family of the poet Nur?' Murad asked in a disbelieving tone. 'I must say, I had expected something different from you, my friend. I thought with your lifelong admiration for his work, your book about him, you were sensitive to his poetry, his quality – '

'I am, I am,' protested Deven. 'Of course I am, Murad. Everything I have written, everything I have *thought* is influenced by Nur, by Nur's poetry. It is only his genius, my respect for his genius that made me come to Delhi and agree to the interview – '

'Look here, *you* don't have to agree to any interview,' Murad broke in roughly. 'It is Nur Sahib who has to agree to the interview – '

'Murad-*bhai*,' Deven interrupted eagerly, 'What I am trying to say is that it will be much more than a magazine interview. He is prepared to give me much more than that. I don't know how it is – whether he has seen in me a disciple, a scholar, a student, or what – or if he is so old now and finds the end close – but he has told me he wants me to do much more than interview him. He is willing to recite his poetry to me, new verse and old verse that he has never written down, it is all still in his head and will be lost if it isn't written – he wants me to take it down. I think I can do even more if I can draw it out of him, if I have time, he may even dictate his memoirs to me . . . ' his voice shook, faded away, and a look crossed his face that made Murad stare.

'You think so?' he queried, seemingly impressed at last. 'That would be a great event, Deven, a great event in the world of Urdu poetry. Perhaps I can give up a whole number to it – a whole number dedicated to Nur Sahib's work – '

'Murad, it will be more than just a magazine number – it may be a book,' Deven glowed. 'If only we have the time -- he and I – to meet and put it all down on paper – ' now he broke off and frowned, worriedly. 'But how? That is the problem. How can I take time off from my work in the college? How am I to take it all down – '

'A tape recording.' Murad said, promptly and emphatically. 'That is the answer: a tape recording.'

Deven gave him a disgusted look. 'What are you talking about?' he snapped. 'You think this is going to be some song for the cinema, or radio, perhaps? Hunh – tape recording! You Delhi-wallahs and your big ideas.'

'You village pumpkin,' Murad exclaimed. 'You are still stuck in the age of the printed page, hypnotized by Gutenberg, I suppose. Don't you know it is over? Don't you know the written line is nearly extinct? If you can't add sound and sight, it won't do with the public. The public wants to see and hear, not put spectacles on its nose and learn the alphabet. These days everything is put down on film or tape. Haven't you seen, or heard, you donkey?'

'Look, don't use all those animal names,' Deven said sharply, growing hot about the ears.

'All right, all right, I will call you by flowers' names if you like – only listen. Get hold of a tape recorder. Then go and sit beside his bed. Give him a drink – buy him a bottle – and ask him to start reciting. Everyone knows he needs to be oiled, so do the oiling and he will recite. Switch on the tape recorder, sit back and listen. That is all. You will have it all on tape, for the whole Urdu-speaking world to listen to, not only Nur's words but Nur's own voice!' His voice rose in triumph at this serendipitous idea and he practically laughed in self-congratulation. 'Then you can take home the tapes and take dictation from them. You can do that at home. See, it will solve all your petty family-man problems: get Nur's memoirs on tape, carry them home and transcribe them at your leisure. So you have a book as well at the end of it. *My Days with Nur Shahjehanabadi* – how do you like the title? Deven-*bhai,* when you have a head like a pumpkin and live in a field, then it is better to come to someone like me for ideas, no? Would such an idea have entered your head, there amongst the grains and grasses of your village? No, you have to come to me for it. At least pay me the compliment of looking intelligent, looking as if you understood and felt grateful – '

'Murad-*bhai,*' Deven confessed at last, 'it is – it is a brilliant idea. Brilliant. But a tape recording, a tape recorder – how? From where will I get such things? I don't have one. I have never used one. I have not even managed to buy a radio yet for my family and you are telling me to get a tape recorder and tapes.'

Murad slammed the flat of his hand down on the table top and got up, pushing away his chair. 'Try to use your own head sometimes – give it a little exercise – it will get stuck with rust otherwise. Is it so difficult to get a tape recorder? To find someone to use it? To get hold of a few blank tapes? This is the age of electronics, haven't you heard? Or hasn't the news travelled to Mirpore yet? Go and get one,' he roared suddenly, 'and then come and ask me what to do next.'

CHAPTER SIX

All that week the college had been undergoing its annual spring cleaning – its walls washed and splashed with lime, its floors and corridors swept, fresh red gravel brought and spread on the worn and dusty driveway, and in the absence of flowerbeds and lawns, truckloads of potted plants arrived and were arranged on either side of the stairs, their burly, shaggy heads given a shaking and a sprinkling in an effort to make them look fresh and sylvan. A man on a ladder unscrewed all the fused bulbs from the ceiling lamps and screwed in new ones, his long face morose with the knowledge that within a week all would be stolen or smashed again. Money was unexpectedly found unspent and a water cooler bought for the students and set up at the end of a long corridor where it was destined to leak and rust in the centre of a permanent puddle that students' shoes tracking through turned to liquid mud. The first graffiti were scratched into its blue metal flanks the night before the annual board meeting. No one noticed because that was the night when the frenzy of activity reached its zenith: a striped cotton marquee arrived on a lorry as if for a wedding and was erected on the sports field so that the early risers next morning, out for their constitutionals in their tennis shoes or off to fetch the milk in clattering cans, saw it risen from the dust like a magical balloon striped red, yellow and blue.

It was in its shade that tea was served, at an unaccustomed

hour of the morning, when the board meeting was over. Punctually at ten o'clock the members of the board had arrived in cars owned or hired by the college for the occasion, and up those flowerpot-flanked steps they had hurried, quickly and neatly folding their hands and bowing to the Principal who stood at the bottom of the stairs in a newly dry-cleaned grey suit, and then hurrying on like important public figures with not a moment to lose. The staff, given the day off from teaching, hung around the corridors, not knowing quite what to do with themselves. They had to be present. They were all to be introduced to the board after the meeting, but till then they could only cluster around the long windows that were slits cut into the veranda walls, gossiping and joking as the students did on other days. Today the students had a holiday and were away, except for those who lived in the hostel. A few of these had come out of curiosity and a lack of anything better to do, although that was all they discussed: that something better to do that they did not have.

At last the weighty matter of the board meeting was over. Out streamed the members of the board, the Principal, the Registrar, the administrative staff – relaxed now and smiling – moving leisurely down the corridors and the stairs. They had to be urged to come along for tea. It was not polite to rush, they hung back while the tea-makers in the marquee waited beside the smoking charcoal fires, the tin trays arranged with pink-flowered crockery, the plates of dry biscuits and saucers of nuts.

Under the marquee, the ladies stood up from the three-piece sofa set that was reserved for the guests of honour, and the straight-backed chairs that had been brought out of the classrooms and arranged along three sides of the enclosure for the lesser guests. The Principal's wife, in a new sari of Japanese nylon printed all over with sprigs of brown and violet flowers, came forward with folded hands to greet the chief guest. The Principal was perspiring as he introduced his wife to him (she was going through a difficult time of life and one could never tell what she might do or say; she had turned overnight from bovine and placid to unpredictable).

After an anxious moment he allowed himself to smile – the chief guest had made a joke about it being a hard day for the ladies who had done so much to make the occasion a success, and his wife had smiled and said exactly what she ought to have said, i.e. not at all, it was a pleasure. So that was all right. They stepped aside from the flapping entrance of the tent to make way for the others who now streamed in, no longer required to postpone their thirst.

There was such a sound of splashing and spilling then, of clinking and clattering, of sloshing and giggling, one might have been quite misled as to the seriousness of this annual affair. None of the staff ever quite forgot themselves – it would have taken something much stronger than sweet milky tea to do that – and they tingled with the possibility of the long arm of the administration reaching out and hauling them up to be introduced to Someone High Up. Every now and then they whipped out their handkerchiefs and wiped their faces or looked over their shoulders to see how close they were to, or how far from, those important guests of honour and even more importantly, the Principal, who was after all of a more direct concern to them. Their scholarly spectacles glinted, nervous hands smoothed down hair and tried to keep away from the cigarette packets in their pockets, throats were repeatedly cleared and a conscientious effort made to seek out ladies and be ostentatiously polite to them – in a relaxed manner, of course, as though they did it every day, without thinking. Then the tea tray was passed around, cups handed out, and the sounds and movements they made began to resemble those of children on a beach or, more accurately in view of their hopeless shabbiness, children collecting water at a municipal tap.

Deven felt this transformation go through him as well, a pleasantly relaxing, self-forgetting process, but when he realized that the Principal was just behind him, he grew tense again, quite still, holding the tin spoon upright in his cup of tea, forgetting to stir in his fear of a hand upon his collar: the summons. Then, feeling the crowd press against him to make way for the royal progress, and seeing the backs of their heads

95

as they moved on towards the table where the Principal's wife stood smiling, one arm outflung from under the brown and purple Japanese nylon folds towards a dish of charmingly arranged biscuits beside a vase stuffed with charming marigolds just beginning to die, he relaxed, he stirred his spoon blithely round and round in his cup and looked up to greet whoever came his way.

Fatefully, it was the head of the Urdu department, Abid Siddiqui who, in keeping with the size and stature of that department, was a small man, whose youthful face was prematurely topped with a plume of white hair as if to signify the doomed nature of his discipline. It was perhaps unusual to find a private college as small as Lala Ram Lal's offering a language such as Urdu that was nearly extinct, but it happened that Lala Ram Lal's descendants had not inherited quite so big a fortune as to endow the entire college on their own, and had had to accept a very large donation from the descendants of the very nawab who had fled Delhi in the aftermath of the 1857 mutiny and built the mosque as well as some of the largest villas in Mirpore. They had been absolutely determined however not to allow this family's name upon the signboard over the gate. The Muslim family had felt slighted and threatened to withdraw its donation. A compromise was therefore made and it was promised a department in which its language would be kept alive in place of the family name. Being occupied with more interesting matters such as the purchase of land and cement and steel and the tenders to be floated and the profits to be made therefrom, the college authorities had disregarded the probability that very few citizens of Mirpore would opt to study, or allow their offspring to study, a language that had become doomed the day the Muslims departed across the newly-drawn border to the new country of Pakistan. In fact, if a few Muslim families had not stubbornly remained behind and had had young ones to send to the college to study Urdu, the department would have remained as empty as the cell from which the condemned prisoner is extracted to be hanged. Abid Siddiqui made up the entire staff of the department and even so found he had scarcely any work to do on account of the size of his classes. Perhaps this was why he tended to wander about the college grounds, his head slightly to one side, looking inquiringly about him as if he were a small bird in search of a modest worm. This made him one of the few people in Lala Ram Lal College from whom Deven did not shrink. He turned to greet him with a smile.

Catching his eye, Siddiqui said, 'Sharma Sahib, the annual day tea is better than the daily tea, isn't it?' and Deven responded with an eager laugh, thinking a conversation so brightly begun might well end as cheerfully.

'The annual day tea is different from the daily tea in every way,' he laughed – giggled actually.

'No, it is not a representative day, a typical day,' agreed Siddiqui. 'Look, we are being served nuts by ladies who do not normally recognize us.'

'And whom we are not prepared to recognize daily either,' said Deven with an unaccustomed roguishness as he stretched out his hand towards a saucer of salted cashew nuts before it was whisked out of his reach. 'Expensive eatables,' he said, munching. 'Cashew nuts, forty rupees a kilo, at least.'

Siddiqui looked after the disappearing tray a little sadly. 'Hard times,' he agreed in a murmur. 'Hard times.'

'Even in your department?' Deven asked, with a slyness that quite shook him by its originality. 'No, don't tell me, Siddiqui Sahib. It may be the smallest department in the college but it is better so – the quality is the finest.'

'Like the cashew nuts?' Siddiqui gave a painful smile. 'Yes, Urdu is becoming a rarity – it is only grown for export. To Pakistan, or to the Gulf. Have you heard, Faiz has gone to Beirut, to edit an Urdu magazine there?'

'But why?' Deven looked concerned. 'That will not help the Urdu cause. Why not write for magazines in India? We still have some, Siddiqui Sahib, and it is a good cause to support.'

'Good causes are also lost causes, Sharma Sahib.'

'No, no,' Deven protested. 'Here is the leading Urdu journal in Delhi planning a special number on new Urdu poetry - it can surely not be a lost cause.'

'Oh? Which one is that? Do they hope to get any worth-while poetry to publish?'

'Of course,' Deven exclaimed, quite shocked by Siddiqui's ignorance and lack of confidence in his cause. 'Even – even Nur Shahjehanabadi is going to have some of his previously unpublished poems in it: it will be a great event.'

Siddiqui cocked his bushy white eyebrows when he heard that – he was clearly impressed, and being one of the nicer members of the staff, he did not mind showing it. 'If Nur Shahjehanabadi produces any poetry after fifteen years of silence, that will be a great event certainly, in this small world of Urdu poetry. He is a whale in a pail of water, I have always thought.'

Just then the Principal and his chief guest, having filled their teacups at the table and talked to the ladies who clustered there, safely on the other side of the table, turned back to the crowd and made their way towards the upholstered sofa set. People fell back to make way for the royal progress, and Deven found himself pressed into a closer proximity with Abid Siddiqui than he had ever entered before. It made him more confidential in his manner; there were, after all, only two teacups between them. Dropping his voice and speaking into his ear, as if it were a secret, he murmured, 'And I have been asked to interview him so that the interview may appear along with the poems.'

Now both the eyebrows crawled upwards in incredulity. 'You are going to meet him?' Siddiqui asked, a little disbeliev-ingly. When Deven had come to him a year ago as a prospec-tive lecturer, in anticipation of better days in the Urdu depart-ment, he had not detected much of note in that craven young man: he now wondered if he could have been mistaken. 'You are going to see him?'

Deven smiled. 'I have been to his house on many occasions,' he pronounced slowly, for full effect, and for the first time in his life felt that the occasion called for pomposity, a state to which he had always secretly aspired. 'I have had many conversations with him. In fact,' he plunged on recklessly, 'I may do more than an article for *Awaaz* – I might write a biography. He has even said he might dictate his memoirs to me.'

Siddiqui too began to smile. This was clearly a fantasy, to be humoured but not trusted. His manner became appropriately facetious. 'To you? A-ha. The great poet came to Mirpore and asked you to be his official biographer, I suppose?'

Deven was hurt. It was clear that his words were not being taken for the truth. He became aggressive. 'How can he be expected to come to Mirpore at his age, to see anyone?' he protested. 'Of course it is I who go and call on him. The matter of his autobiography came up just like that – I did not suggest it, or plan it – but he wants someone to listen to him and take down his memoirs.'

Siddiqui had lowered his head to the teacup's lip, reflectively, like a bird regarding a dot inside that might, or might not, turn out to be an insect. It was not possible to see his expression when he said, after a minute of silence, 'Stranger things have happened, I suppose.'

Deven was not sure if he ought to laugh or feel insulted. He made a snorting sound that could have meant either. 'I know you don't believe me but I will prove it to you, you will see.'

'You could always turn it into a work of imagination,' Siddiqui murmured. 'You know, a few facts and some fantasy. It is said to be a fashionable form in – in other parts of the world,' he became a little vague: his connections with those parts was tenuous.

Deven was stung. 'I am not going to write it at all,' he retorted. 'I am going to record it. Tape it. Yes, I am looking for a tape recorder. The editor of *Awaaz* has told me to get a tape recorder and put it all on tape. That is how it is done these days – in other parts of the world,' he added, a bit viciously. 'And one day, when it is done, I will invite you to come and listen. Then you can see if it is the voice of Nur – or a fantasy.'

Siddiqui was clearly intrigued. When Mr Trivedi, the head librarian, came up to them to chat, he brushed him aside and, taking Deven by the elbow, said, 'You must tell me more about this, Sharma Sahib – it is the first time I have heard of a biography on tape. You have to admit, it is not done like that in *our* part of the world. What is this, please – the age of electronics entering the royal court of poetry over which the Moghuls once presided? Tell me, what is this all about?'

In a corner, sheltering behind one of the poles that propped up the striped canopy over their heads, Deven babbled the whole story as if it were a stream of water from a tap turned on by a sympathetic hand. He did not care much if Siddiqui believed him or not, he was not concerned about persuading him, he was merely relieved to be able to talk about it and hear someone else's opinions and comments on what seemed even to him sometimes a fantastical and improbable project. Describing it to someone else gave it lineaments and dimensions, a certain substance and reality that he himself occasionally doubted. When Siddiqui listened to him closely, stroking his small spade-shaped beard as he did so, and watching his face with sharp, bird-bright eyes, and finally said, 'Strange, wonderfully strange, Sharma Sahib, but even stranger things happen, it is true,' he felt sufficiently relieved of doubts and hesitations, at least for the moment, to cry out enthusiastically, 'Siddiqui Sahib, won't it be a great thing for Urdu literature? Don't you think every reader of Urdu will find it interesting? What about your department, eh? Won't they want to listen to the tapes? Perhaps I will have copies made and send them to the Urdu departments of all universities in India. Murad Sahib says it is the rage in Delhi – people tape record music recitals, poetry recitations, everything. Perhaps your department will buy a cassette player one day, and a library of tapes for its students. And whenever you like you will be able to switch it on – and hear the poet's voice reciting his own poetry.'

Now Siddiqui threw back his head and laughed – not derisively, but disbelievingly. He laughed like a boy, delightedly. Clasping Deven's arm, above the elbow, he cried, 'Wonderful! Wonderful! Truly all our poets will become singing birds to us then. We will be able to hear the voice of the *koel*, the *bul-bul*, whichever songster we wish to hear –'

'Yes, Siddiqui Sahib, why not make a proposal to the Principal? Why not ask him to buy the department some equipment? Today they must have discussed the budget of the past year and the new year; why not suggest to them that they allocate some funds for buying your department a tape recorder, tapes, a cassette player, and to begin the era of electronics in our college?'

They laughed like children at an absurdly funny joke. Some of the staff and guests who heard them turned to stare. This was an occasion of some formality after all, and few people forgot themselves to such an extent as these two in their inadequate hiding-place behind the bunting-wrapped pole under the *shamiana*. Neither of them noticed: they were enjoying themselves too much.

'Sharma Sahib, how can a timid rabbit like myself approach King Leo in his den? And that too on the day of the royal *durbar*? But I will tell you what we can do,' Siddiqui added, nodding his head brightly, 'Let us go together and try to corner King Leo's chief minister, Mr Jackal, and put it to him. As you say, with the new budget under discussion, this may be just the time to find Mr Jackal in a good frame of mind, seeing his treasury full.'

'Mr Jackal?' Deven giggled, mopping his face which was quite heated and red. He had begun to feel as if he were suffering from a hallucination: never in his life had things gone so smoothly, so spontaneously, the various counters falling into place quite fortuitously, without plan or scheme. He had only just begun to see the pattern of the board before him and discern the direction of the game that he had been playing so thoughtlessly and carelessly.

'Yes, yes, the registrar of course, the registrar,' chuckled Siddiqui, and clasping their spare hands together as if they had just signed a treaty and were posing for the photographers, they both burst into laughter.

The laughter faded away when they found him sitting alone on a straight-backed chair behind the upholstered sofa set, quite left out of the *tête-à-tête* the Principal was having with the chief guest and indeed any other conversation in his vicinity. Looking gloomily into space and wagging the leg he had laid across one knee, he looked very much the extra

101

in the game, one who belonged to no department and had no part to play.

But Siddiqui had his reasons for approaching him. Rubbing his hands together he stepped briskly up and exclaimed, 'How are you, Rai Sahib? Tired by your taking down of the minutes? Tired by all those discussions about the budget? Exhausting subject, finance.'

'No, no, not exhausting at all, there is not much finance to be discussed,' returned Mr Rai, uncrossing his legs and bending forwards cordially. He appeared quite relieved to have his solitary reverie interrupted. 'The Board only informs us of cuts in the budget, not of any grants. That is how it is.'

'Rai Sahib, that is bad news,' Siddiqui said, grimacing as exaggeratedly as an actor. 'Here we are, two lecturers from the language departments, coming to you with an earnest request – and you are threatening us with a cut before you even hear our plea.'

'I am not threatening you with cuts, Siddiqui Sahib, it is the board that threatens us,' protested Mr Rai, smiling happily at this bit of flattery.

Deven remained in the background, his hands clasped behind his back, not quite certain why Siddiqui should think it necessary to flatter a minor functionary of the college administration on that day of all days, but feeling he ought to leave the matter to Siddiqui since he had no clue himself as to how one went about making requests for finance. Not being sure either what the status of the Urdu department was, he could not predict how the proposal would be met. He was perfectly aware that funds were being made readily available to the science departments, that the sciences were the rajas of the empire with the humanities pushed to the dustier and more neglected corners where they languished. If any of the humanities departments received any attention, it was usually those of economics and political science. The languages were not considered departments worthy of any attention of the financial kind beyond the meagre funds allocated to the library. Deven did not have much confidence in the status of the Urdu department, seeing how small and precarious it was, there on sufferance merely, and perhaps that was why Siddiqui did not feel he could approach anyone of importance about something that concerned only it, and chose to speak to bored Mr Rai instead. Perhaps, also, he felt it was essential to begin at the bottom of the ladder if he meant to rise to the top. Anyway, anyone watching Siddiqui's delightful performance and hearing his exquisitely ornate use of the language could not help feeling a small stir of hope.

He was standing there stiffly, fingers locked behind his back, his head respectfully lowered as he listened to the two of them exchange reminiscences of Lucknow – both of them had been students of the university there – and of old stalwarts of the Urdu academic world, when he felt an arm slide around him and he was pulled around to face Jayadev of his own department.

'Where were you last Sunday, Deven-*bhai*?' Jayadev shouted in his ear while pounding him on his back. 'And the Sunday before that? Eh? Tell us where you go off every spare moment you have? You have been observed, you know – '

'Shh,' hissed Deven angrily, but Jayadev would not let go his arm and dragged him away into a knot of junior lecturers and readers who were eating the last of the biscuits and nuts and drinking cold tea rather than leave a crumb or a drop behind. 'Sharma Sahib,' they called, 'come and confess – who is this fair beauty of Delhi who lures you away every Sunday? The whole college is talking about her. You thought you hadn't been seen slipping away, eh? Come and tell us all – '

When Deven finally tore himself out of their grip, he turned in despair to find the sofa set and the straight-backed chair empty, Siddiqui gone, Mr Rai gone. Instead, his wife stood there, her hands folded before her, waiting, her face heavy with distress and sulkiness: she never liked meeting his colleagues or their wives and had had to be coaxed into coming that morning. Scowling, she asked, 'Can we go home now? Manu will be hungry. He will be crying.'

Deven was not unacquainted with disappointments and anti-climaxes, with delays and diversions. It did not surprise him at all that the unusual success of his conversation with Siddiqui, passing with such unfamiliar rapidity from doubt to interest and enthusiasm, should have been dashed within minutes upon the stony insensitivity and crudity of his colleagues who had forced them apart and prevented them from pursuing this new association. What did surprise him was the note from Siddiqui brought to his classroom by an Urdu student while he was teaching next day, and the cryptic line scrawled on it to say Mr Rai expected him in his office at twelve o'clock.

Seeing that line waver and break up and come together again upon the sheet of blue paper, Deven felt as if he were seeing all the straight lines and cramped alphabet of his small, tight life wavering and dissolving and making way for a wave of freshness, motion, even kinesis. In openness lay possibilities, the top of the wave of experience surging forward from a very great distance, but lifting and closing in and sounding loudly in his ear. What had happened to the hitherto entirely static and stagnant backwaters of his existence? It was not the small scrawled note, not Siddiqui or Rai or anyone to do with the college who had caused this stir: it was Nur, Nur's poetry and Nur's person; Nur who had caused this thrust, this rush that was sweeping up from outside and making him step forward to meet it, asking it to pour over his feet and mount up his legs to his waist and then his chest and finally carry him right away.

It made his step uncertain as he hurried down the corridor to the registrar's office. Here the wave came to a standstill, dashed against the stained wall and the rusty steel furniture and boiled with frustration, but it would have been too unnatural if there had not been some little obstruction after all. Mr Rai was not in his office at twelve o'clock. After Deven had sat on a chair in the corner for fifteen minutes he rose and asked the doorman if he knew where he was. Of course, was the answer, he was at a meeting in the Principal's room, there was no telling how long it would go on, Deven could wait if he liked – or go. The doorman shrugged, implying it was all one to him but suggested, by the way he spat out the

104

dead butt of a leaf cigarette, that he would prefer it if Deven went. He waited – he could still see the white crest of the distant wave, not very clearly any more but still – until it was time for his next class, then left, drooping with his familiar despair. Yet, on his way home to a late lunch, he decided suddenly to look in on Mr Rai and found him there.

Rai looked up from his files without a smile but not quite with a frown either, simply the everyday pursing of his lips. 'Oh Mr Sharma,' he said, 'here is the paper Mr Siddiqui asked me to give you – a sanction to buy audio-visual equipment for use in the languages department. Please ask for tenders, they have to be submitted before entering into any agreement. This should have been done at the highest level of course but Mr Siddiqui tells us you are in touch with people in Delhi who can help you to obtain the best equipment. Perhaps it is more readily available in Delhi,' he admitted, and Deven felt almost shattered by his agreeableness, by Siddiqui's clever-ness, by the success of the whole mad venture in which he himself had scarcely dared to believe. But the piece of pink official paper was in his hand, a barely legible carbon copy of a pencil-written note from the Principal sanctioning what seemed to Deven a more than princely sum for the 'audio-visual equipment'. True, it was only a piece of paper, not a cheque or a roll of banknotes that would have made it seem more substantial and reliable, but even a note such as this had never come his way before. He had never summoned up the courage even to ask his bank manager for a loan, and he doubted if he himself would actually have found the nerve to make such a fantastic request of the college, had Siddiqui not made it for him. What had made Siddiqui do it?

Nur, of course, the magic name of Nur Shahjehanabadi of course, thought Deven, walking out into the brassy light. It was a name that opened doors, changed expressions, caused dust and cobwebs to disappear, visions to appear, bathed in radiance. It had led him on to avenues that would take him to another land, another element. Yes, these college grounds, these fields of dust, these fences of rusted barbed wire, these groups of hostile and mocking young students at the gate and the bus stop, all would be left behind, and he would move on into the world of poetry and art. Then he corrected himself: it was not Nur's name that was bringing about this transformation, it was his genius, his art. And Deven now had the wherewithal to capture and preserve that art, that verse, for posterity. He had been allotted a role in life.

Crossing the street, Deven murmured a verse of Nur's:

'The breeze enters, the blossom on the bough wafts its scent. The opened window lets in the sweet season, spring.'

Stumbling on a pile of coiled wires, Deven backed into a corner of the small shop, giving Murad more room in which to circle as he examined the radios, television sets, cassette players, speakers and tape recorders for sale or hire. He seemed to be on familiar terms with the shopkeeper and Deven kept a sharp eye on them, determined to catch them out if they tried to strike any private or shady deal that would not be to his advantage, or rather, to that of his college.

'We must be very careful,' he had emphasized as he hurried through the Darya Ganj streets after Murad. 'Only the best equipment, Murad – don't let them swindle you. Do you know anything about tape recorders? Shouldn't we ask for advice?'

'Look,' said Murad, stopping on the pavement and planting his hands on his hips. 'I know one thing about tape recorders and that is their price. And I know that what your college has agreed to pay for is only the cheapest and worst model. So how can I let you in for anything worse than that, please tell me?'

Deven was so offended he said nothing more but pushed sullenly on through the Saturday afternoon crowd of shoppers. He was only slightly mollified to find that once they were inside the shop Murad did not behave as though he could afford only the cheapest and the worst. On the contrary, he acted as though he had unlimited funds at his disposal, and the dealer would be wise to pay extra attention to this important customer. The dealer, however, seemed to know

Murad too well: his manner was unpleasantly familiar. He even offered them betel leaves with his fingers. Deven shook his head with a frown, refusing, but Murad took two and stuffed them into his mouth and munched appreciatively, releasing the heavy perfume of their ingredients into the already overloaded air.

'The latest model – show me the latest model,' he said through his full mouth, swinging around to the shelves and counters again.

'Sahib, if it is the latest model you are looking for, why come to me? Why not go to Hong Kong, Singapore or Manila? You are a man of means, your father is the King of Kashmiri Carpets, a wealthy man, he can send you. So why not do what everyone else does these days? Go on a luxury cruise to the Far East and come back with the latest models – one for you and one for me, heh?' His round belly jumped with laughter under the pink bush shirt and snakeskin belt.

'We are not prepared to pay fancy prices,' Deven said nervously from his corner.

The dealer threw him a contemptuous look. 'No fancy price? Then how will you get your fancy goods, hah?'

Murad, too, laughed. He and the dealer exchanged winks as they laughed. Deven frowned.

'Come, let us go and take a look elsewhere, Murad,' he said angrily, but instead Murad sat down on a folding chair by the dealer's desk.

'Sit down, Deven-*bhai*,' he said, with a curt gesture of his betel-stained fingers. 'I have already talked this over with Jain Sahib. He knows exactly what your needs are. His nephew is bringing us the best model, secondhand, in prime condition, Jain says. Sit down till he comes, why don't you?'

'What?' stuttered Deven, turning cold at the thought of this newest deception of Murad's. 'You have already fixed it up with Mr Jain? Where is this model coming from? Why secondhand? I will not buy secondhand goods, it will only break down, it will give trouble – '

'Sahib, you are saying you want best model. I am getting you best model, at cheap rate. How can it be firsthand also?'

107

Again the dealer and Murad exchanged looks, not quite winking.

Deven began to walk angrily towards the door. The way was blocked by a young man coming in with a large carton in his arms. He smiled at Deven over the top of it, with great artificiality. 'Ah-ha!' cried Mr Jain, 'see, it has arrived, and Chiku also. Please meet my nephew Chiku, he will be of great help to you.'

Deven could not bring himself to rudely ignore Chiku. He waited till Chiku had set down the carton on top of the desk and shaken hands first with Murad, then with him, while Mr Jain beamed with avuncular pride, and when that was done, the deal seemed as good as signed and there was nothing for it but to resign himself to the consequences.

Beaten, he stood by the desk, leaning on the edge of it and peering into the carton despairingly. The other three appeared not to share his presentiments at all. As Chiku lifted out the machine proudly, the others looked at it quite rapturously, exclaiming when they had verified that it was indeed just what Mr Jain had promised, a Japanese model. Japanese: what could be finer?

'Japanese goods mean cheap goods – phut – they break in your hands,' Deven said gloomily.

'*Aré*, Sahib, what are you talking about? Pre-war days? Wartime? You haven't heard about Japan's progress? They are leaders in industry now, Sahib, leaders. Such clever people. If only we had clever people like that in our country – *hai, hai* – what progress we would see! We too could be rich, friends of America. But look at us – *hai, hai,*' he lamented, but briefly, then went on quickly, 'Now look at this model. Chiku, show it to them.'

But Deven turned his face away and sank on to a chair, refusing to look and leaving it to Murad to examine what was already their purchase for it seemed that the three of them had discussed the matter and decided the issue between them, without consulting him at any stage. He knew nothing he said would make a difference to them. And then, what could he have said? He knew nothing about electronics, had no contribution to make to the conversation that was going on, and they knew it. Of course Murad did not seem to know anything either. After beaming down at the unpacked machine, he simply dusted his hands as if the job was satisfactorily completed, and shouted, 'Very good, very good. As good as new, Jain Sahib, and Japanese also. Deven, this is the machine that is going to help you in your project; it is better than a secretary or a typewriter or even both together. Why are you looking so angry? At least come and look at it and listen to Chiku explain –'

'I know nothing about tape recorders,' Deven sulked, 'and don't know how to use them, so what is the use?'

'But Chiku is going to help,' cried Mr Jain, clapping his arm over his nephew's shoulders. 'He will be your assistant – technical assistant. Just completed a course in electronics at the Sethi School of Electronics in Connaught Place. He has been working in my cousin's repair shop in Ghaziabad and came to Delhi to study only, no, Chiku? They gave him a diploma even, na, Chiku?' He squeezed the boy as if he were a sponge.

The boy nodded and tossed a lock of oil-slicked hair out of his bright, kohl-rimmed eyes. Murad gave him a speculative look – he did not seem to know Chiku as he knew Mr Jain – and Deven caught it. He turned away in despair. 'Now what is this, Murad?' he hissed through clenched teeth.

'It is all right, Deven, it is what you need – a technical assistant,' Murad assured him, but with something less than total confidence. 'I explained to Jain Sahib the whole situation – the purpose of this deal. Such a serious, such an important purpose, I explained to him. You need technical assistance with it, isn't it? Here is a young man, provided by Jain Sahib himself, to give you that help. You have just to tell him when you are ready to use the machine and he will come. Give him the address where you want it, the time when you want it, and he will be there. Isn't it, Chiku?' Chiku nodded, but also more doubtfully. 'So now you will not need to worry about the technicalities, all those problems. You can concentrate on the interview, on your conversation with the poet, yes? Yes, Deven, it will be all right.' His voice was a little slow and thoughtful though.

CHAPTER SEVEN

The time and the place: these elementary matters were left to Deven to arrange as being within his capabilities. Time and place, these two concerns of all who are born and all who die: these were considered the two fit subjects for the weak and the incompetent. Deven was to restrict himself to these two matters, time and place. No one appeared to realize that to him these subjects belonged to infinity and were far more awesome than the minutiae of technical arrangements.

Nor did anyone know how much courage it took to slip through that narrow wooden door in the alley again with the intention of hurrying up the stairs to the top of the house and finding Nur there alone. Deven had carefully chosen an hour when he could be expected to have no visitors.

He was therefore taken aback to find the courtyard full of people, and others hurrying up and down the stairs and the verandas that circled the courtyard, all busy and intent, but quiet except for a child crying in the background, petulantly wailing and being quieted by someone shaking a rattle or a tambourine to amuse and distract it and not succeeding but only adding to the atmosphere of discord.

No one stopped him or paid him any attention as he crept up the stairs with his head lowered respectfully – most of the people around were women although there were also some of the young men he had seen on his first visit, more informally dressed in pyjamas and *kurtas* and lounging around idly as if they were waiting for the hour when they could go up the stairs to Nur. They gave the impression this time of being not visitors but members of the family, of belonging, if only to the fringes. He arrived at Nur's door, as usual hung with a thin bamboo screen to keep out the summer light. He coughed to announce his presence and was relieved to hear a deep groan from inside which he took to be permission to enter. As usual it took a few seconds for his eyes, so recently seared by the sun outside, to adjust to the heavy gloom in the green-tiled and curtained room. In those seconds he could hear that heavy, laboured breathing that he knew to be the poet's: it was strange how the lowered shades kept out not only the light but also the din of traffic and even the household sounds. This casting of a spell of silence around him was further proof, Deven thought, of Nur's magic powers. A moment later he discovered the poet's disconsolate figure hunched upon the edge of the divan.

'Nur Sahib,' stammered Deven, once again overcome by his own presumption in appearing before so great a man, and by the poet's graciousness in allowing him to do so. How was it possible not to become a *chela,* a disciple, when in the presence of such an undeniable *guru*?

'Is it you, Deven?' the old man murmured tearfully. 'You have heard? You have come because you heard?'

'No, Sahib, I haven't heard,' Deven said nervously, wondering what new and fearful element had entered upon the scene when he was not watching. 'I – don't know – '

'That she's so ill? Imtiaz Begum? Lying ill in her room and no doctor able to help?' groaned Nur, rubbing his forehead back and forth across the palm of his hand as though faced with the great dilemma of his life.

'Oh?' said Deven, trying to sound shocked and frightened but actually brightening with quick relief. 'Is that so? Is it very – very –?'

'You see what has come of that mistaken celebration we had for her birthday? I did not want it at all – I am superstitious –

but she insisted – and it proved too much for her. She is not strong, you see. She never was very strong, and she breaks easily – under strain –'

'Strain?'

'Yes, yes, *terrible* strain – having to face an audience, having to perform before it – according to the standards she sets herself. She collapsed that very night, you know,' he snivelled into his hand.

Deven stood respectfully at the door, hands clenched before him, but allowed himself the thought that it was more likely the beating she had had at the hands of the older woman – older wife? – that had brought about this 'collapse'. Nor could he entirely quell his rejoicing at hearing who had lost the battle. It was fortunate the room was so dark that he could conceal his expression. Yet it was the darkness that made the sound of the old man snivelling more pathetic, like a child's crying in the night. He came forward to soothe him, tentatively.

'Perhaps, sir,' he murmured, 'it is only a passing - passing ailment. My son, too, is down with a fever. The doctor says it is a virus. Maybe the begum is also ill with a virus.'

To his relief Nur seemed glad to accept this prosaic explanation. 'You think so? You think it can be?' he asked at once. 'Then we should take her to a hospital. I am wanting to – I was saying she must go – she has been ill for so many days, ever since that night – '

'Ever since that night?' repeated Deven, exulting.

'She is wasting away, poor woman. She has had no food, she refuses to eat unless I go and feed her, spoon by spoon, and even then she won't swallow more than a few spoonfuls. I told them all – I keep telling them she must go to the hospital – '

'Nur Sahib, that is an excellent idea!' Deven called out elatedly, much too loudly: he could not help that; he thought of that threatening presence withdrawn from the house, leaving it to Nur and to him so that they could conduct the taped interview in peace, without her evil interruptions. It seemed like a piece of pure gold, such fortune as had never come his way before. Naturally he could not suppress the ring in his voice.

Nur suppressed it for him. 'Of course she would not agree,' he moaned. 'She refused. She cries and weeps if they come to take her to the hospital, and then her temperature rises. It was a hundred and one yesterday, you know. Also she is having diarrhoea. I got so frightened that I begged them to leave her – I told them I would nurse her myself – and she wept in my arms when I said that, you know, wept in my arms – '

Deven withdrew, frowning, feeling more than a little impatient with the old man's weakness and gullibility. It might be a good idea to give him a stiff drink to make him more aware of his own powers, his own individuality and commitment and vocation. He looked around the shadowy room to see if he could spot the bottle, a tray and a glass. Since he could not, he decided to try to distract the poet from this dismal subject. But he had little gift for speech, for conversation, so little practice in it, and knew only how to stumble awkwardly to the point, gracelessly. 'Nur Sahib, you remember I spoke to you of this special issue of Urdu poetry in *Awaaz*? I had hoped that today – since I have come so early – we might be able to discuss it a little – '

Nur stopped rubbing his nose in the palm of his hand and peered through his fingers at Deven. Deven could not make out if it was with interest or amazement, so he continued, 'I hoped you would give me some time and that we could begin – '

'Yes,' murmured Nur, lowering his hands to his knees, straightening his back and growing quite calm. 'It is certainly time to start. Before Time crushes us into dust we must record our struggle against it. We must engrave our name in the sand before the wave comes to sweep it away and make it a part of the ocean. Only yesterday I was thinking about an old poem of mine that I wrote in the days when I was a student, when I was starving, when I was facing the same certainty that the hand of Time was descending to crush me like a fly, and I remembered those lines. They have never

113

been published – but they all came back to me and I wanted to write them down. If only I still had my secretary, that poor boy. If only I had time – '

'Please give me some of your time, Sahib,' Deven begged in an urgent whisper. 'I cannot take dictation, I haven't learnt shorthand but I have arranged for a tape recorder so that your recitation can be recorded. We will not need to write out questions and answers. I will switch on the machine and you can recite and speak and say all you wish on any subject and it will be recorded on tape for everyone to hear – '

The old man was frowning, his mouth pouting in the centre of the tousled beard. 'A record, you say? Record – like in the cinema? For songs? I am not one of those singing poets, you know, some performer at weddings and festivals – '

Deven lowered himself on to a stool beside the bed and prepared to explain whatever he himself understood of the technicalities of a tape recording. He suddenly realized – Nur's protests made him realize – that he was undertaking something of which he knew very little and which ought to be done professionally if at all, and certainly not as some dilettante's self-indulgence. If it was really to be of professional standard, it ought to be done in a studio, by technicians. Strange – he shifted uncomfortably – that neither Murad nor Siddiqui nor Jain nor Chiku had ever mentioned a studio. What made them think that he, who scarcely knew how to turn on a radio, could perform a task of such a highly specialized nature? He was seized by fear that he was completely unfit for the project, the wrong choice for it: this was evidently no matter for amateurs, and he was less than one. With its many facets, some literary and artistic, others technical, who was he to take control of them all, put them all together and then in a manner worthy of the poet and his verse, of the universities and the students who studied his work in them. Where was such an expert to be had? There was only he, totally inadequate, incompetent and unconfident. But now it was too late to withdraw. He would have to stretch himself as he had never stretched before, reach for something he had not been trained to reach nor was qualified to reach, and use whatever capacities he had to the fullest in order to achieve something worthy of his hero. But what were his capacities? Like sandflies, they disappeared into the shadows, first tormenting him and then withdrawing and vanishing.

Nervously spreading his hands, he tried to convince both Nur and himself. 'If we could spend a few quiet mornings together in this room sir – if you could give me a time when we would be left undisturbed – I could bring the tape recorder with me, and also my – my assistant who will work it – and then you could speak or recite, as you liked. I could perhaps begin by asking you a few questions about your life and work, your ideas, too, and you could answer those you wanted to answer, briefly or at length, just as if you were writing your memoirs. If you prefer, you could recite your poetry instead, and it would all be taken down on tape. Later I would take it away and edit it and prepare it for the *Awaaz* article, or your memoirs, or a new volume of verse, anything you want. It would take only a few sessions. If you can tell me when it is possible – '

But after listening very intently and attentively, his head lowered so that it was very close to Deven's, and seeming to consider the matter very seriously, the old man shook his head and withdrew, sighing, 'You do not know what you are saying. I recite the story of my life here, in this house, when she is so ill in her room, there?' He pointed through the door to the room across the courtyard. 'She would hear – it would disturb her – and then, you know, she does not like me to recite any more.'

'Why?' burst out Deven furiously, pressing his fingers into the edge of the divan. 'Why will she not allow you to recite your poetry when she recited hers in – in public? We all come to hear *you* – poetry lovers come only to hear *you* – why does she stop you then?'

Nur grimaced with horror. 'Shh, shhhh,' he hissed at Deven. 'Don't speak like that, we will be heard. I am forbidden. You don't understand. She is right – absolutely right – I only make a fool of myself – an old man, my day is over –

and people laugh, or feel bored, they want someone new, and young, you see –'

'*Who* told you that?' Deven cried in a passion. 'It is a lie. We all come to this house to hear you, only you – it is your poetry we love, Nur Sahib.'

'Don't shout! You are mad, you will be heard,' the poet cried, throwing himself about in fright. 'You had better go. I told you – it is impossible. No, no, we can't – please put this idea out of your head – don't talk to me about it any more,' and he covered up his ears with his hands and refused to listen.

Deven sprang up, sending the stool flying in his indignation. He had come so close! He had come so close to convincing not only the poet but, what was almost as hard, himself, and now – 'Nur Sahib,' he began, when the bamboo screen in the door lifted and Ali came in, saying, 'Nur Sahib, the begum is calling you. She has something to say to you, very important – she wants you.' Then, staring at Deven, he added, 'And your visitor also – she wants to speak to him too.'

Deven and Nur exchanged wild looks. How had she known he was here, when he had crept in so quietly and secretly? Was everyone in the house a spy, set to keep an eye on the poet? Deven realized there was no question of holding the interview or getting the tape recording done in this nest of her spies where they would not be safe for a moment from her jealousy or her vengeance – if these were indeed, as they seemed to be, her motives in persecuting him.

If similar thoughts went through Nur's head at that moment one could not tell. There was only a pathetic resignation in the old man's posture as he rose to his feet, supporting himself on Ali's shoulders, and shuffled towards the door, clutching at his loose pyjamas like some intimidated schoolboy. The pyjama string dangled beneath the hem of his shirt, somehow adding to his look of helplessness. 'She is so ill, and wants me,' he said to Deven as if in an appeal for understanding.

But Deven could not bring himself to trust her even if she were on her deathbed, and found himself cowering a little

116

behind Nur, remembering vividly the scene in which she had flown at the older woman across the prostrate body of the poet.

Outside her door an old woman sat holding the small boy on her lap, rocking him. Nur stooped over them for a moment, murmuring, 'Poor boy, poor boy, he had only his mother – his father much too old – too old for such a pretty baby, pretty boy – and his little mother, too, his mother now –' but the old woman drew back, tightening her hold on the child and grimacing with annoyance so that he moved sadly on and went in.

Deven was relieved to find that she was lying in bed – reclining upon it, propped up against large pillows with frilled edges. Her thin and perfectly triangular face, lined and furrowed with fever and fretfulness, was as small as a sick child's between the lank folds of her horrendously dyed black hair. Deven's eyes shifted uneasily from the sight of these black loops to that of similar coils strewn around her bed on the floor. Had there been another fight, he wondered in panic, as between jealous tigresses? Was this a common scene in this home of ferocious felines? Would they not, between them, devour the helpless quaking flesh of the poet and his as well?

'Come closer,' she said weakly and, stepping carefully over the clumps, he realized they were only the black thread plaits that she used for thickening her own hair which was quite thin and hung over her shoulders like two rats' tails. Wearing a broad bandage across her forehead, she looked like the victim of an accident, or of a sacrifice that had left her with nothing.

Her acolytes hovered around her. One young girl knelt at her bedside and massaged her feet, rhythmically. Another stood at her head, stirring a cup of milk and fussily blowing on it, for it was steaming hot. The odour of chewed straw, of cud, rose with the steam. Deven recognized her as the woman who had sung the accompaniment that night in the courtyard.

Weakly lifting up a hand that was narrow and long and painted all over with a henna pattern that made it look like a

117

glove of snakeskin, she said very clearly in a high-pitched voice that boded ill, Deven knew boded ill, 'Before you persuade that confused old man to appear in public, take one look at one who has done so – and suffered.'

'But,' said Deven, taking one step backwards and nearly falling over Nur who had somehow contrived to get behind him instead of in front of him, 'but I was not planning – I had no intention –'

The reptilian hand swayed in the air, warningly. 'You do not deceive me even if you have thrown dust in his poor weak eyes. I have made my inquiries – I have found out about you. I know your kind – jackals from the so-called universities that are really asylums for failures, trained to feed upon our carcasses. Now you have grown impatient, you can't even wait till we die – you come to tear at our living flesh –'

'Bibi, my heart,' interrupted Nur, coming forwards agitatedly, 'I don't know what your spies – ah, friends – have told you about Deven. I can tell you he is not trying to murder you, or me, or anyone – ' he broke into a nervous giggle, and fell silent under her contemptuous look.

'Jackals don't murder,' she said coolly. 'They wait for others to murder, because they haven't the courage. Then they come to feed on the flesh.'

Deven felt a prickling up his spine and Nur tried unsuccessfully to laugh. 'What flesh, *bibi*, my heart? Dear heart, you are ill –'

'Yes, I am,' she cried, sitting bolt upright in bed so that the sheets slipped off her and the women who attended her stepped backwards, and then hurried forwards to adjust them. She waved them aside - nervy, irritable, imperious, inconsiderate and frantic. They trembled as they tried to soothe her with little sucking sounds of their lips – they feared her as much as they admired her, keeping at a distance as from a poisonous snake, a snake that was also an object of worship. Yet there was gentleness in their ministrations that showed they pitied her as well, that they found here much to be pitied. She glared past them at the two men. 'Still my eyes can see more clearly than yours. You,' she said, spitting at Deven

118

from between her very small, sharp teeth, 'you – tell me why you keep coming here. What are you here for?'

'I? I come as – as others come,' Deven tried not to stammer and to hold his ground, feeling he was beginning to understand her a little. 'To pay my respects to – to a distinguished poet, to hear him recite – '

'He will *not* recite,' she hissed, making small white bubbles of spit fly.

'Dear heart, I will not, no, I will not recite,' Nur assured her, coming closer to the bed with his hands outstretched. 'I am giving no recitation again, ever, please don't think I am.'

Suddenly her eyes turned from hard black beads to liquid and tears streamed down her cheeks, blackening them with kohl. 'Yes, you will,' she wailed like a child, 'you may. Call your friends. Call for drinks. Sit and recite your poems. Sing, let everyone clap and dance while I – while I lie here, *dying*.'

Nur clucked with horror, '*Bibi*, how can you think – ' he protested, lowering himself to the edge of her bed while the women attendants rose up and began to fuss. 'Please calm yourself – please don't think such things – please lie still – you are ill – '

She threw herself back into her pillows and more black cotton came undone from her head, leaving her scalp very nearly bald. She looked much thinner and smaller suddenly, like a child who has fever, and her hands tore at the sheets in what might have been feigned or else very real anguish. Nur reached out to catch them and still them between his, making small consoling sounds with his lips, and Deven stumbled backwards until he sensed he was near the door, fresh air and sunlight, then turned around and, restraining his impulse to flee, walked out with dignified deliberation.

Out on the staircase his feet could be heard to clatter in rapid descent, although his relief was actually mixed with a large measure of regret at having left without making any arrangements or even an appointment with Nur for the interview he still hoped passionately to record. The question was – where, and how? Perhaps it was as well he was giving himself time to ponder the matter. It was quite obvious that the recording could not be done in this house: even if the begum were genuinely ill, she would somehow become aware, her long needle-like nose would make her aware, of what she would definitely consider an act of treason and no doubt she would find some scandalous way to sabotage it. So he must somehow spirit Nur away, and take him elsewhere – to Murad's office? Murad's house? and arrange for the recording to be done there. Deven had still enough wits left about him to realize that this was an opportunity no poetry lover, still less a lecturer hoping for a promotion or at least a confirmation, could possibly forgo. Only the practical details of arranging such a session – or a series of such sessions – remained. Nur, whom he had never seen outside the walls of his house, had to be bodily transported out of it, and that too invisibly, without the venomous begum observing it . . . Deven chewed his lip and clutched his fists to his sides, worrying. Might Siddiqui, that resourceful little bird with the black, bright eye, come to his aid once more?

He was at the courtyard door, trying to let himself out without making a sound, when a small voice called him. Not by name of course, but it was without doubt a summons, an invitation, and since there was no one else in the courtyard, which had been returned to the sleeping cat and the leaning bicycle, it could only be meant for him. He turned, keeping one hand on the door in case it needed to be opened suddenly and quickly, and looked about him cautiously. There was still no one else there – the cat slept, the bicycle stood, the tap dripped. Whatever sound, light and activity there was in that tall house was concentrated on its topmost floor, out of reach. Or was it? He hardly dared lift his head to look upwards but no, there was no one on the verandas and balconies, leaning down, preparing to spit or launch a missile at him. Dropping his eyes, he noticed that one of the doors in the back wall, usually tightly shut, was ajar, and a small girl stood clinging to the post, almost a part of it – that was why he had not noticed her before. Her pigtail hung over one shoulder, tied with a red thread, and she regarded him through slightly squinting eyes. Then the voice called him again and since the child had not opened her mouth, he realized the call came from behind her, on the other side of the door. He walked slowly towards it and sidled past the gravely watching child.

The door led into an inner courtyard, a small and private one that he had not known lay behind the outer one into which all visitors were admitted. It seemed scarcely to belong to this tall house in the congested lane off one of the main bazaars of the city. It had the air of a village courtyard about it, a rural scene, and not only because of the *pipal* tree that grew in its centre, throwing its heart-shaped shadows on the brick flooring, or because of the two goats, one black and one liver-coloured, tied to the legs of a string-cot dragged out beside the water pump. Clothes hung out to dry on a line, a grinding stone stood in a corner where it had obviously just been used for grinding grain, for the powdery white flour still lay scattered around it. A woman crouched before an outdoor stove, trying to light a fire with a bundle of twigs. Her head was covered with a thick brown veil and she had to lift it off her forehead and push it back over her sparse henna-dyed hair before Deven recognized her as the old woman who had come into Nur's room to silence the young begum during a previous tantrum.

'More tantrums going on up there?' she asked drily, looking up from the stove.

Deven gave a cautious nod, unsure if he wanted to be drawn into another vulgar family quarrel. It was true that it was Nur's family – Nur's wives, he imagined – and therefore no ordinary one, but it was still vulgar, and he had quite enough of that at home to want any more.

'A fine actress, that one,' chuckled the old woman, breaking up the twigs and stuffing them into the earthen stove. 'She used to be a dancing girl out there – ' she jerked her sharp chin at the high wall beyond which lay the city and its bazaars – 'and she knows all the dancer's tricks. Now she's persuaded

121

them she's really ill. It is always like that when she wants something from him, always.'

In spite of himself, Deven could not help asking, with dry lips, 'What does she want?'

She gave him a shrewd, sidelong look from under the fold of her veil. 'She wants to get rid of you,' she smiled mischievously.

Deven gave an involuntary twitch of fear. He had an instant vision of a dagger, a blade, slicing downwards. That was not so very preposterous – he had seen her in a rage, and knew. Then he regained his composure and felt quite flattered to learn that he had been chosen by that terrifying woman as her adversary, the cause of her jealousy and rage and even illness. He could not quite suppress a smirk at the extravagance of this compliment.

The old woman, intently watching, frowned at the smile fluttering foolishly across his face: perhaps he did not believe her. But she knew better than anyone else. 'All his followers – all his disciples, his *chelas* – are hated by her,' she insisted. 'She is always trying to stop those evening gatherings on the roof when he recites his poetry. But they only come for the entertainment after all, and because he feeds them. *You* have come for more than that.'

Deven's eyes dropped to the ground. He felt humble again, and nervous – his old self.

'*You* are serious,' she continued, cracking some more twigs between her fingers. 'She has heard that you have come to write a book.'

'No, no,' he mumbled. 'Only an article, an interview. I am not going to write it, I am going to tape it – with a tape recorder,' he said loudly, as much to convince himself as to convince her. 'My college has bought it for me so I can record his voice – '

She was clearly impressed, in an uncomprehending way, for these were not words this lighter of fires, washer of clothes and keeper of goats might understand. That made them more impressive to her. 'Hmm, yes – that is what she must have heard. And she wants to stop it.'

'But why? No harm will come of it,' he urged her, 'only glory for Nur Sahib – glory which should be, must be recorded for all time.'

'Don't tell *her* that,' the old woman cackled, then bent forwards, struck a match and held it to the twigs. An incredible amount of thick, odorous smoke began to leak out of a small heap of kindling. She began busily to smother it with pieces of wood. Deven choked and coughed. 'That is just what she wants to take away from him. She has taken much away,' she said bitterly, 'and she wants his fame as well, his glory.'

'But,' said Deven earnestly, 'she can never take that. She is not a poet of the same quality – she can never have his fame or glory.'

The words did not seem to impress the old woman; she was blowing at the fire, making it thrum. Then she looked over her shoulder at the child still clinging to the post, watching and listening, and called, 'O Munni, go and get me the *dal*,' and watched sharply while the child ran to the veranda to fetch a cooking pot and bring it to the fire. Setting it on the earthen stove, the old woman clanked a lid on top of it, then sank back on her heels with a sigh, evidently preparing to wait till it boiled. It struck Deven as incongruous that he, a college lecturer, should be discussing the quality of Nur's poetry with this old woman cooking in her courtyard, watched by two goats and a child with a squint. He shifted on his feet, wishing to leave the scene as an unworthy one.

Noticing, she gave him that sidelong glance again and beckoned him to come and sit beside her. He looked about for somewhere to sit – he was not going to squat on his heels like her. The child saw and ran and brought a low wooden stool. He lowered himself on to that, unwillingly and awkwardly.

'Don't let that woman stop you,' she hissed as soon as he was on a level with her. 'You write that book – '

'It is going to be a tape recording.'

'Yes, yes, you write that,' she repeated sharply. 'It is important, nah? For your college? For the professor people there? They will want it, nah?'

'Oh yes,' he breathed solemnly, 'it will be very, very important. It will be placed in the library. Students and scholars will listen to it. Other universities will borrow it – '

'Yes, yes,' she interrupted impatiently. 'I know. I know he is a great man. They all tell me so. *Is* he a great man?' she asked suddenly.

'Of course,' he cried, amazed that she should ask. 'The greatest poet alive – the greatest Urdu poet,' he qualified, 'in India.'

'Then do it, son, do it,' she urged him.

'But when?' he asked desperately. 'How?'

She sat silently for a while, trying to understand his needs. They were novel ones to her, she did not comprehend them at all, but felt the urgency. The pot on the fire began to bubble and she leant forward to remove the lid. Steam poured out, bringing out beads of moisture on her upper lip. All her clothes gave out an odour of woodsmoke and cooking. 'Hmm,' she said, letting the lid slide halfway back so that the steam was diverted from her. 'You need a room – you need to be alone in it with him, eh?'

'Yes, and the technician, too. Maybe one or two other people. We will be a small group. We need three, four days with him in private, maybe a week.'

She understood now, precisely. 'Then you will have to leave the house,' she said. 'It can't be done while she is here.'

'Can't she be sent away?' he pleaded. 'If she is ill – can't she be sent away to the hospital? Or to her family?'

The old woman laughed soundlessly. 'Don't you try that. If you say "hospital" she will jump out of bed, perfectly well. And family – you think she has a family, that one?' The laughter became audible, a kind of hollow crackling, like the sound the fire made.

'She will not leave,' the woman went on. 'She has planted herself in our house – like a witch. You will have to take *him* away – through this door,' she pointed to a small door in the wall behind the goats. 'He will come down to visit me – he does that sometimes – then you can take him away by that door. Why not find a room – not far from here, a little up the lane, he can't go further, the old man – take a room and do your work there. Bring him back through the back door, I will send him upstairs again. She will fume, seeing him come to visit me, but she can't stop that, I am the older one, the first.' She laughed again, showing her blackened teeth. 'Even if I had only daughters and she the son, I am still first,' she brooded. Then, sharply, 'And your work will be done, hah?'

Deven bit his knuckles, thinking. 'If that is the only way – '

'It is the only way,' she assured him. 'You want me to arrange a room for you? I can.'

He stared at her, wondering if he had underestimated her after all. 'Can you?'

'Of course,' she waved her hand casually, with a surprising elegance. 'It is easy for me, I have lived here all my life, know every house, everyone who lives in this lane. I can arrange a room. If you come tomorrow morning, at ten – no, eleven o'clock – and stand at the back door, I will let him out – '

'No, not tomorrow,' he burst out in a panic. 'Give me time – '

'Then when?' she snapped.

'Soon. I will let you know soon. I have to discuss this – I will send you a postcard – '

'*She* will read the postcard, not I,' said the old woman, contemptuous of his poor thinking powers.

'All right, a message then. I will make all the arrangements, then send you a message and come and fetch him as you say.'

She nodded, then turned to the child to give some instructions about the food she was cooking. The girl scurried off to fetch things, and the woman took a spoon from her and began to stir with it. 'His favourite *dal*,' she said with a satisfied smack of her lips. 'Only I can cook it as he likes,' she smirked.

Deven got up from the wooden stool, creaking painfully at the joints. Making a kind of bow, he turned to walk away and leave her but she called him back sharply.

'Listen,' she said, in a direct, uncouth way that startled him. 'You will not forget about payment, will you?'

'Payment?' Deven stopped short. This was a new demand, an unexpected one for which he had made no provision. Panic rose inside him, scattering his words and thoughts in its stormy approach.

'Yes, yes, payment,' she said, jerking her head and gesturing with her henna-stained hand at the same time. 'Payment – payment. You think he can do all this for you – give you so many hours of his time and write and recite for you and tire himself out – for no payment at all? What is this – you think the poet has not to earn his bread? You think he has no family to feed? Are poets and poets' families to starve while you and your kind from the colleges feast?'

'No, no,' he mumbled, flushing with shame at her speech. 'That can never be – '

'It must not be,' she flashed. 'So when you send that message of yours, make sure you send a message about the payment that will be made for his labour as well. If I find it is insufficient, you will not find him at the door when you come to fetch him. You will wait and wait but he will not come. Now go. Go.'

Walking away with her crude speech ringing in his ears, so unlike the flowery Urdu spoken upstairs, Deven wondered if this was why the poet had turned from an uneducated country wife to the kind he had upstairs. He himself would not have known how to choose between them. He had no way of satisfying or evading either. He would have to abandon the project.

CHAPTER EIGHT

Deven did not go to Delhi for a long time after that.

Sarla sat watching him, scratching the side of her nose in an offensive way as she watched. Finally she gave her lips a sarcastic twist and said, 'So, no more Delhi for you? What happened – you were thrown out?'

He threw her a murdering look, then raised the newspaper an inch higher to block out the maddening view. From behind the stiffly held, nearly tearing sheets, he said in as controlled a voice as was possible in the circumstances, 'I go to Delhi on work. When I do not have work, I do not go. But,' he added deliberately, 'when I have work, I will go.'

'Hunh, *work*!' she said under her breath and then removed herself to the kitchen where she did not need to restrain herself but could find expression in shouting out of the window at the child or over the wall to the neighbours since it was not possible to shout at her husband, at least not without danger of retaliation.

It was only when she had disappeared into this narrow, cluttered fastness of hers and could be heard freely rattling and clattering in there that it occurred to Deven that it might have made a greater impression on her if he had allowed her to think he really had someone – female – to visit in Delhi. But that was how it was with him, he sighed: his reflexes, sluggish out of a habitual timidity and indecisiveness, were slowing still further; tardy in both thought and deed, he was never ready with the apt word or appropriate action; both seemed to trail him at a moody distance. He sighed again and drew out a cigarette from his shirt pocket and lit it up for comfort. Strange how, with all the world around in its stupefying profusion, there was nothing in it that could be counted upon for solace as much as a cheap cigarette.

Solace. He turned the roll of paper between his fingers and wondered if that had not been his error – to search always for solace when there was other game to hunt in the forest. Had he had more spirit, more nerve, more desire and ambition, then perhaps he would have instead hunted for success, distinction, magic. Perhaps he would have followed in pursuit of an art, published a book of poetry, earned a name for himself, a little fame, even gold bangles for Sarla . . .

But the thought was so puerile that it made him spit out a bitter shred of tobacco. Every effort he had made had ended in defeat: most of the poems he had written and sent to Murad had been rejected, his monograph never published; his wife and son eyed him with blatant disappointment; nor had he won the regard of his colleagues or students. The inherent weakness in his father that had made him an ineffectual, if harmless, teacher and householder, had been passed on to him. He felt it inside him like an empty hole, one he had been staring at all his years, intimidated by its blackness and blankness. Even his attempt to fill it with a genuine and heartfelt homage to a true poet, a man who had distinguished himself as he would have liked to do, had been defeated by all the obstacles that sprang up in his life like shards and pebbles sent up at every step. It was one more blow, and perhaps the bitterest of all.

He sat bent double in his cane chair, his arms hanging between his knees, his cigarette dangling from between his fingers, its smoke curling upwards in a spiral.

Peering through a crack in the kitchen door, Sarla watched, thinking: is he dead? is he alive? without concern, only with irritation. It was only men who could play at being dead while still alive; such idleness was luxury in her opinion. Now if she were to start playing such tricks, where would they all be? Who would take Manu to school and cook lunch for them?

Deven would not have known how to answer her.

Leaning back in his chair and putting his cigarette to his lips again, he laid his head back against the lace anti-macassar made by Sarla in her bridal days and much blackened by use, and shut his eyes. The room became as dim then as Nur's room with its bamboo screens and green-tiled walls and invisible pigeons that cooed so comfortingly. He recalled their first meeting on that afternoon – how he had recited Nur's poetry aloud to him:

'My body no more than a reed pen cut by the sword's tip,
Useless and dry till dipped in the ink of life's blood.'

while Nur lay on the bed, curled up like a gigantic baby, listening to him, and he had felt as though Nur were his child, he the parent, and they were both enclosed within the circle of some intimate, instinctive embrace.

Out on the road the earthen jar seller was walking past with his donkey loaded with his ware, calling in a high-pitched wail: '*Su-ra-hi*! *Su-ra-hi*! – a sure sign of approaching summer. Opening his eyes, Deven saw that his cigarette had burnt down almost to his fingers and having dropped it on the floor beside him, he crushed it under his foot, rubbing backwards and forwards till there was nothing left but a smear of ash. Looking down, he made sure: that was all, just a smear of ash.

But Sarla, walking in noisily, handed him a postcard that had just come, a yellow postcard marked Delhi with the small precise handwriting he recognized. 'My dear sir,' it said, 'you will be happy to know I have composed a new cycle of thirty-six couplets. My dear wife has inspired me to write on the subject of the suffering of women. You will be interested to copy same. Kindly report at earliest instance. Yours faithfully – ' and the Urdu flourish that was his name.

That night the small room in which all three of them slept

129

seemed suffocating. Summer was here and it was time they moved their cots out into the courtyard but Sarla resisted the move each year – she had nightmares about robbers climbing over the wall and attacking them in their sleep. When Deven gave a short laugh, saying, 'What can robbers find in *our* house to steal?' she hissed, 'To them college teachers are big men, important men; how can they know that we *starve*?' He was both startled and offended by the ferocity of that verb and thought of asking her if she had ever gone hungry but did not care to engage in an argument with her, knowing she could beat him. He recalled the time he had refused to buy the child toffees when they were out shopping and she had said, through pinched lips, 'For your own son you have no money; only for going to Delhi to enjoy yourself there is money.'

But he was not going to Delhi again: that was all over now.

He slipped off the bed, he thought quietly, but Sarla instantly gave an irritable twitch, groaning, 'Can't you let us sleep?' He sat on the edge of the bed, scratching his neck and shoulders where the mosquitoes had bitten him, then muttered, 'Going to get a drink of water' and shuffled out of the room. The door opening on to the courtyard creaked as he released the bolt, making him fear he would wake up the child as well and anger Sarla, but there was silence from both of them and once he was out, he felt relieved after all. In place of some emotional release from all that choked him, this simple physical one from the small, stifling room into the open night air would have to do.

He paced up and down the uneven brick paving, avoiding the line where Sarla's washing still hung, the corner by the pump where water had collected in a muddy puddle and the corner where the boy kept his toys: tin cans, sticks, buckets and balls. A *neem* tree grew outside the wall, its branches spreading over half the courtyard. Sarla often threatened to cut the branches, especially in the winter when she said it kept out the sun, but he would not let her, reminding her that it gave them shade in the summer. Now he had to admit it shut out the air as well, acting like a dusty canopy over the small, walled courtyard. Yet it made him feel cooler and fresher simply to be out in the open, to be able to see a few dim stars embedded in the purple felt of the summer sky. What was it Nur had said about those distant planets? Ah, 'Beacons in the ocean of sky, O my ship let them set your course . . . ' No, he would not, would not –

Turning his mind decisively away from these dangerous shoals, he paced up and down in his bare feet, his pyjamas and the vest full of holes, scratching at mosquito bites, smoking an occasional cigarette, refusing to entertain poetry and thinking in strict prose that he must look like a caged animal in a zoo to any creature that might be looking down at earth from another planet. And that was all he was – a trapped animal. In his youth, he had had the illusion of having free will, not knowing he was in a trap. Marriage, a family and a job had placed him in this cage; now there was no way out of it. The unexpected friendship with Nur had given him the illusion that the door of the trap had opened and he could escape after all into a wider world that lay outside but a closer familiarity with the poet had shown him that what he thought of as 'the wider world' was an illusion too – it was only a kind of zoo in which he could not hope to find freedom, he would only blunder into another cage inhabited by some other trapped animal. Being an illustrious poet had drawn people to the zoo to come and stare at him but Nur had not escaped from his cage for all that – he was as trapped as Deven was even if his cage was more prominent and attracted more attention. Still, it was just a cage in a row of cages. Cage, cage. Trap, trap.

Then where was freedom to be found? Where was there fresh air to breathe?

He looked up at the dusty pelt of the sky for some chink that promised, or assured, escape but even the stars were smothered in murk. No message came whispering on a nocturnal breeze; every leaf on the *neem* tree hung still, lifeless. Out in the lane a bullock cart creaked by, the wooden wheels lacking oil and shrieking dismally. Across the canal a stray dog barked in a long monotonous howl of protest. Then there was silence. A long while later it was broken by the sharp, shrill whistle of the Janata Express from Assam clattering down the railway line. He bit down on a cigarette, cursing it: why was there always a train whistle in the dark, calling over vast spaces to all who longed to travel and move on? It promised nothing, it merely reminded prisoners of their bars, mocked them in their cells.

It was time to stop pacing: he was exhausted, perhaps sleep would come to him now. He returned to the room where the air was as flat, used and unfit for consumption as before, and stretched out on the bed. Covering his eyes with an arm, he began to fall through successive grey layers of consciousness towards the last one where grey would sink into a blur of black. But consciousness still had its fine, twisted hooks in his flesh and gave another and another tug, bringing him back unwillingly to the surface. Shuffling through the chalky dust of the lane where night was parting to make way for them came a band of dawn singers – women in white, widows, ascetics and pilgrims – hurrying by with candles and lanterns in their hands, singing in the quavering voices of the righteous:

> 'O will you come along with us
> Or stay back in the pa-ast?
> O will you come along . . . '

Sarla woke to the sound of a strangled groan, like a dog's sob. Raising herself on her elbow so that her hair streamed down on either side of her yellow face and her eyes stood out from between the strands, she hissed, 'Shh! It is only Mrs Bhalla and her friends, going to the temple to pray.'

Although everything around him announced defeat and a tired return to everyday routine, Deven found himself walking, quite against his judgment and only out of a masochistic desire, he told himself, to repeat the dirge for what he had lost, towards Siddiqui's house at the other end of the bazaar.

Siddiqui lived in one of the last of the large old villas of Mirpore, being distantly related to the nawab from Delhi who had built them for those of his family who had fled with him from the scene of the mutiny. Of course the sprawling bazaar had stretched and grown and crowded it from all sides but inside the four high walls of the compound, now breached in many places, the house still stood, decrepit but spacious, set in a large neglected garden of leafless trees and dying shrubs and dust where there had once been lawns and flowerbeds. Siddiqui was sitting out on the terrace in a cane chair, very much in the attitude of a grand landowner, a man of leisure and plenty.

Deven's feet came together in hesitation at seeing Siddiqui seated in such unexpected grandeur. It was unexpected because in order to enter the compound he had had to slip through a gap between the gate and the gatepost: the rusty wrought iron was sagging and held together by a bundle of wires, equally rusty. The banana-seller and the peanut-seller who had built their booths against the two gateposts had encouraged him to use the gap since no one ever opened the gate; it would fall down if anyone were rash enough to try.

'All their motor cars, their carriages, were sold long ago – what is there to open the gate for?' they explained when he looked doubtful, not willing to enter like a thief and unable to believe that this was how Siddiqui entered or left his own house.

Eventually he had edged his way through and now stood in the wide, gravelled driveway, looking up at the dilapidated villa and the recognizable yet unfamiliar figure of the little professor of Urdu seated on the terrace. Siddiqui was equally astonished to see him squeeze through the opening and appear in the middle of the driveway like one of the stray dogs or the chickens that occasionally escaped from the bazaar into his premises. He stood up, dressed in the light white muslin he wore after his evening bath, holding an empty pipe in his hand, and called, 'Come up, come up here, Deven-*bhai*. What an honour, what a pleasure, what an occasion.'

Deven, encouraged by this welcome, gave himself a little shake and came trailing up with a limp, exactly like one of those stray dogs uncertain of whether to expect a blow or a bone, wondering how he had dared intrude on the privacy of a man of such property without warning or permission. But then, he had had no idea Siddiqui lived in such splendour (the darkness added to the dimensions of the villa rather than subtracted from it). He had known that Siddiqui was a bachelor, lived alone in his ancestral home of which he was the sole guardian and which was why he had not applied for a better job in a bigger university, a bigger city: this much at least was college *gup-shup*.

Embarrassed, he stood at the foot of the stairs, murmuring, 'I didn't know, I didn't think–'

'What didn't you know, Deven-*bhai*?' Siddiqui asked, drawing him up the steps by one hand and placing him in the cane chair, then clapping his hands loudly for attention and calling 'Chotu! Chotu!'

'That you lived like this, here, alone,' Deven murmured.

'What! Did you think I had a family, wife, children, relatives? Or did you think I lived like a nawab in a nawab's palace? Take a look, my friend, take a look – have you ever seen such a ruin?' he laughed and waved at a grimy boy who emerged from one corner of the derelict house. 'Another chair, Chotu,' he called, 'if we have one. And a glass and a bottle – a drink for our visitor. We have that, nah? Be quick, too.'

Deven took in the house without any lights, the griminess of the retreating boy, and gave a small sigh of relief. Having been momentarily overcome by the scale of Siddiqui's ancestral home, he was relieved to see that it was in such an advanced state of decay as to be very nearly reduced to the state in which everyone else lived in Mirpore. He felt vaguely pleased as he looked about him and saw that the cane chair Chotu dragged out was tattered and broken, that the house was blackened by neglect as much as by the night, and had clearly not been painted for decades, that there were neither lights nor curtains to colour the gloom. The only door that stood open and had a glimmer of light, flickering and non-electric, was the servant boy's kitchen, unspeakably filthy and charred besides, while others were locked and looked as though they could never be opened. Then, not to seem too inquisitive, he turned his face to what had once been the garden but could no longer be called that – the flowerbeds and paths, although still marked by triangular pieces of brick, were merely areas of dust. Only a few trees remained – mango, pomegranate, tamarind – looming around the compound wall like shaggy guardians even if they were drooping from drought and pollution.

Siddiqui's manner as a host was as impeccable as if all were still in order, still functioning in another, more opulent age. After pressing a glass of rum into Deven's hand, he gave orders to the servant boy and sent him out to the bazaar for kebabs and *pilao*. (Deven shifted his knees uneasily – the scene recalled too vividly Nur's manner of conjuring up a dinner at a soirée.) What was this style of living? It was an unfamiliar one to Deven, so drearily domesticated and thrifty.

Siddiqui appeared to notice his unease. 'After the kitchen roof fell in, we've almost given up cooking at home,' he explained comfortingly, in a kind of pigeon's coo. 'Most of the pots and pans were buried under the rubble and Chotu said what was the use of digging them up, they were all broken. So you see, it is quite convenient to have the bazaar right at your garden gate: I send Chotu to fetch my tea, snacks and, for guests – kebabs and *pilao*.'

'It must be expensive,' Deven could not help saying, with alarm.

'But, my friend, who am I to spend my miserable earnings on except myself?' asked Siddiqui. 'You see before you a man without connections. No, that is not true – there is Chotu. I must, I will provide for Chotu, he is a boy of great talent, you know. When he returns, I must ask him to sing for us. You must hear him sing. I am having him trained. His voice is excellent – it only needs training. I am certain I can find him employment in All India Radio. Don't look so surprised – even a dirty little boy who fetches my rice and meat can have talents given him by God, you know – ' his voice rose, becoming aggressive.

'Of course, of course,' Deven hastened to agree, although dubiously.

'You don't believe me, but you will hear him, I will make him sing. Deven-*bhai*, how happy I am you have come. It had seemed the usual dull, lifeless evening like all others in Mirpore, but now – we shall have a concert. I will ask Chotu to sing and call some friends – another advantage of living in the heart of the bazaar, no need to go far for company – and we will dine here in the light of the moon – is there a moon? ha ha – and perhaps play a game of cards after we have eaten – ' He seemed released from his usual university self – neat, trim and circumspect – now transformed into a hedonist, a sybarite, a connoisseur of music and food and even a gambler, an unfamiliar persona unguessed at by the unimaginative – or uninformed – Deven.

They sat there on the terrace, like a pair of nawabs stranded in the backwaters of time, thought Deven, as he reached for another kebab on the greasy plate brought by Chotu, or held out his glass to be refilled, while Siddiqui talked of history, politics, poetry and philosophy in his ornate Urdu that contrived to build not exactly a wall but a trellis between this to him historic house and the bazaar beyond, so that the tinkling of cycle bells, the hooting of motor-car horns, the blaring of film music from a loudspeaker and the din of hawkers bawling their wares seemed no more than the howling of jackals in the surrounding wastes. It was a strange experience to have here, in the Mirpore whose every dusty furrow and dull contour Deven had imagined he knew, and he wondered how he had remained unacquainted so long with Siddiqui's talent for remaking fact into more acceptable, more attractive fiction: it had never displayed itself in college where he was only what he was, nothing else.

'It was an ancestor of mine who was thrown into disgrace at the time of the mutiny – caught by the British, he was punished and made to crawl on his knees the whole length of Chandni Chowk, and all his property seized and destroyed. He fled to Mirpore with his family and the clothes on his back – and so passed on the curse of living here to all succeeding generations,' he was saying with his lips pressed against the edge of his glass. He added wistfully, 'I have often wished someone would do me the favour of seizing and destroying my property here so I would be free to make the return journey to Delhi where at least within the walled city the Urdu spoken is chaste, unlike the yokel dialect one hears here . . . '

Deven gave a start, spilling some grains of rice down his lap. The reference to chaste Urdu at last reminded him of the subject he had come to discuss – Nur – and that they had somehow avoided mentioning at all – deliberately? It had been such a relief to forget, temporarily, that threatening topic. Deven had been quite willing to be distracted by spicy bazaar food, strong drink, and even the list of Chotu's virtues and merits, now and then catching the professor's eye and hastily looking away again. But he had begun to sense that Siddiqui, although still talking to him, was really ignoring him, and seemed to regard his presence as quite negligible. There was a certain insolence, was there not, in the way he spoke only of himself all the time? 'Siddiqui Sahib,' he began hesitatingly, 'now you have reminded me - of Urdu, of poetry – '

'Ha!' exclaimed Siddiqui, slapping his knee. 'Forgotten! How could I forget when Chotu is standing here at my side? Chotu, leave these plates and go and fetch some of the boys. We are going to play a game of poker, and after that you are going to sing for us – for my friend, a connoisseur of music and verse like us – ' Was he mocking?

'I have to clear the table,' muttered Chotu, starting to pick up the greasy dishes and clatter them together in a heap.

'No, no – leave all this, don't worry about it tonight – you go to the bazaar, go and fetch Anwar and Mehtab – tell them we are going to have a card game tonight – '

'I told them already,' mumbled Chotu, shuffling off. 'They will come.'

Siddiqui looked hurt at the lack of enthusiasm and was quiet for a little while, like a bird feeling a cold blast, but Chotu had been speaking the truth after all and there were some shadows straggling through the gap beside the gate and shambling up the driveway, their shoulders stooped and their toes turned inwards as if trying not to be seen. Chotu, transformed, raced out of the kitchen and sped down the stairs to greet them. They stood laughing and clapping each other on the shoulders, clasping each other in their arms and Siddiqui, watching fondly, murmured, 'Only a boy, so talented, so hard-working, I keep forgetting he is only a boy after all.'

Deven threw him an apprehensive look. He did not really want the evening to develop along these dangerous lines – it was too like the *mehfil* at Nur's house, the signs were undeniable. Was there not every possibility of it turning into a rout? Was the discreet and cautious Siddiqui not inviting disaster by allowing Chotu to turn from servant boy to singing star, and letting the riff-raff from the bazaar enter these imposing, albeit impaired, gates?

Nor had he any wish to join a game of poker and risk losing the little money he had with him. A mat was unrolled on the terrace flags. The boys seated themselves and began to deal out a pack of cards while Chotu bustled about fetching everyone the drinks Siddiqui called for grandly. Having served them in thick, smeared glasses which he carried out in bunches at the ends of his fingers, he sat down cross-legged on the mat too. Siddiqui could barely contain his excitement and anticipation. He played poker as if he were on a drinking spree – uninhibitedly, recklessly. Watching him lose hand after hand in horror, Deven circumspectly withdrew, insisting that Chotu take his place. He sat holding his knees and wondering how much Siddiqui would lose before he came to his senses: he did not seem in the least put out by his losses. On the contrary, they made him laugh and stretch out to fondle Chotu's knee, saying, 'Just wait – I will make you pay back. Take all the money you like off me, I know how to get you to make it up to me.' The boys from the bazaar sniggered and winked at each other and at Chotu who only hung his head morosely and threw down his cards to go and fetch more rum and refill everyone's glasses or go and blow his nose over the edge of the terrace into the bushes, then return, wiping his fingers on his pyjama leg, to continue the game.

It dragged on and on. Even the bazaar outside seemed stilled, half-asleep. The loudspeakers were silenced, traffic had come to a halt. Owls chuckled in the watchful trees. Deven's head dipped lower and lower, swinging from the knob prominent at the back of his neck; often he was away, swimming through sleep slowly, only to be brought back to the scene by a slap on the knee by the excited Siddiqui crying, 'Drink up, Deven, have another. At least drink with us if you won't play with us. Do you see how Chotu plays? Oh I will make him pay, I will make him pay for this!'

Deven had begun to fear his head would come off the knob and roll when the game broke up for what Siddiqui promised would be refreshments. Siddiqui helped him down the terrace steps and along the inky drive to the gate: the lateness of the hour and the uncounted glasses of rum had had a debilitating effect on Deven and surprisingly little on Siddiqui who was only a little dishevelled. While clawing at the iron scrollwork of the gate in search of the exit, Deven remembered to say, thickly, 'But Siddiqui Sahib, Nur – Nur – '

Siddiqui, slightly askew himself, his white hair rising in a peak above his head, clutched Deven by the elbow and whispered, 'Have you got it? Can I hear it?'

'Hunh?' Deven clung to two iron bars, feeling the rust come off on the palms of his hands. 'I don't – understand, Siddiqui Sahib.'

'The tape, Deven, the tape.'

Deven's knees softened and collapsed against the gate which sagged under his weight with a jarring sound. Nearly in tears, he sobbed, 'No, no, no. There *is* no tape.'

'But,' said Siddiqui, pulling himself together and holding his unbuttoned shirt at the neck in an effort at propriety, 'but the money was given, the tape recorder bought. You went to Delhi. Then where is the tape?' He sounded crisp, interrogative.

'No tape,' Deven groaned, 'no tape,' struggling to lift himself off the gate in which he had got entangled. Swaying

139

on his feet again, he planted his hands on Siddiqui's shoulders to steady himself and decided to blurt it all out. 'No tape. I could not begin recording. Nur – his wife – family – demanded payment. They want – they want money first.' The word 'first' came out in a fusillade of spit.

Siddiqui drew back. He freed himself from Deven's grasp. Then he went and stood by the gatepost, leaning on it with one hand. 'Hmm,' he said.

Frightened by his coolness, Deven stumbled after him, clutched at his fine muslin shirt as if he would tear it. 'I can't – go on, Siddiqui Sahib. Will have to – give up. It can't – be done. Nur, you see, Nur – '

'Look,' said Siddiqui, standing upright now and speaking very clearly in a glass-thin tone. 'It must be done. At my request, the funds were made available for a tape recorder. You purchased it. If you do not use it for the purpose for which it was bought, I will be held responsible for your – your deception. That tape is the property of the college, paid for in advance. You must make it. The college must have it.' He looked at Deven with small fierce eyes like lit embers.

Deven stumbled around Siddiqui in a full circle, clutching at his head which felt like a bag of broken glass. He must have become giddy and fallen, he found himself close to the ground, scrabbling in dust, seeing Siddiqui's small pale toes in their sandals. 'I can't,' he whined, 'I can't. Where is the money to pay his wife? And if I don't bring the money, she has said she won't let me enter the house. You don't know, Siddiqui Sahib, you just don't know about her – and the other – and the house – how it is – '

'No, nor does the college. You have to deal with all those matters yourself since it was your idea and your proposal,' said Siddiqui very severely. 'That is your business, how you go about it. But the recording must be done, the tape has to be handed over to the authorities.' Some lawyer in his family seemed to have passed on to him this new severity, this tone and attitude of a prosecutor.

Deven was weeping – at least his face was wet when he felt

it with his fingers. 'How?' he howled, jackal-like, on his knees, 'Siddiqui Sahib, *how*?'

Siddiqui was a small man but looked down from his height with all the contempt of a giant for a worm. For a moment it seemed he was preparing to utter his true opinion of Deven, of all craven, cringing creatures on earth. But the evening held better kinds of entertainment for him; appearing to lose interest in the spectacle at his feet, he only said, 'If you need more money, we shall have to request the authorities.'

'Can you do that, Siddiqui Sahib, can you – will you?' babbled Deven, so crazy with relief that he quite forgot he had sworn to give up Nur, give up the house in Old Delhi, give up the entire idea of the interview and the memoirs and the recording in exchange for the calm and safety of his old uneventful non-existence.

'Since you are incapable,' said Siddiqui cruelly, 'I will have to, won't I?' He turned away from the abject creature at his feet and looked over his shoulder at the house, the terrace. Out there, Chotu and his friends were laughing and singing something in chorus. Siddiqui smiled with a little tremor of his lips. 'You had better go, you had better leave it to me and go,' he said and shoving Deven aside with his knee, he turned and went briskly, almost running, towards the house where his own private Eden was being staged.

Later Deven could not understand how it had all come about – how he, the central character in the whole affair, the protagonist of it (if Murad were to be disregarded), the one on whom depended the entire matter of the interview, the recording and the memoirs, to which Siddiqui was no more than an accessory, having arrived on the scene accidentally and at a later stage, and in which he played a minor role – how he, in the course of that evening, had relinquished his own authority and surrendered it to Siddiqui who now emerged the stronger while he, Deven, had been brought to his knees, abject and babbling in his helplessness. *How*?

What had Siddiqui and Chotu given him to drink that had brought him down to such a despicable level? He suspected

141

the drink because his mental misery was accompanied by a physical wretchedness – he now spent his time running to the lavatory at the end of the courtyard, doubled up in pain, and emerging with his white face glistening with perspiration.

Yet, when Sarla gave him some herbal tea to drink and went off to fetch some powders from the homoeopath in the bazaar, he had only to take a sip of the hot, spiced and aromatic infusion to know it was not the food or drink or even anything malevolent about Siddiqui, but only his own panic. Shaken by it as by a physical disorder, he could not even control his body any longer. How did others control their lives, manage and organize and arrange and even succeed? He was still doubled over by the table, taking small sips of the tea and trying to keep his hands away from the packet of cigarettes that lay on the table, when his son brought him a yellow envelope. It was a telegram and he opened it with nervous fingers.

'Inform immediately when recording will begin and transcript sent to *Awaaz* office stop entire issue held up on account of delay stop explanation demanded Murad.'

He crumpled it up and threw it across the table but so weakly that it did not fall off but lay there in full view. To get away from it he had to leave the house.

He was standing outside the canteen door and feeling in his pocket for some change when he heard Siddiqui calling him. He went up slowly, trying to compose himself as he did so, very conscious of the dignity he needed to assemble for this encounter. Siddiqui gave him a cold smile and said, 'It's done. You are a lucky chap, Deven, I've noticed how things come your way while the rest of us have to go out and work for them.'

'What do you mean?' Deven asked bleakly, certain he was being mocked. All his life he had never even glimpsed the beautiful face of the goddess of Luck. Sarla regularly performed *puja* before a tinted oleograph of the goddess Lakshmi that hung in the corner by her dressing table, offering it flowers, incense and candles, but the flat pink face of the deity

142

in the blue sari never responded. Neither he nor Sarla had ever had a smile from her in return.

'I mean, the registrar has come to your rescue again. I spent the whole afternoon with him yesterday, you know – why don't you come and have a cup of coffee with me and I'll tell you all about it.'

He did. It seemed that Siddiqui had called on the registrar and by talking of their college days in Lucknow and by recalling all the prizes Rai had won in cricket and tennis had put him in such an excellent frame of mind that when it was explained to him that the money sanctioned by the Principal for the tape recorder was not sufficient to cover the entire project and that more funds were required, the registrar promised to forward their case and see that it was dealt with 'sympathetically'.

'And what is more, he has,' Siddiqui exclaimed, once more the bright bird who did no one any harm. He was chuckling with pride and delight.

Deven stared open-mouthed. He could not see why anyone should help him. He no longer knew if he ought to be – or even if he wanted to be helped. Were these people really helping him to succeed in a unique and wonderful enterprise or simply locking him up more and more firmly in a barred trap? And was the trap set by Murad, by Siddiqui, or by Nur and his wives? All he knew was that he who had set out to hunt Nur down was being hunted down himself, the prey.

'Can't you look more pleased? You wanted money to pay Nur for the recitation and the Principal has even sanctioned that. Actually it is money presented to the library by a benefactor – one Lala Bhagwan Das – but it has not yet been used, so can be spent on the recording since the tapes will eventually be placed in the library as a nucleus of a future collection. The librarian objected at first that since the tape would be of benefit only to the Urdu department, it was not fair to deprive the other departments of their share of the library funds. But of course that is absurd because what good are books on bridge-building, agronomy and chemistry to

143

Urdu students? Also, if he starts this library of tapes, he can encourage other departments to take up audio-visual methods of teaching. So the librarian has been persuaded and the Principal has agreed to release funds for payment to Nur for the recording. You are to go to the registrar's office and collect them – and then off to Delhi again, eh, Deven-*bhai*? Your luck is too good, my friend, *too* good,' hooted Siddiqui, and burst out laughing at the baffled expression on Deven's face.

There were still two obstacles to be cleared before he could begin to move towards Nur, poetry, success and immortality. They lay before him like two heaps of debris, of rubbish piled up in the way, and he knew he would have to tackle them before he could proceed.

One was the interview with the head of the Hindi department, a small vicious ferret of a man called Trivedi who had long ago published a few short stories in a women's magazine now defunct and which no one remembered, and had been teaching at the Mirpore college since long before Deven joined. He looked at everyone with the same expression of manic hatred and as if he were calculating the right time to dart out and bite. Deven had faced it so often, he had even come to expect it, and merely hunched his shoulders a little as he mumbled his request for a week's leave.

As was expected, Trivedi bawled, 'A week's leave? Just before the end of term? What for? Why can't you wait till college closes? Two months are not enough for you? Is there no limit to young men's laziness these days? What sort of example is this to your students? Are they also to be let off a week early?'

Deven stood his ground – being firmly seated on a chair across the desk from Trivedi and with his hands clutching the edges of it helped him to do so – and mumbled a long incoherent explanation while Trivedi pulled dreadful faces, like an actor practising the *rudra rasa*, the furious temper – opening his mouth, baring his teeth, narrowing his eyes, cupping his ear with one hand and scowling; his students

144

found these a subject for hilarity but Deven's risibility had long ago been numbed and paralyzed.

'Eh?' Trivedi said at last. 'An Urdu poet? *His* memoirs? *His* poetry? Tape recording?' he screeched. 'What are you talking about? Why can't it wait? Why can't it be done in the summer vacation?'

'Sir, many other people are involved. The publication of the journal is being held up. Nur Sahib himself is eager to begin before the heat grows worse as he is in poor health. His wife is needing the money for the household, sir. And the – the other wife who was ill and is beginning to recover and may refuse to let him do the recording if she hears about it – '

'What? What? What?' sputtered Trivedi, shaking his pen and making large drops of ink fly from it across the desk. 'What rubbish is all this? Have you gone mad? All of you? I always thought a mad dog must have run through this college, biting staff and students alike – you are all mad, rabid, that's what it is,' he foamed at the lips. 'You had better get out of here – '

'On leave, sir?' cried Deven, jumping up and trying not to get any more blobs of ink on the front of his white bush-shirt. 'One week's leave, sir?'

'One week? It would be a relief to me if it were one year,' bawled Trivedi, 'and I did not need to see your stupid mug again. I'll have you demoted, Sharma – I'll see to it you don't get your confirmation. I'll get you transferred to your beloved Urdu department. I won't have Muslim toadies in my department, you'll ruin my boys with your Muslim ideas, your Urdu language. I'll complain to the Principal, I'll warn the RSS, you are a traitor – '

'Yes, sir, I'll go, sir,' Deven said and left just in time to avoid the inkpot that was hurled at the door, hit the wall and smashed in an explosion of black ink. Being treated like a schoolboy made him feel like one. He gave a little smothered laugh.

Dealing with Sarla was a different matter. Sarla never lifted her voice in his presence – countless generations of Hindu womanhood behind her stood in her way, preventing her from displaying open rebellion. Deven knew she would scream and abuse only when she was safely out of the way, preferably in the kitchen, her own domain. Her other method of defence was to go into the bedroom and snivel, refusing to speak at all, inciting their child to wail in sympathy.

Which would it be this time, Deven wondered, as he informed her, while eating his breakfast of last night's cold, dry *puris* and a cup of tea, that he would not be accompanying her to her parents' home after all, that he was going to be too busy to join her there later, that in fact he was starting the vacation a week early in order to take up some extra work that had come his way in Delhi, and that it would suit him if she took the boy and departed for her parents' home a week earlier, in which case he would see her off before leaving himself.

Sarla had not had so many words addressed to her for a long time. She stood open-mouthed at his side, holding a bowl of yoghurt aslant so that it dripped on to the table and splashed.

'Take that away, see what you've done,' Deven told her sharply.

She moved a step backwards. 'And – and what am I to tell my parents? How am I to explain all this?' she finally managed to say in a strangled voice.

'Tell them what I've told you – that *is* the explanation,' he said, glaring at her.

'They – they will ask where you are, what you are doing,' she stammered.

'How can I tell them? They are illiterate, how can they understand *my* work?' Deven yelled and rose from the table, pushing away the metal tray with a new forcefulness. He was impatient now, a man short of time, needing to hurry. When would he clear all these heaps of rubbish out of the way and see the open stretch of road before him? And where would it lead him – to yet another pile of refuse, or to the clear shining horizon at last?

CHAPTER NINE

Then began a period when events moved at such a pace and images and sensations packed themselves in so closely that Deven quite lost the earlier vision of the shining horizon and the empty road, hurled as he was upon the flying horse of a merry-go-round that turned upon its axle with such rattling speed that he could decipher no one image, follow no single sequence and was merely aware of the rush of things as they sped by, now mounting by stages, now descending, in circles around him, leaving him giddy, somewhat sick, and almost giggling with exhilaration.

'So, Deven, at last you've arranged it,' Murad said as he stuck his head in at the door with a cautious air. 'No wonder you are grinning from ear to ear.'

Deven snapped his teeth together. 'No, I'm not,' he muttered, also cautious.

'You look as if you've just had twin sons, or published that rotten book of your poetry at last.' Still standing outside with his hand on the doorpost, he wrinkled his large pock-marked nose so that the pock-marks all merged together into a dark scowl.

'What is wrong, Murad?' Deven asked nervously. 'It is a big room, a quiet house. Nur's begum arranged it, you know.'

She had been waiting at the other side of the door when he

147

timidly struck it with the palm of his hand. Opening it a crack, she had whispered in the exaggerated manner demanded of melodrama, 'Have you brought it?' and Deven had inserted the bulging envelope through the crack, proudly instructing her, 'Count it – it's all here.' But she had only slipped it into her blouse, lifting her faded veil to do so and revealing the dyed hairs combed sparsely across a nearly bald scalp. She looked older and shabbier in the glare of the summer morning. She had hardly any teeth left and they were quite blackened. Shutting one eye, she pointed over his shoulder down the lane at one of the tall houses that backed on to it. Jerking her chin, she said, 'There, the last one in the row, that pink house. Go in by the back door, the woman will meet you and take you to a room upstairs – I have arranged everything, she is known to me, an old friend. The room is at the top, quiet, with a separate entrance, and no connection with the rest of the house. It will be all right. Go and wait there and I will send Nur Sahib.'

And that was how he had come to this pink house in the lane, so unusually quiet, pleasantly decorated, apparently deserted. To begin with, he had had a fright for the back door was guarded by a man who looked like a champion wrestler, black whorls of hair springing out of the openings of his red, gilt-buttoned shirt, gold studs in his ears, a large mouth swilling betel juice, and oil leaking out of his curly hair that glinted blue in the light. Deven had had to swallow the impulse to mumble, 'Sorry, a mistake,' and flee. Instead, he murmured Nur's name, whereupon the man moved a step back and shouted to someone. A woman appeared – tall, surprisingly well-dressed in a flashy way, adorned with pearl rings and glass bangles, clothed in some light gauzy material that almost veiled her pock-marked complexion and heavily-powdered face. Lifting her hand to her forehead, she greeted him silently with no more than a twist of her lips over a piece of scented betel nut that she held between them, and then gave her permission for him to be led upstairs. He had asked for a minute, and gone out to whistle for Chiku, who sat morosely in a cycle rickshaw outside with the tape recording equipment on his knees, waiting sullenly in the heat. Deven had helped him to carry the various pieces of equipment up the tiled staircase which smelt unpleasantly of both urine and cheap perfume, to the top of the house, past doors hung with flowered curtains through which he glimpsed beds, sleeping figures, mirrors and toilet articles – but of course he did not stop to investigate. Chiku, on the other hand, mounted the stairs slowly, stopping before every door and staring in with open curiosity, his mouth slightly open, breathing heavily in his adenoidal way. Outside the doors were shoes, or empty glasses, littered trays. Was this a hotel? Deven gave a slight twitch of apprehension at the thought that there might be a bill to be paid.

'Come on, come on,' he snapped at Chiku, 'we must have everything ready by the time Nur Sahib arrives – we can't waste time – it is to be done in three days flat.'

Three days.

'How long will it take you, Deven-*bhai*?' Murad asked, reflectively chewing a wad of *paan* while his eyes swivelled around, taking in the scene – the bolsters and cushions scattered on the mattress laid out with white sheets, the spittoon, the silver box of *paan*, the glasses and jars of water in one corner, the recording equipment piled in another, the garlanded oleograph of a shock-headed saint from the South hanging on the wall, beneath a tube of blue fluorescent lighting, and the idle figures seated on the mats, slouching or sprawling as they waited for the poet to make his appearance.

Deven frowned a little, as though he had a slight headache. He did not care to answer. He could not. The days were slipping by like some kind of involuntary exudation, oozing past. He seemed to have no control over them, or what occurred during them. 'This is not something that can be done to a timetable,' he muttered and was enraged by the way Murad slowly nodded his head as though his suspicions had been confirmed. 'Coming in?' he asked testily.

Murad gave a snort. 'Don't often come to such places,' he leered. 'Not in this quarter of the city anyway.'

'Oh, what is *your* quarter then?' Deven challenged him, infu-riated at having his so painfully made arrangements derided.

Murad looked momentarily surprised at such a show of spirit. 'Well, my friend, I had no idea it was yours,' he said, shifting the wad of betel leaves around his mouth and starting to chomp on them again.

'It isn't mine – it is Nur Sahib's,' said Deven defensively, 'and we are occupying it only till the recording is done.'

'Yes,' said Murad, putting one foot into the room at last after having debated the matter for so long. He was dressed in white leggings and a loose *kurta* already mapped with perspiration. 'That is just what I came to see – how it is getting on – so I can get an idea how long it will take.'

Deven waved his hand with a fine carelessness he did not really feel. The gesture faded on the air from lack of convic-tion. 'How long? What does it matter? Can a poet be pinned down by time? He can't be expected to keep an eye on his watch, Murad-*bhai* – he is immortal and belongs to all time.'

Murad made a disgusted face. 'What's the matter – are you drunk – at this time of the morning?'

But Deven did not need to drink in order to feel this hazardous euphoria trickling through him – it was not drink that caused it, but Nur.

To begin with, Nur had spoken only of drink and food. Tucking up his feet under him – the white corpse-like feet of the aged who walk little – he had chosen this as a topic of primary interest to the dismay of Deven who had just sig-nalled to Chotu to set the machine going and begin the recording of Nur's imperishable words.

'The *biryani* will have to be sent for from the bazaar, Deven Sahib,' he said at once, panting as though he had hurried here to give instructions. 'I would like a good mutton *biryani* from Jama Masjid for my lunch. There is a man, a refugee from Peshawar, at the back of the mosque, who makes it the way I like – with real saffron, the kind that gives rice not only colour but fragrance as well, and of course the rice must be the long fine kind from Dehra Dun. Do you know, he left

150

Peshawar and came here because he could no longer get that kind of rice there? He said he couldn't make his *biryani* without it so he came and settled down here. A good neighbour for me to have. If you send someone to him with my order, he will have it sent here – he knows this house,' he beamed at his court, in the best of humours. 'I have often had it sent,' he laughed in happy reminiscence. 'At the end of a long night, dawn breaking over the mosque, I would go out on the balcony and shout – it was a race between me and the mullah, who called first, I for my *biryani* or he for the first prayers of the day. Oh how I would shout, the whole house would wake up, *bibi-ji* would be so angry and come and scold,' he waggled his toes with delight, like pale worms weaving out of the grave, 'but she would send the boy to fetch it and I would sit down and eat it while others were unrolling their mats and preparing to pray, infidel that I was in my youth. Ah, that *biryani*, that aroma of rice and saffron at dawn, it made me remember Allah more acutely than the mullah's call could.'

And Deven, who had been frantically gesturing and grimacing at Chiku across the room to halt the machine, dropped his head and listened, certain that now Nur would begin to quote from his poetry, possibly the verse sequence about his profligate youth, the one that played on the many words for wine, goblet, and server of wine . . .

But Nur had moved up another rung of the ladder to the subject of drink. 'There are those who think whisky is the only drink to be had with *biryani* – so Rafiq used to think who so often shared that *biryani* at dawn with me – but I have found,' and his voice dropped to the dark brown level of profundity, 'I have found that rum will do as well, if not better,' and he turned towards Deven and fixed him with a sly look. 'So a bottle of rum you must get, Deven-*bhai*, if I am to eat your *biryani* – it cannot be washed down with anything less, not Khan Sahib's *biryani*. What do you say?' he turned to the young men who had accompanied him up the stairs to this room – the same rabble that surrounded him every night on the terrace – and rolled his eyes at them so

151

comically that they shouted with delighted approval. To turn him senile seemed their sole object, Deven bitterly noted.

'Rum!' they called, while others howled '*Biryani!*' and Deven, flustered, looked around to see who would finance all this festivity. They all looked back at him in smiling anticipation.

He had then had to make his panicky appeal to Murad. 'Murad,' he had pleaded on the telephone, 'without cash, I am sunk. All the college gave me, I handed over to his begum. It is payment to Nur. I had not – not expected all these expenses, these incidentals. I can't go back to my college – there are limits, after all – but without cash, I can't get Nur to perform even for five minutes.'

Murad made exasperated sounds at the other end of the line. Was he angry? Amused?

Deven was dancing from foot to foot in agony. The chemist from whose shop he had telephoned watched him with hostile suspicion, ignoring a pleading customer at the counter. Deven had told him he had to phone for news of a patient who was in hospital and required some rare and costly drugs. He dropped his voice to a murmur. 'Bring some cash. After all, it is for your magazine. You must have some funds. I tell you, it will all be useless, this setting up of all these arrangements, if I don't have cash for – for incidentals. At least provide me with enough to feed him his meals, and some drink, that's all.'

He had been able to elicit no more than a few grunts from Murad who seemed not to like to communicate on the telephone and made no response apart from these stifled sounds. But he had come next morning after all and stuck his head in at the door with the look of a doubtful gargoyle, and when Deven asked, 'Have you brought – ?' he gave a grim nod or two and said menacingly, 'Yes, but I am going to cut it from your fee, you know,' and then surveyed the room in order to make an estimate for himself.

The feasting and drinking did not continue without pause, blessedly: Nur, at his age and in his poor state of health, could not sustain his expensive whims. The boy servant who accompanied him to the house every morning saw to it that he was indulged as befitted his status, but not beyond that.

To Deven's relief, there were times when, without undue prompting, he fished out his metal-rimmed spectacles, searched for the school copybooks till they were brought to him, cleared his throat with painful exaggeration and then read his verse to a rapt audience. Then Deven beckoned joyfully across the room to Chiku, like a trainer flagging off a race, and Chiku would stir himself and begin to fiddle and twiddle and carry long wires and short microphones about the room, switching the sullen frown on his face to a self-important one. He would raise his hand imperiously, demanding that the electric fans be switched off as they were making a disturbing noise or the sparrows chased out of the room. Nur would be irritated beyond endurance by such interruptions and begin a peroration upon the evils of technology – 'You say it has freed him from the law of gravity and sent him into space – but in what kind of vehicle? A vehicle that is made of steel is only a steel trap. Man is not set free by the aeroplane, he is trapped in it. And how is the soul of a poet to rise and float when you keep trying to catch it in a box between your knees?' – so that Deven would be obliged to offer him a drink and make a signal to switch on the fans in an effort to cool him down. Grumpily he would agree to forgive them and recite a verse sequence he had written in his youth on flight and that was familiar to his audience, easy and loved.

Ravished by its sweet tones and murmured sibilances, Deven would sink back on his heels and shut his eyes, nodding gently in agreement with the poet's sentiments, and fail to notice that Chiku was still fumbling with the machine and not taking any of it down. When his clumsy impatient fingers had finally put things in working order and switched on the machine, it was too late: Nur had come to the end of his recitation and was reminiscing about his pigeons and the races and combats and competitions he had held with them on the roof, about pet fantails and prize tumblers, failing to notice how his audience yawned and muttered and winked.

When he did notice at last, he turned melancholy. 'None of you know this royal game of course. In the old days the sky of Delhi was like a shining tapestry – not the thick quilt of smoke and fumes it is now. The air was as brilliant as a piece of silk, the sun sparkled upon it like a huge gold pendant fashioned by a jeweller, and when the fantails flew towards it, they turned into gems and dazzled the eyes. Even with only two rupees in my pocket, I was a rich man then,' he mused, and related a long, involved tale about a neighbour, a greedy rogue, who had coveted them and tried to rob him of them. He began to curse as if the theft had taken place that very morning instead of fifty years ago.

Deven realized belatedly that he was now speaking in prose, of the commonest variety, and tried to convey to the oblivious Chiku that the recorder might be switched off, but Chiku appeared to be dozing and every now and again Nur did throw in a line or two of verse, like a well-polished blade of steel cutting through the tangled thread of his reminiscences, making it seem worthwhile to keep on recording. It could all be edited later, Deven thought hazily, and gave himself up to trying to follow Nur's long and intricately technical description of the training of a champion; he had never imagined there was so much to the hobby of a pigeon fancier and wondered what bearing, if any, such sport could have upon the art of poetry. He therefore listened intently but the others made it obvious that they did not.

Making a face, Nur wound up, 'Useless to talk about it – it is like pulling out the tail feathers of my beauties to show you and leaving my pets naked. Urggh,' he exploded, waving his hands before his face as if to blot out the view. 'I can only bear the sight of you if you give me some rum – no, plenty of rum because there are plenty of you.'

They laughed indulgently and filled his glass from the bottle Murad had brought with him and planted behind the earthenware jar of water provided by the establishment. Then of course the others wanted a drink too and there was much

154

running up and down the stairs, fetching and carrying and passing around. Only when a glass was passed to Chiku was it discovered that he was fast asleep, the tape recorder still on, doggedly recording all Nur's abuses and expletives. Horrified, Deven snatched back the glass and hissed at him, 'Brought you here to drink and sleep, did I? Can't even stay awake on the job.'

'What sort of job is this that goes on for twelve hours a day?' grumbled Chiku, rubbing his bleary eyes and snuffling.

'Let him have a drink, poor lad,' said his neighbour, an obese and jovial fellow who was looking on, amused: to him Chiku was an addition to the entertaining spectacle, the *tamasha*.

'No,' hissed Deven, 'he is *not* to have a drink,' and sat down beside him to make certain he did not: the boy would have to be prodded into doing his work, manually.

It was not Chiku's ineptitude alone that threatened to sabotage Deven's painstakingly constructed project: all the idle men, buffoonish and heedless, attempted ceaselessly to turn it all into a drinking party, edging closer to the poet, coming between him and Deven with their proffered bottles and glasses. Time and again they would deflect him from any attempt to get work done and induce him to speak on matters Deven felt could not be of interest to academic circles. Yet the matter was not a simple one of separating prose from poetry, life from art: at times, when Nur was relating a story of his youth, of his education, his travels, his loves or quarrels, it would occur to Deven that this had some bearing on his art after all. Jerking into action, he would urge Chiku to switch on the machine only to have Nur come to the end of his tale, abruptly. A pause would follow, not exactly of silence because outside the traffic blared and bleated and in the room the electric fans clicked wildly and a nestful of sparrows in the skylight flapped and twittered, but certainly of silence from the poet.

Frantic to make him resume his monologue now that the tape was expensively whirling, Deven once forgot himself so far as to lean forward and murmur with the earnestness of an interviewer, 'And, sir, were you writing any poetry at the time? Do you have any verse belonging to that period?'

The effect was disastrous. Nur, in the act of reaching out for a drink, froze. 'Poetry?' he shot at Deven, harshly. 'Poetry of the period? Do you think a poet can be ground between stones, and bled, in order to produce poetry – for *you*? You think you can switch on that mincing machine, and I will instantly produce for you a length of raw, red minced meat that you can carry off to your professors to eat?'

Deven hung his head, shamed. Chiku sniggered. The tape whirred, recording adversity and humiliation.

Yet there were times when Nur would quietly, soberly recite his verse without any cajoling or prompting at all from Deven. This happened occasionally early in the mornings, as soon as he arrived, when he was fresh enough to be brisk and attentive to his business, and before the waves of dissolute idleness sent out by his aimlessly indolent audience reached him and overcame him. Settling his spectacles upon his nose with a fine scholarly gesture, he would open out one of his child's copy books on his knees and begin to read in a voice that was sing-song yet powerful, breaking off to give Deven the background for the writing of a verse or point out the similarity of his ideas and images to those of the poets he chiefly admired. To Deven's astonishment, these turned out to be Byron and Shelley from whom he liked to quote frequently and fulsomely.

'O wild west wind, thou breath of autumn's being,' he would intone in a voice like an approaching thunderstorm that made even Chiku look up and pay attention, or more gently and trippingly, with affection:

> 'Hail to thee, blithe spirit,
> Bird thou never wert . . . '

Once he broke off the recitation of his own well-known verse sequence on the enticements and frailties of women that the world knew as the Rose poems, to ask Deven for his own preferences in poetry and while Deven mumbled and cast around wildly for one title or one line that would save him from giving the impression of total illiteracy, he raised his hand and said, 'Listen! Listen to the greatest lines that were ever written by anyone,' and intoned dramatically:

'O what can ail thee, knight-at-arms,
  Alone and palely loitering?'

The recitation was so long, so filled with finely timed pauses and gestures, that Deven had begun to wonder if it did not have some bearing upon that aspect of the poet's private life into which he had unwillingly had such a terrifying glimpse, and had even begun to see certain psychological connections before he realized that Nur was just winding up a third rendering of what was evidently his favourite poem. Fortunately, a hoarse cough overcame him at this point and while the servant boy ministered to his throat with a glass of suitably warmed water, Deven turned aside discreetly to suggest to Chiku in a whisper that the second and third rendition could be erased from the tape, only to discover that Chiku, once again napping, had forgotten to turn the tape in time so that there were three renditions of Keats's long narrative but not a line left of Nur's own poem that he had recited later. Deven felt a crimson tide rising inside his ear and threatening to implode within his head.

What saved Chiku – apart from the need to keep this amateurish bumbling disguised from Nur himself – was a commotion that broke out downstairs just then, such screams and yells and sounds of beating that not only could Deven not get beyond a choked exclamation but even Nur had to refrain from reciting, for a fourth time, 'La Belle Dame Sans Merci'. The quarrelling voices were clearly female, their tongues like whips used with practised artistry. Someone appeared to be resisting eviction, then a man's footsteps were heard thumping purposefully up the stairs, the screams became shriller, the sounds of beating more violent and eventually there followed a sound like the muffled roll of a

157

body falling heavily down the stairs, to which everyone listened with their mouths open.

Deven got to his feet and went towards the door, slightly shaking at the prospect of getting involved in a scene of violence but feeling he owed it to Nur to protect him from such vulgarity. He did not go out, however, because everyone called him back, quite jovially. 'Let them be, *bhai*, such things go on here all the time,' said a young man with a mouthful of *paan*, in a squeezed kind of giggle, 'only not usually in the day. Someone has overstayed.'

'How do you know?' Deven asked him sharply; he particularly disliked this character who came dressed in clothes so loose as to be almost indecent and sat against the wall with his legs stretched out casually so that his dirty bare feet pointed at Nur, insultingly. 'How do *you* know?' he repeated.

Everyone laughed but no one answered. Nur, who had been listening with his head to one side like a canny old bird's, winked and began to tell of a brawl in which he had been implicated. The men laughed so much that the story became too garbled and broken for Deven to follow.

That evening, when Nur had left and the others were collecting their belongings and preparing to follow him down the stairs, the young man in the loose clothes and with the dirty feet sidled up to Deven and said, 'Do you know if he comes here to do the recording for you or is he hunting for a new wife?' Deven stared, stupefied. 'Didn't you know,' the man went on, nudging him in the ribs with a right-angled elbow, 'don't tell me you didn't know – he found his second wife here, in this brothel. Who knows, he may be looking for a third!' Doubling up with laughter, he rolled away before Deven could catch him by his throat and silence him. Looking down at his helplessly shaking hands, Deven felt it all beyond his grasp, his control. In taking Nur's art into his hands, did he have to gather up the stained, soiled, discoloured and odorous rags of his life as well? He knew he could not.

Chiku, watching, broke in upon his thoughts by asking, 'D'you want me to play the day's recording for you? Shall I play the tape?'

Deven felt he could not bear that. 'Pack it up. Put it away,' he said.

Thereafter he entered the house with daily trepidation. Even the room at the top no longer seemed private, an enclosed world. Although the house backed on to a quiet lane, it opened out on to one of the main streets of the bazaar and the cacophony of traffic pouring up and down it rose and entered the room through all the open doors and windows. Quite often there was a traffic jam when the angry impatient blaring of horns and bicycle bells grew so frantic that all conversation and recitation had to be suspended, making Nur's face retreat into the shadow of a frown.

There was an occasion when an overloaded lorry backed into the lane, then could not get out again. A crowd collected to give advice which the driver resented and a vociferous altercation broke out. Forgetting Nur, every man in the room went out on to the balcony to watch. Several of the women of the house emerged on to their balconies below, and the young men, instead of looking studiously away as Deven did, leant over the rails to whistle and wave to them. When he tried to pull them away and force them inside, saying 'Nur Sahib is waiting,' they shook him off, and one even snarled, 'Want your milk teeth knocked out, puppy?' The last pretence of the gathering in this room being a *mehfil,* a tribute to the poet, collapsed.

Nur, however, took the interruption as an occasion to give the servant boy instructions for a meal of kebabs and *parathas* that he wished especially prepared at his favourite restaurant. Deven heard him say, 'Go, collect the money from Deven Sahib and then go and give the order.' Deven could not refuse to pay but, turning upon Chiku and seeing that the brainless boy was recording Nur's involved instructions about the kebabs, cried 'Switch that off, can't you? Is this something to be recorded?'

Nur drew himself back and glared briefly at Deven, then said to the young men who were beginning to return to the room from the balcony, the successful exit of the lorry having

159

caused the lower balconies to empty, 'Poets, you know, are not supposed to live on meat and bread. They are expected to be able to survive on verse,' and just as Chiku removed the microphone from before him and began to put away his equipment, he half-rose upon his haunches like some aged lion goaded into protest, and thundered out one of his earliest, almost forgotten poems that had once caused the literary world to be shaken like a straw stack in a storm, so livid and loud was it with dissent.

When he stopped, Deven pounced upon Chiku, almost shaking him by the shoulders, and asked, 'Did you record that? Did you?'

Chiku eyed him balefully. 'Just after you told me to stop?' he asked, then refused to pay Deven any more attention and went into a corner and sulked while Nur sat back in his usual reclining posture and accepted the congratulations and adulation of his listeners.

That evening, when the crowd was dispersing noisily down the stairs in the wake of the departing Nur, Deven went across to Chiku to warn him to perform his duties with some measure of human intelligence, whereupon Chiku turned upon him and gave in his notice.

'My sister's marriage is next week and I must go. I am the only brother. My parents have left all the arrangements to me. I have no time for all this poetry-shoetry. You can get some technician to finish the job . Please give me my pay – I am leaving.'

'You cannot have your pay unless you finish the job,' Deven heard his voice scream shrilly. No one had told him that the boy had to be paid. He had assumed his services were thrown in with the rotten secondhand tape recorder.

'Our contract was for three days – and it is now three weeks, nearly,' Chiku retorted.

'There was no contract.'

'I will speak to my uncle. I will go to Murad Sahib.'

'There's no need. Stay here and finish the job and you will get paid.' Deven fought to control his voice and subdue it to its normal pitch. He turned around to leave before the boy

160

could answer but at the door could not refrain from adding, bitterly, 'Chiku! What kind of name is Chiku? Couldn't your parents even find you a proper name?'

Down in the street he telephoned Murad from the chemist's shop to complain about Chiku. Murad was not sympathetic. 'We told the boy it would take a week at the most,' he reminded Deven, 'and it is now three weeks.'

'Three weeks?' Deven was alarmed to have Chiku's charge confirmed.

'What is the matter with you, can't you count? Poetry gone to your head, has it – Nur's "timeless, immortal" poetry? Of course it is three weeks, and what the bills are mounting up to, God only knows. Of course you poet types don't think about such matters. But now that I am reminding you, will you please wind up your circus, send your star performer home, transcribe that interview and bring it to me so that I can finally send this issue to the press? You are holding it up. My friend Sahay reserved this week to do my printing, he refused three other jobs to take up mine, he is also losing money, we are all losing money.'

'Murad, I assure you I am also the loser in this. I am gaining nothing by drawing it out so long – '

'Then will you please cut it short? I want the interview latest by the end of the week, hear?'

But Deven, as he left the chemist's shop, still felt the vibrations from Nur's majestic roars in his ears and felt loath to put an end to the recording when it seemed Nur had just roused himself to begin reciting in the manner of his fabled youth. Deven felt as if he had at last netted some of the treasure out of that turbid, churned-up ocean he had been drearily dredging. Now he needed only to somehow direct Nur into recollecting the years when he had first begun to write and attract the attention of connoisseurs and patrons of Urdu poetry; he needed his reminiscences of the literary world of that period, of the poets and writers who had been his friends and enemies, and of course the work he had done in those heady days.

161

Given a little more time – another week, or perhaps two – he would have not only a brilliant recording with which to dazzle the Urdu department of his college and, who knew, such distinguished Muslim institutions as the Jamia Millia and the Aligarh University as well – but enough material for an interview and perhaps even a slim volume of memoirs. He could almost see it lyng between his hands – he would have it bound in a soft, sky-blue cover like a sheet of the sky in which Nur's pigeons flew, and its title inscribed in the poet's hand, distinctively.

What he was actually gazing at was the stationery shop in front of which he had stopped to study the shelves filled with copy books of the kind Nur used for his writing, reams of foolscap, school textbooks, geometry boxes and pencils, calendars and coloured maps, and it struck him that if he bought some paper and took down Nur's words, he would not be wholly reliant on the idiot Chiku and his maddening machine. Then nothing would be lost. Nothing should be lost.

He pulled out some money from his pocket to pay for the copy books and was dismayed to find that he did not have enough: he could not afford even the equipment of a small schoolchild. 'Just one, please, not three,' he mumbled shame-facedly and tried not to notice the look of contempt on the shopkeeper's face as he reduced his purchases.

He was grateful, after the ignominies of the day, to creep off to the small flat in Darya Ganj he had chosen to shelter in rather than go to his mother's family home and ask for accommodation. He imagined that must still stand where it had stood in his childhood, inhabited perhaps by a new generation of relations, but a reluctance to resume his relation-ship with them had made him turn into a dark lane remem-bered from his schooldays and find his way up the stairs to an old schoolfriend's home instead. Raj, born with one leg shorter than the other, had been the least intimidating of his schoolfellows. He had lost touch with him after he went to live in Mirpore. Then he had received, to his great astonishment, a

162

postcard from Cairo informing him that Raj was teaching in a school there. The exotic notion of his handicapped friend fetching up in Egypt had struck him speechless; he had not even replied. Now, standing in the doorway and asking the gently smiling old aunt if Raj had returned, he received no answer. Yet she must have recognized him for she beckoned him in with a calm welcome that old ladies do not generally proffer to strangers ringing their doorbells at night. Stepping in, he had seen that she was just serving a meal to a spectacled and skeletal male guest whose sparse beard made him look unwashed and who was seated cross-legged on the kitchen floor. Did she actually recognize him, the schoolboy Deven, or did she take him for another beggar who must be fed in accordance with the rules of piety? She wore not only the widow's white clothes but also the chain of wooden beads and other such insignia of the initiated. It was with the gestures of a trained devotee that she bade him sit down and accept the tray she handed him. Then she proceeded to fill it with a gratifying variety of foods. When he politely protested, the spectacled man who was shovelling in rice and pickles by the handfuls, told him, 'Eat, eat. She enjoys when you eat,' so he did. Later, when she had removed the trays and brought them betel leaves and nuts, he tried to find out if she really remembered him by talking about Raj and asking questions about him, but it was always the guest who replied. He seemed to know the family well. His intimacy with them went so far that it was he who suggested Deven spend the night there. 'You are from outside Delhi? You are needing a room? Then stay here – lie there in the veranda and sleep. No need to go to a hotel when Sister is here to look after us,' he guffawed, throwing her a sly look. 'Na, Sister-ji?' he asked, and since she made no reply beyond nodding, Deven gratefully accepted the offer, thinking it was for three nights at the most and he would write and tell Raj about it, expressing his gratitude.

No one objected to his extending his stay. The old lady continued to smile piously while she served him his meals. The spectacled man grew more loquacious however and

Deven learnt that he was not a relation at all but the tailor who worked in a small shop under the staircase and had moved in after Raj left 'to give Sister-ji some protection, na'. He had his own corner in the flat where he kept his mat and his belongings but the stuffs and materials of his trade spread the starchy, chemical smell of unwashed textiles through the whole flat and snippets and bits of thread and fluff floated around indiscriminately even though his workplace was downstairs, at street level. Deven felt vaguely uneasy to be sharing the restricted sleeping space with a tailor, a man of the working class, but could hardly object or permit himself to act as a superior when their hostess treated them with such benignly equal hospitality. In fact, the tailor's position appeared to be one of slightly greater privilege, and Deven soon found out the reason. The old lady's piety consisted not only in the feeding of whoever came to be fed – large numbers of *sadhus* in white or saffron, carrying begging bowls came regularly for the purpose of helping her to fulfil her earthly duties and earn her merit in her next incarnation – but also in performing long and elaborate *pujas* at dawn and dusk. Possibly at other hours as well but it was these occasions that Deven witnessed. She had one wall of the kitchen turned into a veritable temple, with tinted oleographs of saints, plaster images of her pet gods, incense-holders, fresh garlands, saucers of offerings and lamps ranged along the shelves and in the niches. While she sat, or stood, or bowed, and tended this family of domesticated gods, the tailor played the role she had assigned him – of a devotional singer. It turned out that he had a fine tenor voice quite unexpected in a man so lacking in physical comeliness, and a huge repertoire of devotional songs that he rendered with great emotion. The old lady smiled in appreciation, and after lighting all her lamps and joss-sticks and making all the offerings for the day – or hour – sat down cross-legged beside him and beat time with a pair of tin cymbals, clashing them with intense passion, often allowing the veil to slip off her head and display its pale, bony nakedness, the smoothness contrasting starkly with the withered and drooping skin of her face, while he played on a small drum held between his knees and made the walls resound with the full-throated abandon of his voice in a joyous hymn.

> 'I shall make my body into a clay lamp,
> My soul its wick and my blood oil.
> Ah, the light of this lamp would reveal
> The face of my Beloved to me.'

If Deven came upon them during such a performance, there was nothing for it but to retire to a corner and sit down quietly and wait till it was over when Raj's aunt would get to her feet with a sigh, the only time she appeared a little sad, and go off to cook them a meal, and the tailor would put away his drum, take out a packet of cigarettes and tell Deven about his latest customers and their whims.

'She came in a long, long car with a pile like this – this – of materials. "There is a wedding in the family, I need thirty blouses by Sunday," she says. O Ma, by Sunday? I say, how can I, a poor tailor who has no assistant, and bad eyes also, only just recovering from conjunctivitis? I always say that to frighten people away if I can't take on more work, but nothing frightens her away. She is counting out the materials – two cambric, two two-by-two, two rubia voile, two satin silk, two Benares brocade – and each one a different style. What styles, I tell you, even a courtesan of the Moghul courts never thought up any like them – here an opening, there an opening, what is there left for me to sew, only tapes to hold them together?' he laughed through his sharpened, blackened teeth, making a sound like a whistle. Then he exhaled, 'O Ma-a. Let more such fish fall into my net and I will be able to move out of Darya Ganj. I know a place in Tolstoy Lane where they are wanting a ladies' tailor. If I can become a full partner there, O Ma-a!'

This Deven had to endure if he wished to eat and sleep in the flat and it was so very convenient being within walking distance of the lane where he worked all day, and a place moreover where no one questioned him about his family, job, occupation

165

or anything at all, that he did so patiently. He sometimes felt a twinge of guilt at the expense he was causing the polite and hospitable old woman, but when he once stopped in the market on the way to buy her a basket of fruit, he found that she offered it to the gods instead of eating it and after that distributed it all amongst a band of monks who had come visiting, so he did not buy her any more: he had a fastidious dislike of the monks' soft flesh, unmarked by toil. Lowering himself on to the mat in the veranda that night, he was not able to relax and stretch out and give himself up to what was surely well-earned rest. He felt uneasy at having been so forcefully reminded that day of his initial three days' stay having stretched to three weeks. What must that insufferably loquacious tailor take him for – just another leech? In his role as the widow's protector, might he not one day throw Deven out if he suspected him of having sponged for too long? Crossing his arms under his head, he listened to the tailor's lascivious monologue about a new customer, a foreign woman, fair, droning on in his corner like a trapped mosquito, and tried to discover in him some sign of a poisonous sting. But the tailor seemed as pleased as ever to have a captive listener.

Through the veranda railing he could see the night sky lit to a chemical incandescence by the violet street lamps that shone into the veranda as well as the small park across the road. So late at night, the park was deserted, considered unsafe by the residents of this backwater of Darya Ganj, although by day it was filled with old men sitting in the shade, errand boys stopping for a game of marbles or a quiet smoke, and furtive couples behind the bushes. Once it had also held Deven and Raj, copying down each other's homework or playing a desultory game of cricket – Raj with his shorter leg in a clumsy orthopaedic boot and Deven trying to hide away from Murad's more demanding friendship and avoid going home to his own family. Even then he had always been running away from someone.

Turning on to his side he tried to give the tailor an indication of his wish to sleep. He wanted silence in which to plot his strategy for the recording next morning. How was he to bring

166

it to a fully rounded, beautifully completed and satisfying end? That, he sighed, was the question, and it could not be evaded much longer.

Next morning he was determined to begin the proceedings by opening out the copy book he had purchased and explaining to Nur that he would be taking dictation, but that day Nur had lost all interest in reciting his verse, said he had slept badly and was tired and asked some of his young admirers to recite theirs instead. Deven tried to suppress his dismay and listen patiently, but he could scarcely restrain the trembling of his lips as he sat with his head sunk below his shoulders, plucking at loose bits of cotton in the mat and trying to shut out the sound of some lowly mediocrity's voice reciting banalities. Chiku pointedly leant over and asked, 'You had better tell me – do you want me to record everything that is recited here?'
  Deven was still trying to control himself before he answered the insolent fool when Nur, who had overheard, turned to them and said, looking directly into Deven's face, 'Has this dilemma come to you too then? This sifting and selecting from the debris of our lives? It can't be done, my friend, it can't be done, I learnt that long ago,' and he broke into a verse that Deven had never heard before, that no one in the room had heard before, that entered into their midst like some visitor from another element, silencing them all with wonder. Nur looked about him with a faint, pleased smile, as if amused and gratified by the effect it had on them. Then he spoke the few lines again slowly and this time Deven had the presence of mind to open up his copy book and start scribbling them down. 'Here, give it to me,' Nur told him, seeing what he was about, and seizing the book from him, he wrote in it himself, holding it on his knee, stopping to lick the pencil now and then, peering at the letters with his cataract-filled eyes, while around him the babble broke out again as his audience excitedly discussed this new verse of his, praising it in such exaggerated terms that one might have been hard put to it to decide whether they were being truly appreciative or

merely parodying satisfaction and admiration. This was the audience Nur had always had to try his verses on, Deven saw, revolted by their flattery, and he knelt behind Nur in reverential silence, watching him write, keeping himself apart from the others, the one true disciple in whose safe custody Nur could place his work.

But very soon Nur's hand tired. He threw away the pencil and demanded a drink. 'They are over, my writing days,' he said, drinking noisily. 'My schoolboy days are done.' Putting down the glass, he kneaded his hands together, pulling at the joints, trying to bend the fingers, flexing and unflexing them, with a brooding look on his face as of a driver who wonders if his vehicle has broken down for good, and fears that it has. 'The music, it is over,' he mumbled.

'Sir, you are a musician who has no need of an instrument,' called a young man in a purple shirt and gold chains. 'You can play on even when your hands can no longer move.'

'Such is the glory of a poet,' exclaimed another, striking his full, round thigh.

Nur gave them a look from under his heavy eyebrows, twisting up his lips sceptically. After another drink, he announced 'The blood, it is still.'

A loud protest broke out. Another bottle of rum was opened and a fresh drink poured. Someone shouted hilariously, 'Call up the women. Let us have women and dance. Then let us see whose blood is stilled.' Deven jerked up his head to see who could be so crude, so insolent, but Nur was smiling as he shook his head.

'Women and dance have long since overtaken me and left me behind,' he muttered sorrowfully. 'Now even the glass slips from my hand and spills.' He clutched it so tightly that Deven feared it might break between his fingers and cut him. 'Then what is left, my friends, what remains?'

'Sir, your poetry. Your volumes of verse. They are left. They will be with us always,' Deven whispered passionately at his elbow.

'You keep them,' Nur said curtly in a tone of dismissal. 'You keep them and let me go to what I have waiting for me –

168

six feet of earth in the cemetery by the mosque.' Calling to his servant boy, he rose heavily to his feet with his help, and began to shuffle towards the door.

Nor could anyone stop him, he simply propelled himself forwards so that they had to fall aside and make way. Deven hurried after him, crying disconsolately, 'Sir, please – let us carry on with the recording. If you are tired, I will send for tea, and food. After a rest, we can resume – '

'No, I will not resume,' Nur told him, shaking his head and continuing to shake it as he was led up the lane to the back door of his house, Deven following in an agitated dance. Adamant up to the very door, he said, 'All one can resume, at my age, is the primordial sleep. I am going to curl up on my bed like a child in its mother's womb and I shall sleep, shall wait for sleep to come.'

The door in the wall opened and the servant boy helped him over the threshold and led him in. The door shut.

CHAPTER TEN

The room was empty when Deven returned next morning. He stood in the doorway, holding aside the strings of blue and green glass beads that formed the curtain and saw it bare, stripped, the light from the dust-filmed windows falling on the marble tiles bleakly. Only the sparrows nesting in the skylight twittered and quarrelled, scattering twigs as they rustled about in their nest. Out in the back lane a man was crying his wares – the earthen water jars that were strapped to his donkey's back. '*Su-ra-hi*!' he wailed, as if warning of doom, '*su-ra-hi*!' Stupidly, Deven wondered where he had heard that call before – here, or in Mirpore, or where? The call that had seemed to announce summer, heat and thirst - but summer was already here, devastating everything, laying waste his life, like this desolate room.

Chiku arrived at the top of the stairs, having toiled his way up with his equipment, heaving for breath exaggeratedly. 'Hunh,' he grunted, looking over Deven's shoulder, 'carry it all the way up and they aren't even here.'

'They're gone,' Deven said, still stunned. 'Nur Sahib has gone.'

'Hadn't you better fetch him? It's late – and so hot,' Chiku complained, perspiration welling out of the folds of his neck and oozing down his chest and back.

'I don't think he means to come back.'

'Then – then, it's over?'

170

'Yes,' said Deven, 'over.' He let go of the strings of beads that tinkled glassily against each other, again reminding him of something: Sarla's glass bangles clinking as she worked? Home, Mirpore, quotidian life drawing close, closing in?

'You should have told me,' Chiku burst out in a shrill voice. 'Why didn't you tell me? I've wasted another day – my sister is crying – my mother is saying I have not helped them – I have other things to do and you don't even give me notice . . .'

'Heh, who is there? What is going on up there?' shouted a voice at the foot of the stairs. The tall woman with the pock-marked face, holding a pink veil across it, glared through two huge rims of kohl.

They leant over the banisters and stared back at her mournfully.

'The same circus!' she exclaimed to someone hidden from their sight. 'What is this? Yesterday Safiya Begum sent word the room is no longer required, today you come back to it. Do you think you have bought yourself a room here? What do you think this is – some sort of shelter for vagabonds? I tell you this is a respectable house – I won't have it. Bulu, show them off,' she barked, so fiercely that the veil slipped from her face, which was puffy, swollen with some kind of distemper. She had had a bad night, or was sick, or even afraid – Deven could not begin to guess at the squalors of her life.

Chiku had already begun to crawl down the stairs like a spider with its load. Deven caught him up, relieved him of some of it, and began to follow him down. The bouncer Bulu met them on the landing, clad only in a *lungi* wrapped around his waist, so that his chest was bare and his muscles bulged and glistened. 'Leave at once,' he commanded, unnecessarily.

At the back door the woman stood watching them. As they descended the stairs into the lane, she called after them, 'The bill has been sent to Safiya Begum; see that it is paid. I have friends amongst the police who see to it that no one owes me anything, see?' She did not shut the door after them but stood glaring through the two baleful kohl-rims of her

171

eyes at them as they stood helplessly in the sun, holding pieces of the recording equipment, looking sadly for a rickshaw to take them away.

Murad did not sound at all pleased with the idea of arranging for the tapes to be heard in Delhi before Deven took them with him to Mirpore. 'What is the use if you haven't edited it yet? It will have to be cut, won't it? Why don't you do all that work before you bring it here?'

'Murad, I will do all that later, when I get back to Mirpore – I have to go back immediately, all the examination papers have to be corrected – but at least come down to Jain Sahib's shop to listen to the tapes before I take them away. That will give you an idea of the material I will be sending you for the magazine. Don't you want to know?' Deven pleaded.

Jain, picking his teeth with a matchstick as he watched Deven's face, muttered, 'I told you – what is the use? Take it with you – listen to it at home – what is the use of playing it here in my shop?'

Deven glared at him and shouted into the phone. 'You must come. I am waiting for you in Jain Sahib's shop. At least listen to a part of it – only a small part. We must make sure the quality is good.'

Chiku suddenly disentangled himself from a coil of wires and emerged, dusting his hands, and wiped his face with his sleeve. 'All right, I have set it up and now I am going. Uncle, please play the tape for him,' he jerked his chin at Deven in an insolent way and went off, leaving both Deven and the proprietor to protest loudly and ineffectually at his departure.

It occurred to Deven that it might be preferable to take all the equipment to a more congenial setting – say, Murad's house – and listen to the tapes there. He had never visited it but he felt it would be substantial, even lavish – surely it would have many rooms and offer privacy. But when Murad walked in, frowning with unwillingness, and heard the suggestion, tentatively and weakly made, he brushed it aside. 'No,' he said, throwing out his arms as if to bar the entrance to his father's house. 'We can't go there. My mother will be

172

resting – my sisters will be sleeping. We can't disturb them.'
Flinging himself down in a metal chair and folding his arms,
he set his jaw. 'Jain Sahib, please put it on. Quick. I can't
stay.'

He was obliged to stay for quite a while, however, because
Jain Sahib did not seem to know how to start the machine.
He shook and pummelled the box, pressed all the switches in
a row, fiddled, cursed and shouted for help. Murad sat
scowling and throwing exasperated looks at Deven who grew
more and more agitated. Eventually a boy was brought in
from the courtyard at the back, so covered in grease as
to resemble a motor mechanic rather than an electronics
technician. He brought along his tools, fiddled for long
minutes and at last produced a sudden, loud blare of sound,
cut it short and took what seemed hours before they were
able to settle down to listen.

It was a fiasco. There was no other word for it. Disbelievingly,
Deven had the first tape removed, the second tried and then
the third and the fourth. The cardboard carton that held them
seemed bottomless, there were so many. Everyone's tempers
were frayed by the constant stopping and starting. When the
tapes could be induced to produce sound, there seemed to be
nothing to listen to – long intervals of crackling and sputtering
interspersed with a sudden blare of horns from the street, the
shrieking of nest-building birds, loud explosions of laughter
and incoherent joviality, drunken voices bawling, singing,
stopping short. Where was Nur? Occasionally his voice wandered in like some lost mendicant off a crowded street,
offering a few lines of verse in a faint, foundering voice, then
breaking off to say, much more firmly and positively, 'Fetch
me another glass of rum. What have you ordered for lunch
today? Has someone gone to collect it? I need more rum if I
am to wait for so long.' Or else wandering through some
difficult and involved tale of his vagabond days, stopping to
groan and complain of the agony piles were causing him,
pleading for some relief from discomfort, cursing his age,
calling for palliatives in the way of food and drink, then

173

sinking into silence while some young admirer of his bawled out advice or encouragement with bawdy undertones that made the audience yelp like a pack of jackals.

Deven found himself sinking lower and lower upon his seat, his eyes fixed upon his dusty, cracked shoe-caps, feeling a tightening about his heart. His breath was short and shallow and if anyone had noticed, they would have seen his nostrils turning very pale and waxen.

At last Murad said, 'Stop all this. We've wasted enough time. It's no good. You should have had the tapes played back to you as soon as each was done – then you could have gone back and repeated what was missing and corrected what was wrong. Why did you leave it so late?'

Stung by this devastating and accurate criticism, Deven got to his feet although he could hardly stand, he felt so physically wrecked by the disaster. 'Murad – I will somehow – somehow salvage something from this. I *have* to. I can – I can easily put together enough material for an article for your journal. You will have that – you will. But my college – the college paid for the tapes – ' he began to stammer.

Murad appeared for a moment to comprehend his anguish. Turning to Jain, he said harshly, 'What is all this? What kind of tape recorder did you give us? And what sort of technician is your nephew? He knows nothing about recording – nothing.'

Jain glared back at him. 'What are you saying, Murad Sahib?' he snarled, making a stabbing gesture of his hand at him. 'Take care what you are saying. What is my nephew to do if you don't even get a studio for him to work in but set him to work in the middle of the Chandni Chowk bazaar? He can do wonders with professional artistes – you should hear his recording of Asha Rani's songs – but what sort of artiste was this?' He twisted his head in order to look at Deven with heavy accusation as though facing the true culprit.

Immediately Murad swung around too. 'That is also true,' he agreed. 'What can one expect of a recording if it is not done in a studio? The quality of the performance has also to be taken into account, Deven, you can't say that is not important.'

174

'But Murad,' said Deven in a faltering tone, 'it was Nur. *Nur*, you know . . . ' Then he fell silent. He had had so little confidence to begin with, it was so easily shaken and the two of them had destroyed whatever remained of his faith in this project, in the transferring of Nur's greatness, in which he never ceased to believe, on to the tapes.

Murad appeared to enjoy seeing someone so thoroughly beaten. He threw an arm around Deven's shoulders and said cheerfully, 'The tapes are hopeless as they are now. You will have to do a lot of work on them to get anything out of it at all. You had better take them back to Mirpore and see if you can cut and edit them and put together at least one passable tape for your college. Otherwise that Principal of yours – or is it the board – will have you by the throat, nah?' he laughed unpleasantly.

Squeezed suffocatingly in Murad's embrace, Deven wondered what such a friendship really meant. Without sympathy, without compatibility, what was there under these jests, these embraces? Nothing but familiarity, custom. It was really custom that was the lasting ingredient of friendship, nothing but long custom, and custom could be a well from which one never rose, a trap from which there was no release.

Murad did release Deven however, and marched off, shouting over his shoulder, 'At least send me the article, will you? And some of the verse he recited – that will do for me. Of course your college is another matter.'

The thought of his college, of having to justify the spending of the library funds on something totally unusable, made Deven turn upon Jain with one last unexpected surge of spirit. 'The equipment was bad,' he shouted. 'When I saw it that first time, I told you I didn't want secondhand equipment, it is no good. The tapes also were rotten, cheap. You sent me a technician who knows nothing about recording. It is nothing to do with the performance – or the artiste. The artiste was the greatest – the best –' his voice rose to a shriek, and cracked. He was perspiring from every pore of his body, streaming with the salt fluid like someone mortally injured in a street accident.

175

Even the phlegmatic Jain was impressed. Half-rising from his bent steel chair, he motioned to Deven with both hands, each bearing an array of rings set with large gems, patting the air between them pacifyingly as if to send out the beneficial rays of these gems to his agitated customer. 'Calm down, calm down, no one is cutting your throat or robbing you. It is only a technical matter, nothing more. You can edit the tape, eliminate the noises, leave in only the voice. It can be done, it is not so difficult, not impossible; why get so upset? Can you not find someone to help you?'

'In Mirpore?' Deven tried to laugh, but his voice was all in splinters, he could not assemble it into anything meaningful. 'There are only two or three electrical goods shops in Mirpore – and mechanics who repair radios, irons, lamps, nothing else. Who will know how to handle these tapes and turn them into audio-visual aids for teaching in a college department?'

Jain chewed his lip, ostensibly thinking over Deven's only too evident problems. Then he gestured again with those flashing gems that sent out electric red and blue rays as if from some ejector, at the greasy boy crouching in a corner by the tape recorder. 'Take that boy,' he said, as if he were offering Deven a seat. 'He is Pintu, another nephew of mine. Take him to Mirpore. He will go with you.'

Deven and Pintu stared at each other in silence loaded with hostility and disapproval.

They sat together on the bus, the carton of tapes and the gadgetry to play them at their feet, under the seat. Pintu wore a new shirt of white nylon with green vines printed on it and a single pink rose over the breast pocket that also bore the words *Love Story*, the title of a recent film; it appeared to have started up an itch on the back of his neck for he kept scratching it while he stared out of the window, his mouth hanging open as if with incomprehension, trying to make out the shapes of smokestacks, brick kilns, bicycle shops and mango groves through the stinging yellow dust. Deven leant his head against the seat, closed his eyes and remained absolutely silent.

176

At the bus terminus they staggered off and hailed a cycle rickshaw to carry them and their luggage to Deven's house. It stood sadly empty, the green lattice doors of the veranda sagging but still shut, and the convolvulus creeper that grew over it dead from long dehydration. When they went in, Deven found the floors and furniture furred with dust, as though they had been silently growing pelts in their summer solitude. The heat inside the closed house was almost at boiling point. Deven went around throwing open windows with savagery. Sarla had neglected to empty the dustbin in the kitchen before she left: its contents had turned putrid, and stank.

Still neither of them spoke to the other. Deven could not bring himself to speak to the boy who looked even more imbecilic than Chiku. He merely gestured, pointing out his son's cot to him, ordering him to put his boxes in a corner, telling him to wait for a cup of tea. He found the boy's presence in his house almost impossible to bear; it took all of his self-control to refrain from turning him out and sending him back to Delhi. If he had been alone, he would have howled, one long animal howl after the other, struck his head against the wall, beaten upon it with his fists, and wept.

Instead he went into his room, stood staring at the cots with their bedding rolled up at the ends, and at the empty corner from which Sarla had taken away the tin trunks of her belongings. Eventually he collected the things he wanted and went across the courtyard to the bathroom for a bath. Then he beckoned to the watching, waiting boy and informed him he could bathe, too. It had cheered him that the taps still functioned, warm water trickled into the bucket and provided some refreshment to his wilting soul. He went into the kitchen to see if he could make tea. But of course there was nothing there. It was not like Sarla to leave behind largesse in any shape. The state of dereliction here was only a reflection of the dereliction of their marriage, perhaps even of themselves. He would have to take the boy to the bazaar to eat.

The next day a letter arrived:

177

Since we last met many problems have arisen and made my life unbearable. My eyes have suffered great damage from strain during the recording. The doctor has told me rest is not sufficient remedy and that cataract operation is urgently required. No funds available for same. Please arrange to have me admitted to Government Hospital for Eye, Ear, Nose Diseases and request your college authorities to collect bills for operation. Otherwise I may lose my sight and my profession. Work is at a standstill –

The college seemed as abandoned as his home. He wandered up and down the corridors looking for a watchman to open the staff room. He had arranged with his colleagues to leave the examination papers there for him to correct. Only a few weeks were left before the marks sheet was to be sent in, and the office opened for admissions to the new academic year. In those few weeks, Deven had to make some effort to catch up with his long neglected and almost forgotten duties as well as to put those disastrous, chaotic tapes in order. With Pintu's help. With Siddiqui's help.

Having arranged with the watchman to keep the staff room open in the mornings for him to work in, he fetched Siddiqui in a cycle rickshaw to come and help him and Pintu with the tapes which now lay on the table in the centre of the bleak room where the lecturers usually sat with their tea, cigarettes and books. Now it was scattered all over with the paraphernalia of the recording, with the examination papers shoved to one end, out of the way. Siddiqui watched quizzically while Deven and Pintu struggled to set up the recorder and play the tapes. Now Pintu displayed the extent of his knowledge; as Deven had suspected, it was nugatory. Siddiqui, smiling wanly, made a pretence of helping but really knew nothing about mechanical matters. He did not seem very curious to hear the results of Deven's long labour in Delhi but had become strangely abstracted. It worried Deven that he showed no reaction to the obvious failure of the project. It became clear to Deven that he stood isolated, that

178

no one was going to come forward with help or with a solution, that he would have to correct matters himself or be thrown out of college for false pretences, misappropriation of funds, fraud, cheating and incompetence.

Help came – *why* did it come, only to revive him and guide him deeper into disaster? – in the shape of a moon rising at the grey-filmed window of the staff room. It was the curious face of one of his students, a boy who had been hanging around the college to see when the marks sheet would be put up; seeing Deven going in and out of the staff room daily, he had hopes of finding out his marks in advance. Deven had been too preoccupied to notice him but now the boy ventured to look in at the window and next to sidle in at the door and finally to come and stand by the table and take in the scene. It happened to be very much to his taste: Dhanu had a gift for mechanics, studied radio technology by correspondence course. He watched the incompetent and inefficient proceedings with a brightness Deven had not suspected in him, and seemed to take in all it was about without being told. 'Sir, we must get another tape recorder. I have one at home, I can bring it if you like. Then we must record all the pieces you want to retain on to a master tape and cut out all this – this –' he waved a dismissive hand, then rolled up his sleeves and set about helping Pintu. What was more, he had a group of student friends who shared his interests. With Deven's permission he sent for them. They had all been bored and idle, college still shut, and came readily in the hope of some distraction and entertainment. Siddiqui, observing this with some relief, faded away with a faint, apologetic smile and did not reappear; it was obvious he preferred to wash his hands of an affair in which he regretted having played a catalystic role. Pintu also retired, to the canteen, having first taken money from Deven for cold drinks and cigarettes.

Deven remained in the sepulchral staff room, watching the boys with growing amazement and a gratitude that was almost painful and that he had to hold and nurse quietly while he watched.

He was not allowed to remain entirely passive. It was

179

still his responsibility to buy a master tape for the boys and to do so he had to visit his bank and take out his last savings, hoping Sarla would not immediately discover the withdrawal. Even with this in hand, there was not very much the boys could do to improve matters: they were mechanics and not miracle workers. Although they had some success with cutting out the surface noise, the crackling and rustling in the background that so often drowned out the voice in the foreground, it still did not mean that Deven was left with a tape of Nur's recitation, or memoirs, that could be of scholarly or even of general interest. Connoisseurs of poetry like Siddiqui might be sufficiently interested to crouch by the amplifier with their ears cocked and straining to catch the badly recorded voice that wandered distractedly down the lanes and by-lanes of a weak and failing memory, and find something of interest in his quotations from Keats and Shelley and his opinions of contemporary Urdu poets or reminiscences about the bazaars around Jama Masjid, but it was hardly a performance to be presented to students of Urdu literature. The patchwork that the boys made of the tapes, recording an excerpt from one tape and putting it together with an entirely incongruous bit from another, quite arbitrarily and fantastically, made a bizarre pastiche of it all, completely useless from a scholarly point of view.

Finally it was considered fit to be presented and Siddiqui was invited to come and hear the finished tape – the bottomless box of tapes at last reduced to just one – on the day before the college opened for admissions. He seemed entirely disinclined to come but Deven sent Dhanu in a rickshaw to fetch him. 'Tell him I am waiting in the staff room. Tell him I have ordered tea for him – for all of us.'

He was fetched and set upon a sofa against the wall, a teacup on his knee, looking a little bored, smiling quizzically at the boys who were fooling around, laughing, clapping each other on their backs, well pleased with their effort. Deven, sitting across from him on an upright chair next to the amplifier, watched his expression for reactions.

'What do you think, sir?' Dhanu asked when the tape came to an end and began to spin around soundlessly, because Deven seemed to be struck dumb. 'What do you think of the recording?'

'Charming,' said Siddiqui, smiling and rising from the sofa. 'Charming,' he repeated, and spun around on his heel and went quickly out of the room. Caught by the agitated Deven in the corridor outside, he said in a low voice, 'Deven, is that *all*?'

Deven bit his lip. 'All that is left,' he admitted, 'after the cutting and the editing.'

Seeing the disappointed look on Siddiqui's face, he added, 'Of course, I am writing something also – I am putting together my notes – enough for an article, or perhaps a monograph. Yes, I think it will be a monograph – the college printing press might like to print it, the Urdu department might – '

'Deven, they released the funds for a tape, not a monograph,' Siddiqui reminded him with some severity, and Deven fell silent and stood to attention at the reprimand. Siddiqui had lost his remote air and begun to look quite agitated himself. It occurred to Deven that he probably held himself responsible. He seemed to be having some difficulty in finding the right words to express his feelings, and walked off down the corridor with his head sunk low. 'Hmm,' was all that Deven heard him say, 'hmm, it will be difficult. The board will be meeting the day before college opens. If they ask to hear it, what will they think?'

Deven was still standing at the top of the stairs, watching him cross the blank playing field in the white heat of the sun, when Pintu appeared at his elbow, rolling down the sleeves of the white nylon shirt with the pink rose and the green vines that he had worn every day in Mirpore.

'I want my pay,' he muttered at Deven with a warning flash of his yellowish eyes. 'I want my bus fare back to Delhi. My work is done.'

Deven took out what change he had left in his pocket to give him, then went back to the staff room to lock the tape and the equipment into the cupboard. As he tidied up, dazed and mechanical in his movements, he heard someone come in and turned to see that it was the boys who had helped him, Dhanu and his friends. He looked at them inquiringly, too strained and tired to smile.

They smiled at him broadly nevertheless. They stood in a row against the door, as if blocking off escape. 'Sir,' said one of them at last, 'Sir, they are saying that the marks sheet will be put up tomorrow.'

'Yes?'

'Sir, you are marking our Hindi papers, sir. What are our marks, sir?' they chorused, giggling slightly and jostling against each other.

Deven backed against the cupboard defensively. He looked from one to the other and felt some spittle collecting at the corners of his tightly closed lips. 'You will see them tomorrow,' he said.

'Please, sir, you must give us all first division marks, sir,' they cried.

'Yes, sir, extra marks for fixing your tapes, sir!' one shouted boldly.

'No one else in Mirpore could have done this work for you, sir,' said the fat boy who had done the least work but smoked the most cigarettes and drunk the most bottles of aerated drinks. 'We are the only trained technicians here.'

'How did you get your training?' asked Deven through parched lips, 'when you are supposed to be attending classes here? Your attendance has not been very good. Have you been going to classes elsewhere?'

'Sir, please, sir,' they shouted, 'why should we waste our time learning Hindi when we can pick up some useful skills that will help us find employment?' They seemed to be mimicking some illiterate advertisement in the newspapers, or else someone they had heard on the subject; he was certain they were not all that concerned about employment. But one of them added rudely, 'Hindi does not help get you employment.'

'Then why did you take it up?' Deven asked.

182

'For a degree. We must have degrees, sir,' they told him plainly.

'You must give us a first division, sir. Tomorrow we are coming to see the marks sheet. You must put our names at the top of the list, sir.'

They did not say 'please', they did not plead; the words were spoken with an undertone of threat. But, unexpectedly, they shuffled out of the room after speaking them, and went rolling down the corridor, hooting with laughter as they went. Deven was not sure if he really heard, or if he only imagined the fat boy saying, above the hubbub, 'We will make him pay. How can he not?'

On returning home, he found another letter:

No reply to my request for medical allowance is hastening my early death. Family very anxious. My son will be left fatherless. His mother serious. It is necessary to arrange the future of the boy before I depart for my heavenly abode. The Mirpore College should endow the child with free education in recognition of work I have done for them. This is the minimum payment I request for recording and recitation of poetries. Please arrange to extend all facilities to sole male issue of the poet –

He sat up all night, a wet towel wrapped around his head, correcting the papers. It was as still as death, the tree in the courtyard appeared lifeless. Only a cricket shrilled incessantly in the kitchen, shrilled and shrilled. He worked, grateful to be alone in the house, Pintu gone and Sarla not back. He was relieved to have Nur's tapes out of the way, too, where he did not need to see them or, just tonight, think about them. He had not yet found the strength to deal with them. When he got up to go to bed, he staggered. He lay there wishing he could lead the rest of his life in this near-unconscious state. He hoped his former life of non-events, non-happenings, would be resumed, empty and hopeless, safe and endurable. That was the only life he was made for, although life was not perhaps the right term. He needed one that was more grey, more neutral, more shadowy. He sifted through alternatives like torn pieces of grey paper, letting them fall to the floor of his mind with a whisper and bury him in sleep.

In the morning he carried the marks sheet across to the college. There were many students hanging around the gates: they were not being allowed in, they were to wait for the results till two o'clock in the afternoon. Deven avoided look-ing into their faces but as he pressed past them he heard someone hiss, 'Psst, Sharma Sahib, have you done it?'

'Meeting in the staff room,' the watchman told Deven and opened the gate to let him through.

The meeting was already underway. Deven went and perched on a chair at the back, holding his marks sheet on his knee, listening to the ticking of the electric fan over his head, not to the droning voices. He knew they were only saying what they said every year – how standards were deteriorating, how they must not be allowed to deteriorate any further, how every effort was to be made next term to improve the students' attendance, how laxity in the matter of attendance was leading to poor performance in examinations, what the staff could do about it, should do and must do . . .

Afterwards, he handed the marks sheet over to be pinned on the notice board. Then he stood wondering what to do next. He had to do something to avoid going to the cupboard and confronting the tape. As he looked around for rescue, his colleague Jayadev strolled up and asked him to come to the canteen for a cup of tea. Deven accepted and found himself sitting across the tin-topped table from Jayadev whom he did not like at all: he was a slim and restless fellow with narrow hips and shoulders that made reptilian movements as though he was insinuating himself through cracks.

Jayadev did not seem to sense Deven's hostility or unease. He flashed him a broad smile; one of his front teeth was gold-capped, and gleamed.

'Why are you looking so ill, Deven-*bhai*? Haven't you had a good holiday?' he asked, offering a cigarette.

184

Deven accepted the cigarette but shook his head. 'No, I've worked right through.'

'Why do that? What good does that do? Has it got you a promotion?'

Deven gave a bitter laugh. 'Promotion,' he said. 'I am going to get a dismissal. For my hard work – a dismissal.'

Jayadev clicked his tongue reassuringly against his gold cap. 'Don't talk like that. Dismissal? No, no, you are too good, hard-working, conscientious – '

'But my hard work leads nowhere, to nothing. Nothing.'

'No, no, *bhai*, don't say that. Look what I got in the post,' said Jayadev, fishing a postcard out of his shirt pocket and passing it to Deven who studied it with a puzzled frown. The card bore a coloured picture of a Mickey Mouse figure selling popcorn in a candy-striped booth, pink-cheeked children in lettered T-shirts stood around him, eating popcorn out of mammoth bags; a ferris wheel loomed above them in an amusement park at the back. Handing it back to Jayadev, Deven asked, 'What is it?'

'A postcard, *bhai*, from my friend in America. Did you know a fellow called Vijay Sud who used to be in Mirpore two years ago? He went to Indiana, he is teaching in a state college, he is earning a big salary, having a big house, doing well. See what he writes – ' Jayadev turned over the card and read the cheering message on the other side.

Deven stopped him with a curt gesture. It did not interest him to hear what car the man had bought, or the states he had driven it through on his holiday. 'What is he teaching there?'

'Biochemistry – that was Sud's subject. He went to Indiana on a fellowship, to study, and at the end he was offered a job. Why should we not do the same? Why should we not also leave this dustbin Mirpore and go to America where the women are tall, white, blonde . . . '

'And what will you teach them – Hindi?' Deven interrupted, impatiently. He stubbed out the cigarette in the saucer. 'What are these dreams of yours? America! You want a job there as a *Hindi* teacher?'

185

Jayadev flushed, both hurt and annoyed. He had tried to cheer up a despondent colleague and been snubbed and made to feel despondent as well. He admitted, 'We are in the wrong department. We took up the wrong subject. We should have taken physics, chemistry, microbiology, computer technology – something scientific, something American. Then we would have had a future.'

Deven gave him a pitying look. 'We have no future. There is no future. There is only the past.'

Jayadev made a face. 'What is all this past-fast stuff? I am sick of it. It is the only thing we know in this country. History teaches us the glorious past of our ancient land. Hindi and Sanskrit teachers teach us the glorious literature of the past. I am sick of that. What about the future?' he muttered.

He made no protest when Deven got up to leave. At the door Deven was stopped by a familiar group of boys, eyeing him with suspicion and with threat in their eyes. He brushed past them, roughly.

Pushing open the door to the veranda, he saw two letters lying on the unswept floor, slipped in by the postman. He recognized Sarla's handwriting on one and dropped it on to the table, then opened the other with the more familiar, more compelling writing. He found separate sheets in the envelope. One bore the careful, regular script he knew and dreaded. The other was a piece of greasy yellow paper. Unfolding it, he saw it was a bill for five hundred rupees. 'Rent of room,' it stated, giving the dates during which they had occupied the room at the top of the pink house, he and Nur and the tape recorder. He lowered himself into his cane chair to read the accompanying letter.

'Safiya Begum has begged me to forward the enclosed bill,' Nur wrote, 'to be paid immediately. It was as a favour to her that the rent was not collected in advance as is custom. Please arrange for payment.'

Sarla had not returned. The college had not re-opened. There was still time to go to Delhi once more. One last time. Then he would never go again.

'Cold water, ten *paise*,' yelled the water vendor at the bus depot, wheeling his portable water container up and down the queue that waited for the Delhi bus. Seeing Deven hesitantly step out of line, he stopped and said encouragingly, 'Going out in this heat can lead to sunstroke, Sahib. Fill up with cold water, ten *paise* a tumbler.' Deven reached out for a thick glass and held it to the metal spout. Would it help him to survive this trip?

It was the last fortnight before the monsoon arrived in Delhi. The whole plain around it was laid waste by months of devastating heat. There was nothing to see in it but sulphur-yellow dust, the white sky, the occasional glitter of a tin sheet. There were no stray dogs, no vultures or even crows in sight. Bushes and grasses all appeared to have died; the land was shorn, or shrouded. The bus rattled through the wastes as if taking corpses to be dumped.

Yet, in Delhi, the tea-stall owner boiled his cans of tea, called to the dust-covered travellers as jovially as he had in kinder seasons. Now they all turned away from him and made for the cold drinks stall, choosing between red and orange aerated drinks. Deven did not stop for one but hailed a scooter rickshaw and asked to be taken into Kashmere Gate. The searing wind that blew through the open vehicle felt as if it would reduce him to cinders. Holding one hand over his mouth and nose to keep out the dust, and another clinging on to his dark glasses, he arrived in the walled city and stopped outside Murad's office.

Upstairs the gloom was a relief, like a bandage upon the lacerations made by the heat outside. Murad and the old printer with whom he appeared to be sorting out a tray of newsprint were both startled by his appearance in the doorway.

'Has the sun driven you mad?' Murad asked bluntly.

'Please have some water,' said the printer politely.

Deven sat down and accepted a glass of water brought by the small urchin still tying up bundles on the balcony.

'The journal is not out yet – you sent in your article so late –

187

it held up everything. You can't expect it out till the fifteenth,' Murad said loudly.

Deven put down his glass, wiped his mouth, and then took out the scrap of yellow paper and held it out to Murad.

'What is this?' Murad asked suspiciously, refusing to take it.

'Another bill – '

'Look here,' Murad shouted belligerently. 'Don't you try any more of that on me. I've already spent every *paisa* I could get from my mother on that blasted poet of yours – '

'Murad, it was *you* who sent me to him, *you*,' Deven's voice trembled as he spoke. It made them stare at him. He doubled over in his chair, his arms wrapped around his middle as if to forcibly prevent his sorrow from spilling out. If he had been an old woman, he would have swayed and wailed.

After a moment's reflection, Murad said, 'Yes, but what did it cost *you*? It is I who paid for everything – bought those bottles of rum, sent for food for a whole roomful of idlers and no-gooders, for week upon week. In the end even my sainted mother became suspicious and wanted to know why I needed so much money. She is willing to indulge me so far – but no further. No further, I tell you, so don't hold out that bit of filthy paper to me – take it away. Take it back to Mirpore and show it to your bank manager.'

The old printer stood blinking now at Murad and now at Deven, timidly, like an owl in daylight.

'Look, Murad,' Deven pleaded, leaning forward in his chair. 'I am not going to ask you to pay any more bills. I am only asking you to advance the payment for the article I sent you. After all, you already have it – '

'What?' roared Murad indignantly. 'Those two, three sheets you sent me? You think they are worth – worth *five hundred* rupees?' He shook his fist at the bill Deven had laid on the table before him. Murad's lips were flecked with spit, and purple in colour, he was so enraged.

'I never asked you how much you were going to pay me,' Deven said sadly, heavily. 'I took up the work only because it interested me.'

'Exactly!' Murad sputtered, cutting him short. 'It was an honour – you said it was an honour – something you had never dreamt could happen to you in all your life – going to see Nur, talking to him. You have had all the fun, and all the honour – now you want payment on top of that?'

The printer clicked his tongue disapprovingly. Deven looked to him in appeal, sensing his sympathy. 'Are not all contributors paid?' he asked him in despair. 'Why am I not to be paid for my contribution?'

'Yes, Murad Sahib, he is right, it is only fair, equal treatment for all . . . ' pleaded the old man, his head wagging nervously as he spoke.

Outnumbered, Murad marched away to a distant corner of the room. From there, he shook his fist at Deven and shouted, 'All right, you will be paid. But only when the article appears – that is the rule; all my contributors get paid *after* publication, not before. I have to give equal treatment to all. And don't think, don't you think,' he raised his voice threateningly, 'that I will pay you that sum. It is *ten* times the amount I pay for a two-page interview! You are only the interviewer, Deven, not the poet.'

Deven's head sank so low that his forehead touched the top of the desk before him. He held still, staring at the wooden rim, waiting for its solid darkness to enter his head and turn it to black wood as well.

Now they were all hurrying up to him, bustling around him. The old printer was patting him on the back and feeling his pulse. The urchin was sent to fetch another glass of water. Even Murad was close by – Deven saw the tops of his shoes near his chair. The glass of water arrived. The printer held it to his lips, saying, 'Oh the heat – how long will it go on? The monsoon is delayed. How can we bear it? It is too much. Should not have come in this heat, should not leave the house . . . '

Deven wiped his mouth and put down the glass. Then he got up to go. There was after all nothing left to do. Oddly enough, the certainty that he could expect no more help from Murad had a calming effect upon him. Perhaps when

189

everyone had cut him off and he was absolutely alone, he would begin to find himself and his own strength.

Murad hurried after him and caught him by the arm out on the landing. 'Look, Deven, I know you have a problem. You have run up debts. You let yourself get carried away by the whole thing, you simply lost control over it, you let everyone bully you and cheat you, and now you can't pay the bills – '

Deven swayed slightly on the landing, but said nothing. Murad went on, 'I'll tell you what. The tape you say you have made – the finished one, the cleaned-up one – give it to me. Give me the sole rights. Let me try to sell it to HMV or Polydor. Then I shall clear your debts, pay that hotel bill, pay Nur, pay his wife, pay everyone. In return for the sole rights.' He had his hand on Deven's shirt front and was shaking him lightly to elicit the correct response to his splendid idea. 'See?' he said.

Deven put up both his hands and pushed him back as far as he could on the small landing, till his back was against the wall. 'I can't do that,' he hissed, 'it is the property of the college. The college put up the funds for the tape recorder, the tapes, the recording. It belongs to *them.*'

'Oh?' said Murad, straightening up in the corner and throwing off Deven's hands violently. 'Then get your college to pay the bills too.'

Deven went down the wooden staircase as steadily as he could although his knees shook weakly. Murad's perfidy filled him with the iron of resistance and he felt steady, straight. As he reached the foot of the stairs, he heard Murad call over the banisters, 'One last time I am offering to help - one last time. Sole rights! Only sole rights!'

Deven went towards the exit without looking back.

The temperature that day was a hundred and fourteen degrees. The *neem* trees along the streets drooped, stricken, encased in dust. The horses between the shafts of the old *tongas* stood with their legs sloping under them, their necks swaying between their knees. Even the flies that adhered to their muzzles and flanks had ceased to buzz and crawl and appeared to be stuck on with glue. Traffic continued to move, motor and bicycle traffic, but as if searching for somewhere to go and die. Deven moved through it slowly, like a swimmer in unknown water, stopping often in the shade of a tree or a building, sometimes having a drink of water at one of the many drinking water booths set up by philanthropists. He had tied his handkerchief on to his head by making knots at each corner. He walked aimlessly but late that afternoon found himself in Chandni Chowk, standing outside the jewellery and sweet shops, amongst the shoppers and hawkers and barrows and handcarts, staring.

The green wall of the hospital was visible over the top of the fruit and garland stalls that flanked a pink and white stucco temple with a chased silver door. It was a few minutes' walk to Nur's house. If he went there, he would find Nur stirring after his long afternoon siesta. He would find his servant boy preparing his couch for him on the terrace, amongst his pigeons, for the evening. He would sit at Nur's feet, listening to his voice as he recited his verse and lamented his fate, and then perhaps he would learn if it had been worth all the trouble, if anything of value had been gained. What's it all about, Nur Sahib? he would ask, O what is it all about?

But he found himself wandering on. He walked past the sandstone walls of the Red Fort still incandescent with heat, and across the dusty flat spaces separating them from the great Friday Mosque. He walked on towards Darya Ganj, thinking he might visit Raj's aunt: he had left the house without telling her he would not be back. He ought to explain. She would only smile when she saw him and say nothing. Perhaps she would be seated before her garlanded gods, plying her cymbals while the tailor sang. Then he would ask them, Why? What is it all for? What is it about?

Instead, he veered to the right and entered a small park where royal palms marched in grave rows on either side of a gravel path and benches were set amongst beds of cannas. All was calmly geometrical. It was too early for the city crowds to pour out for a breath of air and Deven sat down on an empty bench. Putting his head back, he found he could see the dome and the eastern wall of the mosque. The sun was behind it, in a great brassy conflagration, dazzling his eyes, but its forms and lines stood out against the heat and light clearly. The white and black marble facing of the eastern doorway made a graceful calligraphic pattern. The enormous arched doorway soared upwards to the dome which rose like a vast bubble that the flat earth had sent out into the dusty yellow-grey sky, a silent exhalation of stone. It was absolutely still, very serene. It was in fact the silent answer to his questioning. Since it was silent, he could not hear it, but he felt it impress its shape upon his eyelids, very gently, very lightly, like fingertips pressing them down to sleep. Gradually the sky disappeared, the sun and the light and the glare, and the shape became clearer and sharper till it was all there was – cool, high-minded and remote.

Sitting there while the dusk gathered, oblivious of the children who were climbing on to the back of the bench and leaping down from it with howls and shrieks or of the women who moved about in twittering bunches under their black and brown and white veils or of the families that sat on the grass around transistor radios and paper cones of salted *gram*, Deven recalled, incongruously enough, the conversation in the canteen with Jayadev, how they had envied their scientist colleagues who had at their command the discipline of mathematics, of geometry, in which every question had its answer and every problem its solution. If art, if poetry, could be made to submit their answers, not merely to contain them within perfect, unblemished shapes but to release them and make them available, then – he thought, then –

But then the bubble would be breached and burst, and it would no longer be perfect. And if it were not perfect, and constant, then it would all have been for nothing, it would be nothing.

CHAPTER ELEVEN

The house stood open when he returned to it next morning. Sarla was back. She was down on her haunches, sweeping the floor with a long, soft broom. Dust lay heaped in small piles all around her. Some contained dry *neem* leaves, others feathers, and all were mixed with torn-up letters. Through the door he could see her luggage heaped behind, still unopened.

She looked up as he came in. She had wrapped the end of her sari around her mouth and nose to keep out the dust as she swept. She pulled it off with one finger, letting it fall, and stared at him. 'So, still spending all your time in Delhi?' she asked heavily.

He stood very still, although he was immensely agitated, and immensely worn out by a sleepless night spent at the bus depot. 'Why didn't you tell me you were returning today? I would have come to the station to meet you.'

'I did write,' she snapped, and pointed at an unopened letter that lay on the small table next to his chair. 'You never opened it,' she accused him, and started sweeping again.

He did not move out of her way but stood watching her crawl about the floor, sweeping the dust into little hills before her. He found he was no longer irritated by the sight of her labour, or disgusted by the shabbiness of her limp, worn clothes, or her hunched, twisted posture, her untidy hair or sullen expression. It was all a part of his own humiliation. He considered touching her, putting an arm around her stooped

193

shoulders and drawing her to him. How else could he tell her he shared all her disappointment and woe?

But he could not make that move: it would have permanently undermined his position of power over her, a position that was as important to her as to him: if she ceased to believe in it, what would there be for her to do, where would she go? Such desolation could not be admitted. So he turned aside, asking, 'Where is Manu? I don't see him. Manu!'

'He has gone to the neighbours to show them his new clothes,' Sarla said, not looking up. 'My parents have given him new clothes. And shoes.'

He nodded, entirely accepting this slap to his pride and dignity as the breadwinner. He deserved their insults. They were perfectly right to insult him. When had he last bought his son anything? And now of course he never would – he was ruined.

He sat down on the cane chair and stared out of the open door at the garden gate, waiting for Manu. At least that was what Sarla thought he was doing. She felt moved to ask, 'Tired? Shall I make you tea?' Contrary to appearances, she was actually quite pleased to be back in her own domain, to assume all its responsibilities, her indispensable presence in it; in her parents' home she had missed the sense of her own capability and position.

Deven only shook his head, saying nothing. She began to get irritated by his inaction. She wanted to get on with the cleaning of the house. She got up and went to fetch a duster, shouting from the kitchen, 'How could you let the house get so filthy? Why didn't you call for the sweeper to come and clean?'

He started to tell her that he did not know where the sweeper lived, but he would have had to raise his voice and he couldn't; he was much too tired. He knotted his hands together and stared at the unopened letters on the table beside him.

It must have been Sarla's hand that guided him, by remote control, because the letter he at length picked up was not one in Nur's familiar handwriting at all. Sheets, closely folded, fell out in a solid packet. Opened out, they proved very fine, very thin. The writing upon them was large, sloping, filled with flourishes and ornamentations. The words ran into each other like one wave upon another merging into a whole flood.

The recording is no secret. Whatever your reason for concealing it from me, Nur Sahib could not conceal it from me. Was I considered incapable of understanding the need to record Nur Sahib's voice for posterity? Was Safiya Begum considered wiser and more capable because of her greater age and her longer years with him? Dear friend, I beg to put it to you that you have insulted my intelligence by your deception.

The elegance and floridity of her Urdu entered Deven's ears like a flourish of trumpets and beat at his temples while he read. The essential, unsuspected spirit of the woman appeared to step free of its covering, all the tinsel and gauze and tawdriness, and reveal a face from which the paint and powder had been washed and which wore an expression that made Deven halt and stumble before he could read on.

'No doubt the men whose company you keep and make Nur Sahib keep have filled your ears with the poison of their gossip. Like them, you thought I was a prostitute who dazzled Nur Sahib's eyes with my dance and so inveigled my way out of a house of prostitution into the house of a distinguished poet. Is that not an insult to the poet you claim to idolize, quite apart from the insult to me? Do you imagine it was possible for a common dancing girl to win the heart of a great poet? Is it not clear that it was my mind in which he was interested, that if I did inveigle my way into his heart it was by my talk, my poetry and whatever wit I have? You should allow me to prove this to you by placing before you my own poetry.

Judged by Nur Sahib's standards, the poems I enclose for you to read may appear to be minor works. Kindly remember that unlike Nur Sahib and unlike your respected self, I am a woman and have had no education but what I have found and seized for myself. Unlike poets and scholars who have won distinctions, I have had no patron apart from my honoured husband, no encouragement and no sympathy. Yet there must have been some natural gift if Nur Sahib himself was impressed by my early verse. It is the reason why he married me in his old age, to have at his side an intellectual companion of the kind he did not have in his first marriage. None of your friends credit him with even so much intelligence although they profess to worship him.

It is therefore necessary that I prove my gifts and abilities to you and to other scholars and devotees of the art of poetry. It is for this reason that I am enclosing my latest poems for you to read and study and judge if they do not have some merit of their own. Let me see if you are strong enough to face them and admit to their merit. Or if they fill you with fear and insecurity because they threaten you with danger – danger that your superiority to women may become questionable. When you rose to your feet and left the *mehfil* while I was singing my verse, was it not because you feared I might eclipse the verse of Nur Sahib and other male poets whom you revere? Was it not intolerable to you that a woman should match their gifts and even outstrip them? Are you not guilty of assuming that because you are a male, you have a right to brains, talent, reputation and achievement, while I, because I was born female, am condemned to find what satisfaction I can in being maligned, mocked, ignored and neglected? Is it not you who has made me play the role of the loose woman in gaudy garments by refusing to take my work seriously and giving me just that much regard that you would extend to even a failure in the arts as long as the artist was male? In this unfair world that you have created what else could I have been but what I am?

Ask yourself that when you peruse my verses, if you have the courage . . .

But Deven did not have the courage. He did not have the time. He did not have the will or the wherewithal to deal with this new presence, one he had been happy to ignore earlier and relegate to the grotesque world of hysterics, termagants, viragos, the demented and the outcast. It was not for the timid and circumspect to enter that world on a mission of mercy or rescue. If he were to venture into it, what he learnt would destroy him as a moment of lucidity can destroy the merciful delusions of a madman. He could not allow that.

Sarla, coming in with her duster, looked at him tearing up a bundle of blue sheets of paper into strips, and cried, 'You're dropping rubbish all over the floor I have just swept!'

In the morning he set off for the registrar's office to ask for an interview with the Principal so that he could explain the whole matter before the board meeting on the final day of the summer vacation. The tape could not be presented before the board, that was out of the question; he would have to engage the Principal's sympathies and prevent such a thing from happening. The tape, the shameful tape, must not be heard by anyone.

'Papa, buy us a watermelon,' Manu screamed from the house as he unlatched the gate. He nodded and waved to the boy and then turned to find the postman thrusting a letter at him. Taking it without a word as if it were an injection being jabbed into his arm, stiffening it and filling it with hot lead, he pocketed the letter and set off, telling himself this would have to stop, it had to be made to stop –

The clerk outside the registrar's office told him that the sahib was busy at a meeting in the Principal's office and he would have to wait for an interview. Deven stood still for a moment, pondering, and then left. How many more bills, more requests from Nur could he place before them after all? Nur would never stop writing, demanding. The letters would keep pouring in the way the tapes had kept on grinding. He had launched himself, and them, upon a course it now seemed impossible to stop.

It was essential to find someone who could bring it to a

halt. He must have had some residual confidence left in Siddiqui for he found himself standing by the wrought-iron gates that led to his house. Only the house no longer stood there. It was a heap of rubble from which dust rose like a ghost, and demolition labour whacked and pounded at whatever remained vertical. While they worked, they shouted loudly and savagely as if they were wrecking it out of personal vengeance. The decayed villa groaned as the last of it collapsed.

'Go in, go in,' said the cigarette and banana vendors at the gate. 'You will find the sahib there – he stands under the tree watching all day,' and they pointed at the dusty *neem* tree by the compound wall.

Deven approached the tree and found Siddiqui under it, holding a black cotton umbrella over his head. When he saw Deven he waved in his direction quite gaily but a little vaguely, turning away to shout orders to some workmen and discuss something with a large moustachioed contractor. Having sent them off, he turned to Deven and cried 'Come to see my ancestral home vanish in the dust of Mirpore, Deven-*bhai*?'

'I didn't know,' Deven faltered, 'you didn't tell – '

'No, no, no. I was so busy, too busy to come to college lately. You see, I was made this offer by a Delhi businessman. He wants to develop this land - build a block of flats with shops on the ground floor, cinema house at the back, offices on top – all kinds of plans for putting this wasteland to use. And as I need the money – you know my weakness – the offer was too good to refuse, so – ' he giggled a little, rubbed at the dust on his forehead, and then turned enthusiastically to the contractor who had returned with a message that weighed down his lower jaw gravely.

Deven was aware that he was in the way. Yet he could not bear to leave without making an attempt, even if badly timed and intrusive. 'Siddiqui Sahib,' he murmured, 'will you be attending the meeting at the college tomorrow?'

'No, no, no, I have no time, can't you see. It is no small thing, developing an area like this,' he said testily.

'Yes,' Deven agreed meekly, nodding, 'but I thought if

you could tell them – the librarian, at least, and the registrar, if not the Principal – testify to the value of the tape – however faulty, however poor, at least authentic, and of historic value,' he pleaded, the sweat breaking out on his upper lip, 'and made at such expense. If they can be persuaded to pay the bills I accumulated while recording it – '

'That tape?' Siddiqui cut him short impatiently. 'That useless tape? But, my friend, it is a disaster, not worth anything. Useless to play it to them.'

'It is poor, of course, Siddiqui Sahib,' Deven replied, 'but it is not without value. It has some importance to Urdu poetry after all. If only you, as head of the Urdu department, could persuade them that the project has been worthwhile, perhaps then the bills – ' he fumbled in his pocket, drew out his unopened letter, put it back, pulled out another piece of paper, this time the bill for the room he had unknowingly rented, and held it out to Siddiqui.

'What is this? Another bill? Who will pay it? The college? Never,' said Siddiqui, but stretched out his hand and took it. With all the riches of his future as a property developer before him, he could afford a little magnanimity to the hopeless failures that peopled his meagre past. 'I can put it up to them of course – but I don't know if it will do any good.'

'Siddiqui Sahib,' Deven cried, 'it was not my fault! I worked hard – I prepared for it and I worked – but I was fooled and cheated by everyone – the man who sold me the secondhand equipment, the technician who said he could do the recording but was completely inexperienced, by Murad who said he would pay and did not, by Nur who had never told me he wanted to be paid, and by his wife, wives, all of them – '

'Oh,' said Siddiqui, giving him a cool look from the heights of his new prosperity, 'and why did you let them all cheat you? Why did you not take care and see that they didn't? Look at me, standing all day in the hot sun, watching every brick fall so that I am not cheated. That is the only way to do it, Deven-*bhai* – hard work, hard work.'

'But Siddiqui Sahib,' said Deven, and his throat was so parched that his voice came out in a hoarse whisper, 'I did –

you know I did. There is nothing to see for it, only a mess, a failure. That is all anyone will see. But underneath it – underneath that lie my efforts, and my – my sincerity. Also my regard for the poet, and my love for poetry, you know. That should be considered, before you judge – ' and then his whisper was drowned by an enormous crash of bricks and plaster on to the terrace from where they spilt and spread, with a sad sigh, over what had been the lawn.

In the cycle rickshaw going home – his legs felt strangely weak, he knew he could not walk – he opened the letter. It was not written in English this time but in Urdu and he read it while wobbling down the streets, so that the letters danced crazily before him, turning him giddy:

> My pigeons are dying. A new disease has broken out, unknown to the doctors of the bird hospital. It has claimed five already, each a champion. On the others, too, I see the grey mould that grows till it caps the bird's head, closes its eyes and seals its beak and then afflicts the claws and feet, so that it slowly suffocates to death. There is no medicine to cure them. I watch them fall and find them lying on their sides, cold. When the last of my pigeons is gone, I will cease to write poetry for ever. I will go with them.
>
> Unless you can arrange for me to go on the pilgrimage to Mecca that alone can save my sinful soul that is now being punished –

The rickshaw swerved suddenly to avoid a collision with someone who had stepped off the pavement directly in front of it, and Deven, lurching to one side, found himself staring into the face of one of his students, tight with hate, and heard him say in a low voice, 'Meet us behind the college and see what we do to you.'

Then the rickshaw driver recovered his balance and pedalled on. 'All right, sahib?' he shouted over his shoulder at Deven.

Deven nodded. 'All right,' he said.

That night, before the board meeting, Deven found himself unable to sleep. The house was more oppressive, the heat more unendurable, than on any other night that summer. He thought he heard thunder in the distance – perhaps the monsoon was coming, perhaps it was drawing close. It had to be because he could not endure any more of this heat, this waiting.

He lay on his string bed in the courtyard, periodically rising to walk up and down, from one wall to another, barefoot so as not to wake his wife or their son. But Sarla woke when he struck a match to light a cigarette and moaned in protest, so he went in to smoke it on the veranda. There was no air here at all, it had all been consumed, leaving nothing. Out in the courtyard, Sarla lay awake, fanning herself and the boy with a palm leaf fan that rattled and rustled. Finally it fell from her tired hand and she slept again.

After a while Deven lay down beside them quietly, straining to hear wind or thunder, but the stillness of the night hung intact and impenetrable. It was finally broken by a dog howling across the canal. A little later, shortly before dawn, he heard steps shuffling through the dust in the lane and voices singing. They grew clearer and louder, and it was obvious they were approaching. He slipped off his bed and went back to the veranda to peer at them through the lattice as the singers passed, all dressed in white, holding lamps. Mostly old women, wagging their heads as they sang with a demented air:

'O will you come along with us – '

The rear was brought up by a priest naked to the waist, pawing at the earth as he pranced along, clashing his cymbals with abandon.

'What is it?' Sarla asked, coming to stand beside him, haggard from broken sleep. 'Why don't you sleep?'

He gave a disgusted snort, gesturing at the band of devotees. 'I can't sleep now,' he said, 'I'll go for a walk,' and before she could protest he slipped out of the door and left.

He walked slowly at first, giving the procession of old widows time to move on, rousing family after family as they went and setting the dogs howling. They turned left towards the temple in the town and he turned right on to the path by the canal. It was not something he had ever done before, he was not accustomed to being out at such an hour, and he felt vaguely excited, hearing his pulse beat inside his ear. Was he actually hoping to meet the student with the grudge, with a knife? No, he would never have the courage to come out here in the night. There was nothing to be heard but the water rushing past the banks, although it was still too dark to see it. He could slip in if he was not careful. He felt weeds and pampas grass brush against his legs and his feet grew dusty and then muddy as he walked. Out in the invisible fields a lapwing gave a wild, startled cry and he could see the pale flash of its wings in the darkness that was growing dilute now in the east.

He watched the sky pale to grey, the feathery plumes of the pampas grass to mauve. He did not want the day to dawn. He had hoped to stretch the night endlessly by walking on and on. Day would bring with it the board meeting, an inquiry, an interrogation, exposure and blame. Yes, and what else? The bills would be returned to him to pay. The tape would be played and declared a disaster, even a hoax. There would be criticism. Who was he to have been entrusted with such a project as well as college funds? He would be sent for, he would have to appear before them, and plead for sympathy, for mercy, for acquittal. If it was not forthcoming, he would be censured, perhaps dismissed. O God, if he was, he would be ruined and Sarla and Manu with him. He would have to pawn, even sell her jewellery to clear his debts, she would have to be sent back to her parents to his eternal disgrace, and the boy would grow up to consider his father a failure – a disgraceful, thoughtless, irresponsible and hopeless failure. Where would it all end? Why, seeing it all so clearly, could he not halt it?

The student leaping out of the bushes with a knife would be a simple solution, one to be hoped for by comparison. But the bushes stood still, still dark with night, no breeze to stir them. There was no release or escape.

Walking on, he kept his eyes on the clay path, a chalky streak beside the dark water that ran deep in its bed of reeds. He remembered how he had walked there with Manu and how a parrot had let fall its brilliant tail feather and he had picked it up and handed it to Manu who had put it behind his ear and laughed so that it had seemed an omen, a joyous, delightful omen. Then they had returned to the house and found Nur's letter, the first of Nur's letters.

Nur – he tried to think of him as separate from his letters, his senile demands, to feel again for him as he had when Nur had first allowed him into his presence, in his still, shaded study. When he remembered the joy of hearing his voice and listening to him quote poetry, then quoting his lines back to him, binding them together in a web, an alliance, he knew this was what he would have to recover, to retrieve. If he could do that, it would give him a reason, and strength, to survive whatever came. He had to believe that.

He was hurrying along the path now, fleeing through the weeds and grasses that caught at him, tearing at the loose pyjamas on his legs, and at his feet in their open sandals. Brushing them aside, he tried to return to his old idolatry of the poet, his awe of him, his devotion when it had still been pure, and his gratitude for his poetry and friendship, that strange, unexpected, unimaginable friendship that had brought him so much pain.

That friendship still existed, even if there had been a muddle, a misunderstanding. He had imagined he was taking Nur's poetry into safe custody, and not realized that if he was to be custodian of Nur's genius, then Nur would become his custodian and place him in custody too. This alliance could be considered an unendurable burden – or else a shining honour. Both demanded an equal strength.

The faintly glimmering path by the black canal was like a thread he had to follow to the end. Where *was* the end? Was there one? He had a vision of Nur's bier, white, heaped with flowers, rose and marigold, bright blazing flowers on the white sheet. He saw the women in the family weeping and wailing around it. He heard the funeral music play. He saw the shroud, the grave – open. When Nur was laid in it, would this connection break, this relation end? No, never – the bills would come to him, he would have to pay for the funeral, support the widows, raise his son . . .

He stopped, panting for breath, on the canal bank and stared at the water that stopped and turned concentrically in a whirlpool at that point. The whirlpool was an opening into the water, leading into its depths. But these were dark and obscure. The sky was filling with a grey light that was dissolving the dense blackness of night. It glistened upon a field of white pampas grass which waved in a sudden breeze that had sprung up, laughing, waving and rustling through the grasses with a live, rippling sound. He thought of Nur's poetry being read, the sound of it softly murmuring in his ears. He had accepted the gift of Nur's poetry and that meant he was custodian of Nur's very soul and spirit. It was a great distinction. He could not deny or abandon that under any pressure.

He turned back. He walked up the path. Soon the sun would be up and blazing. The day would begin, with its calamities. They would flash out of the sky and cut him down like swords. He would run to meet them. He ran, stopping only to pull a branch of thorns from under his foot.